THE
MOMENT

JOHN WOZNIAK

DENVER, COLORADO

All scripture references are from the King James Version (KJV) of the Holy Bible unless otherwise noted.

This is a work of fiction. The events and characters described herein are imaginary and are not intended to refer to specific places or living persons. The opinions expressed in this manuscript are solely the opinions of the author and do not represent the opinions or thoughts of the publisher. The author has represented and warranted full ownership and/or legal right to publish all the materials in this book.

Outskirts Press, Inc.
http://www.outskirtspress.com

ISBN: 978-1-4787-0834-6

Library of Congress Control Number: 2013905524

Outskirts Press and the "OP" logo are trademarks belonging to Outskirts Press, Inc.

PRINTED IN THE UNITED STATES OF AMERICA

1

The spirits toyed with Cliff, mocking him, branding him as a loser. They had never so blatantly entered his private space before; their boldness only increasing his desire to fight them. He was convinced these creatures knew where his wife was. Someday he would enter their world and find her. That moment was rapidly approaching, and he would face it with a vengeance. He stared at his wedding ring and ground his teeth.

"It's your turn." The voice of Ralph Huntley snapped Cliff's thinking back to the real world, the physical world, the one that right now seemed very surreal. Cliff picked up the dice and tossed them, watching closely for any kind of visual evidence of the invisible spirits he knew were there.

"This is nuts!" he exclaimed, as he landed on St. Charles Place again, this time with three houses on it. "Go ahead, take the money." Losing the game didn't happen in this round, but it would happen in the next, guaranteed.

Cliff's mind wandered as he watched Ralph slowly set the bills on their respective piles. For decades they had played these Monopoly games and the action had always been give and take, win or lose. Today it was all give and no take. Cliff only landed on properties that Ralph owned, and only picked cards that said 'pay'. With that sort of luck, he was about to lose his third game in *less than an hour*. "Roll the dice!" he barked at Ralph. "I haven't got all day!"

Ralph gave the dice a quick toss without mentioning that

they actually did still have all day. He then moved the seven spaces from GO to Chance.

"More money I suppose," Cliff grunted.

"No, it's not," he said apologetically. Then he placed an orange get-out-of-jail-free card next to the yellow one he already had.

Cliff grabbed the dice that had tumbled to his side of the board. He shook them quick and tossed them with a 'who cares' attitude, knowing full well something else was controlling the outcome. A stash of cash was waiting at Free Parking, penalty money he had paid, but Cliff knew it wasn't for him. Ralph only owned one property from Virginia to Illinois, and that was New York Ave. If Cliff's theory was correct, that was his next destination. "That's it!" he said as the eight spots on the dice put him right there. No house was needed to take his last twelve dollars. "Set it up again," he barked.

"Isn't three games enough for one day?" Ralph asked.

Cliff glared at him and said, "Ralph, just do it." He did his best to control his anger, because he knew he couldn't explain what he was thinking. So Ralph Huntley--Cliff's employee, friend, and caregiver--just gathered, shuffled, arranged, and dealt what he needed to. Meanwhile, Cliff sat in his wheelchair and scowled. The scolding he gave Ralph didn't get the response he hoped for. Care, comfort, and conversation were fine, and Ralph had provided them well. But today Cliff desperately needed to talk to someone about this board game that seemed to have an evil life of its own.

"It's ready," he heard Ralph say; as if oblivious to the strange phenomena taking place.

Cliff just looked incredulously at Ralph. "Don't *you* think these games have been strange?"

"Well, yeah," he answered hesitantly.

"Something seems to be controlling the roll of the dice."

"Yeah, you've never had such bad luck."

"Forget luck Ralph. There has to be something controlling the game. Can't you see that?"

"Well it's not me!"

"I know it's not you, I never said it was. It's as if I've been cursed," Cliff continued, glancing angrily around the room. "Like a witch doctor has gotten a handful of my hair and is offering some sacrifice to have me destroyed."

Ralph's eyes got wide. "What did you say?"

Cliff ignored the question and yelled, "Whatever you are that's messing with this game, leave it alone and get out of this house!"

Ralph stared as if he was looking at a madman. "Mr. Preston, are you okay?"

The formality of the question drew Cliff's attention back to Ralph and the game spread out in front of him. Still angry he said, "Give me one of the dice." He was determined to beat these spirits at their own game, and beat Ralph at this one. They both rolled. When Cliff saw that his 3 beat Ralph's 1, he said, "Well, I finally get to go first." Then he just shook his head as Ralph moved the combined four spaces and took from him the income tax amount.

Cliff still frowned as Ralph rolled a 10 and moved to 'Just Visiting' the jail. But his attitude changed when he rolled a 7 and landed on St. Charles Place. Ralph took the money from Cliff and eagerly placed the violet property on Cliff's side of the table. This was the first time in four games that Cliff had even been *able* to buy a property, and they both knew it. When Ralph went broke three hours later, they both sat there stunned.

Cliff stared angrily out the window for the better part of an hour. He was aware of Ralph's nervous fussing around him, but he couldn't stifle the anger long enough to speak to him. What frustrated him most was his desperate need to speak to Ralph, and the trust that would be destroyed when he did. Fatigue eventually forced him to speak, but also provided an excuse to avoid the issue. Turning to Ralph he said, "Get me to my room."

Ralph eagerly grabbed the handles of the wheelchair and guided it through the twisting hallway to Cliff's room. As they approached the bed, he asked, "Is there anything you need?"

Cliff knew that Ralph's concern went beyond a glass of water, but he wasn't in a mood to talk about it. All he was able to say was a stern, "We will discuss it tomorrow."

Jack Watchman sat at his computer, studying the first chapter of the latest book to hit his e-mail. This one was a character-driven sci-fi novel, which he hoped would be more interesting to him than the western romance he had just finished. It shouldn't matter, because his job was to critique it, and not necessarily enjoy it. Besides, sometimes it was simpler to provide criticism if he didn't enjoy it.

He was thankful for the Internet because it allowed him to work from his home in the trees rather than commuting to an office in some concrete canyon of a city. When the mood struck him, he could go for a walk, turn on some music, or sit and talk with his wife, Barbara. He could work 14 hours a day, or take 14 days off, whichever suited him. He was his own boss, and Barbara had gotten used to his erratic income.

In fact, the only thing he missed about his former job was the quality of the manuscripts he got to work with. Ghost writing for Cliff Montgomery, one of the best anthropological authors in the world, was far more prestigious than what he was doing now. But at least with this current arrangement his employment wasn't in jeopardy. He would never again have to suffer the embarrassment and financial ruin that his former boss had put him through. And he hoped Barbara would never again witness the anger that he was capable of delivering.

Jennifer grabbed the tarnished brass doorknob and yelled, "I'm going to get the mail!"

A disgruntled voice from the living room asked, "What for?"

Jennifer ignored her husband and walked out the door. 'What for?' she thought to herself as she walked down the driveway. She could think of a dozen ways that God could bless them by something coming in the mail. She fought the negativity that her husband Robert always dwelled on.

For instance, the unemployment checks weren't an embarrassment, they were a blessing. She believed that someday soon God would pour out His abundance on them and all of their creditors would see His majesty and grace. One day the perfect job offer would arrive, and Robert would know that God loves him. All she had to do was to have enough faith to counteract Robert's lack of any. Then she sat down in despair on the top of the railroad tie retaining wall. The only envelope in the mailbox had the words *Second Notice* emblazoned in red across the front.

Cliff sat motionless in his wheelchair, staring out the conservatory windows. He didn't seem to notice the beautiful Western Tanagers eating just outside the windows. As sedentary as he seemed, his mind was churning furiously. He had made peace with the fact that he wouldn't cheat death this time. But then what?

Then what? That question never crossed his mind when the

doctors told him that his cancer was inoperable. Neither did it come up when he shared the news with Ralph. He just assumed that life ends and the world kept turning.

But then there were those Monopoly games. Something, or someone, was controlling those games. There was no possibility that they happened by chance. *'What is out there that I can't see?'* he asked himself, *'and am I about to join them?'* Panic gripped him, and he hated that. He determined to push past the fear and find a logical answer.

The first logical question, he reasoned, was how could anything control the roll of Monopoly dice? More importantly, why would they *want* to? It felt like he was being mocked, but what if something, or someone, was trying to communicate with him? What if someone was trying to guide him or warn him? What if it was his wife, Gloria? What if somehow she was getting closer to him, or he was getting closer to her? Was there some clue in that game, or was it just a cruel joke? Then fear gripped him as he considered the probable truth, that the cancer that was ravaging his body was beginning to contaminate his mind.

That's not true! That thought sounded like another voice in his head and he wanted to believe it. Yes, he *did* believe it. Those Monopoly games *did* happen. Three games were played in an hour and that *is* impossible. Ralph was there; he saw it happen. He was going to have to trust Ralph with the outlandish thoughts that were going through his head. Ralph may be the only person left on the planet who would be able to understand, and would want to try.

Without changing his position, he yelled for Ralph.

"Yes, what is it?" Ralph replied from the kitchen.

"Do you remember the I.P. sessions we used to have?"

Ralph had to think for a minute. "You mean back at the office, when you wanted to take a trip to do another book."

"I certainly didn't mean down the hall on the left."

"What? Oh, I get it. No, I mean, yes, I remember them."

"Do you remember what your job was?"

"I was to be quiet and take notes until you were through talking and wanted my input."

"You do remember! Good, then get your notepad, we're going to do another."

"You're kidding."

"Cliff Montgomery never kids."

Ralph's eyes got big enough to see whites all the way around the pupils. He stared at Cliff for a minute to see if he was joking, but there was no sign of it. He finally realized that Cliff Preston, the wheelchair bound man he had cared for all these years, was planning once more to become Cliff Montgomery, the author. "If you don't mind, I'll use my laptop," he finally responded.

"That would be fine, now get moving."

Ralph sat quietly and took notes. He hadn't performed this job for Cliff in years. 'Investigatory Preparation' was what they used to call it. Years ago these types of sessions spawned literary pieces such as *Creature Comforts in Siberia, Finding Life in the Sahara Desert, The High Life in Nepal,* or *Abundant Life in the Jungles of the Amazon.*

Those books sought to illustrate human struggles in harsh environments. The 'I.P.' sessions laid the groundwork to explore those struggles as thoroughly as possible. Cliff wanted every scrap of information he could find about surviving in those types of situations. Then he would enter them. He would live alongside the people who were native to that land, as they were accustomed to living, with no safety net.

What Ralph was involved with today was totally different.

The struggle was *within* Cliff, and the environment could not be entered. Not with a human life at least. Cliff was dictating to Ralph how he intended to investigate the spirit world and the after-life, if there *was* one. Ralph finally reached the point where he could no longer stay silent.

"May I interrupt, Mr. Preston?"

"Go ahead Ralph, what is it?"

"I'd just like to say…I think you're tackling a subject that's been dealt with before."

"So who has the best information on it?" he asked impatiently.

"Well, uh, that depends."

"Depends on *what*, Ralph, on what I want to believe? I don't want to believe anything! I want to *know*. I *have* to know. My plane may leave tomorrow, and I need to know what I'm stepping into when I get off of it." Cliff quickly spun his wheelchair around so Ralph couldn't see his face. He was embarrassed, but he had finally admitted the truth. He knew he could die at any moment, and he had no idea what came after that moment. Now, even thinking about that moment threatened to scare him into it.

Ralph hated to upset him, but he didn't think the project that Cliff was suggesting was even possible, not in his condition. In a submissive tone he said, "I just thought there might be some information we could glean from the net, you know, just to save a little time."

"Well, you're probably right. It just seems that most of it can't be trusted. You've got religious people talking about an all-knowing God, who don't seem to know anything themselves. Some of the Spiritists I met seemed to know stuff they shouldn't, but even they seemed to do it for profit. I guess when it comes down to it, I only trust myself. But it won't hurt to look. Maybe I'll know what I'm looking for when I see it."

There was an uneasy silence in the conservatory. The only sound heard was the grandfather's clock in the parlor. It too seemed to be telling them that time was running out. Ralph broke the tension by asking, "Have you determined how you're actually going to accomplish this?"

After a moment, Cliff turned around, gave Ralph a sly smile, and said, "Yes I have. I have decided that I'm in no condition to travel around looking for something that I may not be able to travel around and find."

"So you plan to do what?"

"Find it right here."

"Here? In the conservatory?"

"Why not?"

Ralph couldn't answer that question, so he asked one. "What if you can't find the answers?"

Cliff turned to look out the windows and said, "Then I'll die trying."

Ralph spent the next week doing the research that Cliff had requested. From the Internet he compiled a list of authors that had written books about the after-life, about poltergeists, aliens, spirits, and God. He worked tirelessly trying to separate the legitimately informed from the truly bizarre. As usual, Cliff wasn't looking for the information; he was looking for a guide. There was always someone who knew where to find the hidden trails. Cliff would walk those trails himself, if that was possible. Ralph never really knew how Cliff chose the trails and the trials that he did. This challenge was certainly no exception.

Cliff slowly rolled his wheelchair up to the table where Ralph was doing his research. "Are you about done?" he asked.

"It's been exhausting so I hope it's exhaustive enough for

you," he responded.

"We need to do something soon," Cliff stated. "We're on a deadline you know. No pun intended."

Ralph knew what he meant. Even though the cancer was advancing slower than the doctors had predicted, it was beginning to take its toll. He knew Cliff would never admit to pain or fear, so he didn't let Cliff know that he saw them. To divert attention away from his own fears, Ralph pointed to various stacks of information on the table. "What I've done here is to separate the authors into certain schools of thought."

"What might those be?"

"Well, here are the ones that believe in reincarnation, and here are the evolutionists. Then there are the creationists, the New Agers, and the sci-fi guys."

"By that you mean the ones who say we were left here by aliens?"

"Yeah, that sort of thing. I put the Shamans and witchdoctors in this stack, and all of the occult stuff in this one. Then here is a list of people that you wanted to invite that aren't authors."

"All the people that tried to push their religion on me?"

"That's right."

"And this last pile?"

"Those are the ones that didn't fit into any of the other categories."

"Such as?"

"Such as people with interesting ideas that haven't written books, authors that have died, some bloggers, and this guy." Ralph handed Cliff an ad he had copied off a website.

"The Big Picture by J.W. Gilbert," Cliff read out loud. He scanned the rest of the page for a second and asked, "What's his deal?"

"He claims to understand all of the rest of these and to

believe in none of them. He says he knows God and despises religion."

"I'd say you have plenty to choose from. Some of these are obvious, like Dr. Paradox here," he said as he handed the sheet back to Ralph. "Invite as many people as you can, so we have a better chance of getting someone who truly knows something. Don't invite the dead people. Weed out what you can. We can go over the rest later. I'm going to go and lay down for a bit."

As Cliff was wheeling himself out of the library, Ralph said, "Sure Mr. Preston. I should have a list for you to go over when you get up. I'll shrink it down as far as I can." Ralph was surprised that he was being allowed to make these decisions. Cliff usually reserved that right for himself. He contemplated whether Cliff wasn't concerned, or just didn't have the energy to care. Both ideas troubled him. But he was thankful that this project had invigorated Cliff. He was wheeling himself around again and that was a welcome improvement for both of them.

2

Jack usually enjoyed the fifty-mile drive to town to get his mail. Twice a week he would quickly scan through it, deposit any checks he received, and then get a few perishables from the store and head home. On this day though, the ritual ended. The name in the return address of one letter was oddly familiar: Heathcliff Montgomery Preston. It couldn't be possible. Intrigued, he tore open the envelope.

Cliff Montgomery will grant you an interview with him if you desire one. He will accommodate you on October 7, at 2:30 PM at Preston Manor. Please send required RSVP in the envelope provided. No negotiations of time or meeting location will be considered. Upon receipt of your RSVP, directions to the Manor will be sent to you.

Cliff Montgomery was still alive. It had been eighteen years since Cliff went into seclusion, and at least ten since there had been any news about him. The once world famous author was dead as far as anyone knew. Now Jack knew differently, and it was shocking news. It would be a dream for any other author to be allowed to interview the famous Cliff Montgomery. For Jack it would be traumatic.

It had taken years for him to recover emotionally and financially from what this man had done to him. The years that followed had allowed him to forget those days and move on. Now, in just thirty seconds, he was being forced to start the process all over again. He could feel the animosity burning in his soul like a demonic firestorm.

Jack had originally planned for this to be a quick trip so he could get back and finish the book he was critiquing. As he got out of his car in the driveway he was oblivious to the mid-day August heat, but not the fact that he had forgotten to visit the store. He stopped twenty feet short of the front door and collapsed into the chair next to the koi pond.

In a few minutes the front door opened. Jack knew he had to wipe the frown from his face before his wife saw him. If he didn't, there would be questions, and he was not in the mood to deal with questions. Right now he just wanted to be mad for a while. His wife, Barbara, on the other hand, had a distinct intolerance for anger. She didn't understand it, and Jack loved that about her, even if it did at times make him angry.

"What's up?" he heard her ask, but he couldn't answer her. His brain had vapor-locked. All he could do was frown at her with a look that said 'don't ask!' It was the type of look that years ago would have started an argument. This time she just walked slowly back into the house and closed the door. Jack knew that he was only off the hook for a few minutes. He needed to compose himself before he talked with her about the letter, the frown, and the missing milk. It wouldn't be easy to do, especially with *that day* on his mind.

That Day

As he roared up the driveway, Jack angrily mashed the gas pedal to the floor. A split-second later he was standing on the brake to stop the car before it hit the garage door. At the moment he was more concerned with displaying his anger than preserving his new sports car. Barbara was sure to confront him about his irrational behavior. Fine. He needed to vent his frustration on someone. He slammed the car door just as Barbara rounded the corner of the house.

"What's going on?" she demanded.

"I'm soon to be unemployed, that's what's going on!"

"What?"

"Unemployed, out of a job, you know, like in no more paycheck."

"Why, what did you do?"

"I didn't do anything! Why do you assume that something was my fault?"

"Don't snap at me, just tell me what's going on!"

"Cliff skipped town."

"Skipped town?"

"Yeah, just took off. I think he went into hiding for some reason."

"What makes you say that?"

"Whatever it is, it was planned. He left us all notes telling us what we needed to finish before we could be unemployed."

"You're kidding. Was Mr. Huntley there?"

"Yeah. I'm sure he knows what's up but he's not saying a word, and believe me, some of them were pressing him pretty hard."

"So everyone's gone?"

"No, this was the last day for about half the office. Some of us are going to finish the Bangladesh book, the rest are filing away the other projects in case he wants to start work on them again. Not much got done today though. And I really don't know who'll show up tomorrow."

"Are you going to?" Barbara asked kind of sheepishly.

Jack hung his head and then looked at the car. "I've got to. How else am I going to pay for the 'Vette? You know I was expecting a raise. And I was sure that the bonus on Bangladesh would be at least as big as Sahara. Oh man, this is not good…not good at all."

"No, and it's probably not good for anyone else down there."

Jacks eyes got wide as he remembered everyone's reactions. "You should have seen Jenny."

"Which one was she again?"

"The gal that sorts Cliff's mail."

"The one you call 'smiley eyes'?"

"They weren't smiling today. I went to ask her if Cliff had gotten some strange mail lately, you know, like from a lawyer or a hit man or something."

"Had he?"

"Don't know. She told me that the only letter that concerned her was the one she got from Cliff firing her at the end of the day. She dumped the rest of his mail on the floor and left. I've never seen her that mad."

"From what you told me you'd never seen her mad."

"Nope, just smiles and freckles." As Jack recalled the ugly look in Jenny's pretty eyes he walked over and kicked the bumper on the Corvette.

Disgusted, Barbara said, "Instead of getting angry at it, you better figure out how to pay for it."

'Hey, just back off! Go back to your daisies or whatever. I'll take care of it."

'I'll take care of it.' Nothing he tried to do took care of it, not for the Corvette anyway. With two part-time jobs he kept the house and Barbara took a job to keep food on the table. But there was no way he could even afford the insurance on the Corvette. He lost everything he put in that car, including his pride.

He remembered that he wasn't the only one that had been hurt by Cliff. Everyone that worked for him, other than his personal staff, had been spurned to some degree. It added insult to injury knowing that Cliff didn't seem to care. *'But then, why should he?'* Jack thought to himself. *'The rest of the world loved him. They didn't know him like I did. They loved the way he wrote, but I was the one who wrote it!'*

Jack liked to believe that he had personally written a number of Cliff's books, since technically speaking, he had. He was Cliff's penman. He had been the one that put Cliff's adventures to paper. True, they were Cliff's stories, but Jack was the one that wrote those stories down and made them readable. He was the one putting in the long hours at the keyboard. Because of that, he considered himself to be one of Cliff's most important assets. Unfortunately, that particular ego bubble burst on *that* day. As he thought about *that* day, he regretted having remained so faithful to Cliff.

Despite the verbal abuse that he occasionally received, he had actually considered Cliff to be one of his best friends. In fact, Jack was on a very short list of people that were on a first name basis with Cliff. That may have been why it stung so much when Cliff fired him. Jack felt that he was poised just below the pinnacle of a dynasty, with no heir apparent except himself. The next thing he knew he was filling out forms in an unemployment office, where one fact became painfully obvious. It was the name of Cliff Montgomery on all of the manuscripts that Jack had written. It was Cliff Montgomery that the publisher, editor, and public loved. Without Cliff Montgomery's commendation, Jack was a nobody; a bitter, out of work, nobody.

The only person that would have known Cliff better than Jack would have been his staff of one, Mr. Huntley. The employees all called him "the Staff" because Cliff was constantly leaning on him. They all pitied Mr. Huntley, but they also appreciated him. When Cliff felt like pushing his weight around, Mr. Huntley usually received most of the pressure, and held up under it. When Cliff barked out orders, Mr. Huntley delivered them, usually minus the bite. Jack did not recall anyone ever thanking Mr. Huntley for that, and assumed that was why he showed no concern when he had delivered the termination letters. Mr. Huntley never allowed anyone to get near Cliff, who was never seen in public again. Any messages from Cliff were delivered through e-mails, and were probably written by Mr. Huntley.

As Jack stared at the colorful koi, some important memories slowly returned to him. Barbara loved him enough to come back. God loved him enough to forgive him. The housing market turned around and he finally sold his extravagant home. He started a manuscript editing business that was pleasantly successful. He completed writing a book of his own. And he eventually forgave Cliff, or so he thought.

Barbara was not prepared for the response she got to her question, but she wasn't totally surprised either. She saw Jack get out of the car in the driveway. She saw him stare at the mail, take a few steps, stop, shake his head, and take a few more steps. His usual brisk pace to relief from the summer heat was slow today.

What worried Barbara the most was the frown she saw as he passed the kitchen window. He rarely frowned since he had started doing work he enjoyed. She knew he had just eaten, so the hunger-grumpies were out of the question. The other frown initiating activity was the hammer-meets-finger variety. Something like that would have brought him in the house for sympathy after about ten seconds of yelling. No, this was a full ugly-face frown, something she had not seen for a long time.

She had decided to just make her presence available if he wanted it, and found out very quickly he didn't. For him not to want her sympathy was a very serious heart condition indeed. She knew she had to call on the only one she knew that could truly deal with a situation like this. She sat down in the living room and started to pray.

After a few minutes Jack finally stood up and walked into the house. He could not get rid of the frown, but it didn't matter; Barbara had already seen it. She didn't say a word as he slumped into a recliner and tossed her the invitation. Suddenly he heard her exclaim "Oh, no! He's still alive?" All Jack could do was nod. "After all this time, *now* he wants to meet with you?" He didn't even respond to that question. "Are you thinking about going?"

"I *have* to go!" he snapped. "You *know* that." On the inside Jack was trying to reign in his anger. Considering what was going on in his head, he thought he was doing a pretty good job. Barbara didn't see it that way.

"Why can't you just let it go?" she asked.

"Look, I just need to talk to him once, just once. I just need to know why…" Jack couldn't continue. All he could see was his peaceful existence getting shattered. "Dang I don't need this right now."

"No kidding you don't need it," she scolded. "We're going on vacation in two weeks. Are you going to be able to forget about it while we're on vacation?"

"Hon, I can't talk about it right now. Just let me..." Jack took a slow, deep, angry breath, and went back out to the koi pond.

The heat didn't help Jack's attitude one bit, but the koi did as they kissed the surface of the water. And so did the birds as they took turns calling to each other. Then along came a squirrel that slowly jerked its way past Jack to get a drink out of the pond. The antics of these little critters seemed more flamboyant than usual. It was as if they were saying *'Forget that guy, aren't we cute?'* or *'We don't care about him, why should you?'* They probably just wanted food.

Regardless of the reasons behind their behavior, the distractions were working. Even the smoke from the neighbor's barbecue seemed to draw him out of the dark drama taking place in his mind. He was picturing himself ranting and raving and preaching at an old man and trying to justify doing it. He even felt embarrassed for thinking he needed to. But he knew he did, and he knew he would. Between now and then, he decided to pray that somehow Cliff would have a heart to receive the harsh rebuke Jack was going to deliver to him. And boy was he going to deliver it.

He heard the front door slowly open, and saw his wife of 31 years appear in the doorway. "Are you better now?" she asked. Jack just nodded, aware that he was still wearing the frown. "Well that's good, 'cause I've been praying for you." Jack did appreciate her doing that, but it didn't show. "I think you should go and see Cliff," she added. "Get whatever it is off your chest. Besides, after all this time, maybe he's changed."

As Jack thought about that, he realized that Cliff must have changed somehow. There had to be a reason for the invitation. He was curious now to know what it was.

Jennifer had come to dread the trip to the mailbox. What arrived in it only seemed to add red ink to the ledger book of their life. Even the store coupons required spending money to save any. Then her eyes fell on a letter that shocked her. It had been addressed to Jenny Baker and forwarded from her parents address. 'No one has used my maiden name in years,' she thought. The name Heathcliff Montgomery Preston didn't register with her. She opened it up and found a curious invitation.

Cliff Montgomery will grant you an interview with him if you desire one. He will accommodate you on October 7, at 2:30 PM at Preston Manor. Please send required RSVP in the envelope provided. No negotiations of time or meeting location will be considered. Upon receipt of your RSVP, directions to the Manor will be sent to you.

She started walking slowly toward the house. Suddenly she stopped, looked at the invitation again, and shouted, "Mr. Montgomery?" She knew her husband Robert would never believe it. And he sure wasn't going to like it. She knew he blamed Cliff Montgomery for every financial problem they had.

3

Intermittently for the next two months Jack stewed about his eventual meeting with Cliff. He recalled the years he spent working for that driven man. Back then he had a lot of respect for Cliff, especially for his dedication to finding the facts about whatever it was he was currently obsessed with. He envied the adventures that Cliff went on; even though he knew he would have hated the accompanying hardships. He wasn't sure whether Cliff had a death wish or a James Bond type of coolness toward his own mortality. Whichever it was, Cliff probably spent half of his life in harms way.

Jack recalled that Cliff had an interesting philosophy. Whether it was the dangerous jungles of the Amazon, the scorching heat of the Sahara desert, or the bitter cold of Siberia, *somebody* called it home. Cliff was obsessed with knowing how they ended up in such a place, and what possessed them to stay there when they had opportunity to leave. He would live with them, as *they* were accustomed to living, in an effort to comprehend their loyalty to that region.

Cliff's writings about these various people groups were very compassionate. Because of that, his books were wildly popular in the parts of the world he visited. They were also required reading in a lot of anthropological classrooms.

On the other hand, his *conversations* about these native peoples were scathing. He considered their rituals and beliefs to be the cause of more of their suffering than the land they lived in.

Jack couldn't wait to confront Cliff about his hypocrisy.

Jack also wondered if Mr. Huntley was still hanging around with Cliff. He couldn't be sure, but the invitation had a Cliff-via-Mr. Huntley feel about it. There was a rebuke prepared in Jack's mind for Mr. Huntley as well, but it was formed from disappointment rather than anger.

Barbara had done her best to get Jack to ignore his inner warfare. She had wisely suggested a vacation in Branson, Missouri. The Las Vegas style shows were immensely entertaining and not offensive to their Christian values.

The angry make-believe banter still cropped up on occasion in Jack's mind, but it happened less often as the vacation went on. The most peaceful place for Jack, surprisingly, was the bustle of Silver Dollar City. The shops and displays in this theme park pointed to a simpler life that appealed to him. He longed for the innocence of youth that he tried so hard to escape from when he had it. He decided the best way to get it back was to do something, well, youthful. He decided to ride a roller coaster named *Wildfire*.

For some reason he couldn't convince Barbara to join him. The ride took him twice as high as the trees and then dropped straight down. Jack felt the panic from the soles of his feet to the top of his head. When he got off the ride he was so shaken he could hardly walk. So he just had to ride it again.

The invitation from Cliff had tied Jack's stomach in knots for two weeks. Wildfire had brutally untied those knots in less than a minute. Thoughts of Cliff rarely entered his mind for the rest of the vacation.

Ralph wheeled Cliff into the ornately decorated library at Preston Manor. On a floor plan the room shape resembled a football, with only two curved walls that met at doors on each end. Three intricately carved oriental chairs were clustered in the center of the room, arranged in a circle designed for four. In the center of the open circle was a round marble topped table. The natural beauty of the stone was enhanced by a chandelier overhead, and hidden only by one lone book.

As Cliff was pushed up to the table, he pointed at the book and asked, "Is this the faux book?"

"As phony as can be," replied Ralph, with a play on words that got no response. "That's what you want, right?"

Cliff looked the book over and said, "This will do."

"You still haven't told me what you're doing with this book."

"I'm doing something that I've witnessed in almost every culture that I've encountered. I'm casting lots."

Ralph took the book from him and looked it over. "I don't understand," he said.

"It's like flipping a coin. I'm just doing it my way. Remember the contest that I told you we're going to have?"

"For someone to find a book in this library that they think no one else knows the author of."

"Right. Well, this is the book. Whoever finds this book can sign his own name in it as the author. That person will win the contest and hopefully we will have the person we're looking for."

"But, by chance, that could be anyone," Ralph argued.

"After those Monopoly games, I no longer believe in chance."

Ralph nervously thumbed through the blank book as he avoided eye contact with Cliff. He again felt guilty for suggesting they play those games, and he was even more confused about Cliff's intentions. "I don't understand how this is going to help," he said as he tossed the book on the table.

"Do you remember any of the stories I told you about medicine men, shamans, and witch doctors?"

"Well, yeah, some."

"They do this sort of thing. They do something that should have a random outcome, and they expect spirits of some sort to make it happen a specific way."

"Do you think that's what was happening with the Monopoly games?"

"That's the only explanation I can come up with. If it is, then whatever was changing the numbers on those dice is in this house. That's why I think we can find the answers here. We just need to find someone that's enlightened enough to understand it and reveal it to us. If they are in tune with – whatever it is they get in tune with – they will be able to find this book and know what to do with it."

Ralph was silent for a minute as he carefully considered how to phrase his next question. "Do you think yelling at the spirits is what changed that last game?"

Cliff adjusted himself in his wheelchair and then dropped back into a slumped position. "I don't honestly know. I really didn't expect it to, I was just mad. But now—I just don't know."

"And you think this contest thing is going to produce someone who understands what's going on?"

"Ralph, we've been over this before. Like I said, it may or it may not. I have nothing to lose by trying, and something is urging me to try. I don't know what it is or how to explain it to you."

"And you think Mrs. Preston might have something to do with it?"

"I don't think she's doing it, if that's what you mean."

"I guess I still don't understand what you *are* thinking."

Cliff hated talking about this stuff with anyone, but he knew he needed Ralph's help, and his understanding. "The best way I can explain it is, it's like something is trying to torment me, drive me crazy if it could. I know that's not Gloria. She would never do something like that."

"I know she wouldn't."

"I know you do. But whatever this thing is, I am convinced that it's tormenting me *because* of Gloria. I just can't explain to you why or how I know that." In his mind Cliff was pleading with Ralph to drop the subject. He frantically wanted to avoid revealing the dark secret he had kept for so many years.

"And you think some spiritually enlightened religious person will know?"

"No, I don't know. Ralph, just trust me. I need to do this."

"Okay sir. Where would you like to hide the book?"

"On the bottom row behind the door to the foyer. In the middle of some other books about the same size. Place it so the door hides it when it's open."

Ralph followed all of Cliff's directions, trying to make sure it blended in with the other books. Cliff had never acted this strange before. He hoped it wasn't a harbinger of troubles to come.

"Are you sure you're going to be okay?" Barbara asked.

"Barb, please, I need to get going." Jack responded impatiently.

"But we haven't prayed yet," she snapped back.

The realization of what she said hit him as if she had told him he forgot to put on his pants. The extra moments it took to pray would be well worth the effort. The time had come to meet Cliff, and Jack was going to need all the help he could get, even if just to protect him from himself.

As they sat down on the sofa to pray, Barbara handed him the small bottle of anointing oil. As he anointed them both, Jack said, "Father, thank you for another day, and for all that you have blessed us with. We ask that you again surround us with your hedge of protection, for me as I travel to meet Cliff, and for

Barbara here in this home. We ask that walls surround our property and possessions to stop the enemy's attacks against them. By faith we put on your armor, and ask that you inspect it, that it will be proper for today, *especially* today Lord, as I meet with Cliff. We ask for your wisdom, and a special anointing for this meeting today. We also ask that our physical health would continue, and that our day would progress according to your will. Help us to see and hear what your Spirit is trying to show us and teach us. Thanks Lord. In the power of the name of Jesus, amen."

"Amen!" repeated Barbara. Then she looked him in the eyes and said, "Don't worry about it Jack." Then she tapped his chest and added, "And try to listen more than you talk." Jack agreed with her, but he knew it wouldn't be easy. If God had something to say, he knew he had better be prepared to hear it, and more importantly, share it.

4

The road leading up to the security gate at Preston Manor was littered with news crews. Jack was shocked to see several vans sporting satellite dishes, each with a handful of people around them. There was also a field next to the gate with a number of cars. The location of this place was only a two-hour drive for Jack, but it would have been in the middle of nowhere for most everyone else. Seeing the spectacle around him, Jack knew his chances were slim to none of ever speaking to Cliff alone. Regardless of that, the urgency to be rid of the weight on his shoulders kept him moving toward the manor.

When he showed the guard his invitation at the gate, the guard looked at his little Honda Civic and pointed him through the right hand entrance. This took him on a circuitous route through the trees, and to a parking area near the garage. Only a handful of cars were parked here. Jack wasn't sure if he was a VIP, or he just had a small enough car to take the narrower driveway. He tucked his laptop computer under the passenger seat and headed for the front entrance.

Preston Manor stood rather dauntingly in front of Jack. During the past weeks there had been a lot of rehearsals in his mind regarding this place. How he approached it, how the door opened, and how he responded were all played out. With this many people milling about, none of the scenarios worked.

Just as he rounded the corner of the house, a teen-aged boy almost ran into him. "Whoa, excuse me," Jack said defensively.

The kid looked over his shoulder as he continued running and replied, "No problem!"

As Jack continued toward the front door, he thought the boy looked very familiar. His thoughts were interrupted when a rather rotund man stepped into his path.

"Hey, Watchman, remember me?"

Jack took a few seconds and finally put a name to both the face in front of him and the one that had just streaked past him. "Bill White! How are you doin'?"

"I'm doin' great, how 'bout yourself?"

"Doin' good. Hey, was that your kid that just flew past me?"

"Yeah, my youngest. How could you tell?"

"Oh, just a hunch." The Bill White that Jack remembered more resembled the scrawny kid that almost ran into him, than it did the big man in front of him. "What are you doing these days?"

"Workin' for Nat Geo."

"Really? Still doin' research?"

"Yeah, but it's a whole lot different than it was with Montgomery. It's all electronic now. Digital photographs, word processors, you know."

"Not much field work for you then?"

Naa, almost none. But that's okay. It was getting too political anyway."

Just then a boy landed at their side. "Got it Dad," he said, as he handed a camera to Bill White.

"Is the new memory stick in it?"

"Yeah, and I downloaded this one," he said as he handed it to his dad.

"Well, you didn't need to do that, but, oh, by the way, Trevor, this is Jack Watchman. He was a writer for Mr. Montgomery."

Jack took the cue and held out his hand. "Hi Trevor."

Trevor gave Jack a firm handshake. "A writer, huh? Awesome. Which books did you write in?"

"Oh, Sahara, Amazon, Siberia, you know, most of his last ones."

"Did you do the Viet Nam jungle people one?"

"No, that was before my time."

"Trevor, we should get our seats before someone takes them."

"Sure dad. Nice meetin' ya Mr. Watchman."

Jack watched as Trevor skip-stepped through the crowd. "Nice kid, Bill. Lots of energy."

"Well, he's kind of excited to see Mr. Montgomery. He's read most of his books. He can't believe his old man knows the guy. Hey, you wanna sit with us? Tell you what, go grab yourself a cinnamon roll over there and I'll grab you a seat. There's pop and stuff there too."

Jack looked to where Bill pointed and said, "Sure, that'd be great."

Jennifer felt out of place in this fancy house. She had never known anyone who owned a big house, especially one with a name. She wasn't famous or important like many of these people probably were. She wondered if she looked as insignificant as she felt. At barely five feet tall, she was sure she did. As she sat in a seat near the front, she scanned the room behind her for anyone she might know. She thought sure there would be some-one else from Mr. Montgomery's office. That was so long ago everybody must look different. Then she noticed a tall man by the door that she recognized. He was somebody who used to spend quite a bit of time with Mr. Montgomery. She thought his name was Jack something. She decided to wait until he finished talking to the other guy before she introduced herself. '*Of course, he probably won't know who I am,*' she thought as she continued to scan the room.

Ralph walked up to Cliff, who was sitting quietly at the dining room table. "It sure is a motley bunch of people out there waiting to see you. It appears someone must have leaked an invitation to the public, because there are a *lot* more people than what I invited."

"Are you sure there are enough guards to keep them out of *here?*" Cliff asked.

"More than enough. Plus I have the dogs in here. They're a bit nervous, but they shouldn't bark unless they see someone."

"I sure hope this was the right thing to do."

"So do I. One thing for sure. It will be another adventure!"

"Then *you* write about it," Cliff said sarcastically.

"Maybe I'll do that some day," Ralph said as he walked Cliff out to the conservatory. "But right now I need to go out there and get this thing rolling. I'll have Lloyd send his son Steve back here to guard you. He's not only big, but he gets along with the dogs too."

"Okay, that'd be fine. Mr. Huntley, you better get going."

Hearing his name that way, Ralph knew what it meant. It was time to get serious. "Wish me luck," Ralph said as he walked out of the room.

"I don't believe in luck," Cliff mumbled.

Miss Kempler had seen Jennifer looking around the room. "Would your name be Jenny?" she asked.

"Yes it is. Miss Kempler? Is that you?" Then she held out her arms and gave her a big hug. "It's so good to see somebody I know!"

"Ain't that the truth? Who are all these people anyway?"

"Haven't the foggiest. They look like they're from all over the world. Must be a bunch of people Mr. Montgomery met over the years. Can you believe all the news people? Do you think he's going to talk to all of these people privately? I don't see how he could. I don't see that he's ever going to have time to talk to me. Course, I don't know why he would want to in the first place. Were you surprised when you got an invitation? I sure was." As Jennifer was unloading her entire repertoire of conversation on Miss Kempler, she was interrupted by a rustling sound from one end of the room. It looked like someone was preparing to address the crowd.

Jack had just started dribbling coffee into his cup when a voice behind him said, "Could everyone please find a seat?" He quickly grabbed some sugar and creamer and his once-bitten cinnamon roll and looked for Bill and Trevor. "Could I please have your attention?" boomed one of the hired Pinkerton security officers. Pointing with his thumb to the door behind him, he said, "As I read your name, please proceed to the library through this door." He then read off names in random alphabetical order, as if whoever made the list tried to do it alphabetically from memory and kept having afterthoughts.

At the reading of "Mr. Jack Watchman", Jack finally got to wiggle out of the crowd, past the guard, and into the massive library. It was a huge oblong room with a very long teak table in the center. Both the room and the table were shaped like a football with the ends cut off. The table was plain and there was nothing on it, which was a stark contrast to the ornamentation around the library. There were no chairs at the table, or anywhere else in the room. Jack assumed this had been done to accommodate this number of people, which was about half of the crowd that was in the foyer. As he tried to drink in the surroundings, and for the life of him understand what was going on, he heard an old, but still familiar, voice say "Thank you all for coming."

The voice came from Mr. Huntley, who was still undoubtedly Cliff's main man. Jack and a number of others started to move to greet him, but he held up his hand like a traffic cop. "I am pleased to see a number of faces I recognize," he said, "and I do look forward to catching up on a little bit of lost conversation. However, there are things we need to tend to first, and Mr. Preston would like me to proceed." This was typical behavior for the Staff. He was not a big conversationalist, but when he did talk to you it was with warm consideration and concern. He was the type of person that you could pour your heart out to and bare your soul. That is, until Cliff spoke, at which time Mr. Huntley abruptly ended the conversation, and walked away as if the conversation had never been taking place. It always tended to make one wonder if he had even been listening. Since he was rarely out of earshot of Cliff, most of those in the office seldom gambled to speak to him, though Jack believed many desired to.

"I am sorry to say that Mr. Preston does not have the energy to speak to each one of you personally," said Mr. Huntley, as he slowly walked around the room. "Nor can he meet with you to answer any of your questions. He would like to meet with one of you however. There have been so many requests to speak with him over the years, that he could not decide whom to allow that privilege." It appeared to Jack that the years had not stolen Cliff's egomania completely.

"Mr. Preston has decided to have a sort of contest to see who might be deserving of this honor." At that statement a number of groans were heard around the room that was met by a half irritated, half knowing glance from Mr. Huntley. Speaking a bit louder, he said, "Anyone not willing to participate in this event may leave at any time during the instructions for this contest that I am about to give. When you do, someone from the room you just left will take your place. Those people are being briefed just as you are, and will be prepared to replace you when I am finished." That threat seemed to quiet most of the groaners.

"This contest is specifically to obtain an interview from Mr. Preston, whom you all knew as Cliff Montgomery. If you are strictly on a fact finding mission, Mr. Preston has prepared a half hour long DVD regarding the reasons for his seclusion for the past 18 years. This DVD will begin playing ten minutes after this game officially begins. If you are merely seeking a story, the DVD will provide you with the information you desire in a timelier manner."

At that statement 13 people left, muttering "I don't have time for this!" and "Who does he think he is?" as well as certain unpublishable remarks. After they were gone, Mr. Huntley quieted the remaining attendees and proceeded.

"The rules of the contest are this. First, I will pass around a hat, filled with wooden discs. On each disc is a number. Once you have your number, you will have 10 minutes to negotiate with others in the room to get either a higher or lower number, whichever you think is more important."

"So which *is* more important?" said an older man Jack didn't recognize.

"I am sorry I can't answer that or any other question. The importance of the numbers will become evident after we start. Now, if we may proceed, take a disc and pass the hat around to the others in the room." He then handed the hat to the man with the question and left the room.

One by one they carefully took what looked like a wooden poker chip out of the hat. Actually, the hat made it through about ten careful people, then one person started fishing through the hat looking for a particular number, then another person grabbed it, and finally someone else just dumped the hat on the table where it became a free-for-all. Jack decided that he didn't know whether a high or low number was better; so he just grabbed one, number 54. When he turned it over, a quick, snorting type of laugh overtook him. On the back of the chip were the words "TO IT". It brought back a lot of memories of Cliff yelling, "Whenever you get around to it, Mr. Huntley." Jack didn't think Cliff ever saw these chips. Most people just looked for a chip that suited them, but it did sound a little like the floor of the Stock Exchange just as Mr. Huntley returned to the room.

"Quiet please," he said, to get everyone's attention. "Around this room you will see many books by famous and not so famous authors. Your job is to locate a book whose author you believe to be unknown by anyone else in this room. When you think you know, raise your hand. When I recognize that individual, the rest of you must face the table. When all eyes are facing the table, that person will state the name of the book. Once we have heard the book's title, I will ask if any person can name the author of that book. If no one can name the author, the individual who named the title will have the honor of interviewing Mr. Preston."

After hearing that, a number of people started glancing at the books around them and moving closer to the shelves. "However," Mr. Huntley continued, "if anyone *can* name the author, the person who suggested the title must leave." That statement caused a gasp from some, a curse from others. It also caused 7 more people to straggle out the door, throwing their chips on the table.

"So what are the numbers for?" asked Bill White. Jack remembered that Bill usually was the one to ask the questions that the rest of Cliff's employees either wouldn't ask, or were not quick enough to spit out.

"If five minutes passes," Mr. Huntley continued, as if he hadn't heard the question, "and no one has raised his hand, I will begin to call on you to give the title of a book. You will then have two minutes to do so, while the others continue to scan the library. If you have not given a title within those two minutes, you will be required to leave, and I will call another person. If someone raises their hand, then we will proceed as mentioned before, facing the table."

"So what about these numbers?" asked Bill again.

"I will call on you in the order of the numbers on the chips." Mr. Huntley responded.

"Starting at the top or the bottom?"

"Both actually," answered Mr. Huntley, with a quick smirk on his face. "I will call the lowest remaining number first, then the highest."

At that, everyone looked at each other, many with a vocal noise included, then looked at the remaining chips on the table, that the Pinkerton guard was scooping up.

"By the way," continued Mr. Huntley, "Who has two chips?"

"Watcha talkin' bout'?" said one man. "Someone's got two chips?" asked another.

"Twenty people have left the room, and there are nineteen chips remaining. We have found none on the floor. Who has the missing chip?"

"This guy has it," said Miss Kempler, Cliff's at-the-time young but none-the-less capable personal secretary. "I saw him stick one in his coat pocket. He took one out of the hat, stuck it in his pocket, and then grabbed one later from the table."

While she was talking, Mrs. Hanley, another former researcher standing next to the man, stuck her hand into the coat pocket Miss Kempler had pointed at. The man swung around to hit the pickpocket, until he realized it was a frumpy older woman who looked like she would enjoy hitting him back. She quickly pulled out the chip and tossed it on the table, and then waddle-jumped away from him.

"What do you have to say for yourself, Mr. Bernard?" said Mr. Huntley, in his most condescending tone.

"Make it twenty-one," he snapped, throwing his other chip on the floor, and storming out of the room. "Outta my way!" he yelled at the Pinkerton guarding the door. "Don't waste your time," he told others as he left. Over a dozen people quickly followed him from the foyer, probably reporters wanting to know what just took place. Then the library door closed again.

"Well, I see Mr. Bernard had number 74 and number 9. Being a photo-journalist and not a part of the literary community," Mr. Huntley said, as he paused for effect and for the laughter to die down, "I believe he would have been eliminated soon anyway," at which they all saw a rare Huntley guffaw, stopped just shy of a knee-slapper. It was short lived, but Jack enjoyed it.

"If there are no more questions," he continued, recovering quickly, and indicating in his own way that he wouldn't answer them if there were, "we will bring in the remaining chip recipients." He then waved a crooked finger at the guard, who went back into the entry. No sooner had the door closed than it opened and in came 21 more people, each picking a chip out of the hat that the guard held out to them.

"Lloyd, does everyone now have one chip?" Mr. Huntley asked the guard.

"Yes, sir," he responded, and then handed Mr. Huntley the hat.

"Are there any more questions before we start the contest?"

"Yea," said Mr. Johnson, a reporter from the Times. "What if someone just makes up a title? Or what if the book is real, but isn't in this library?"

"In order to engage in conversation with Mr. Preston, one must produce the book from this library that he used to obtain the interview. Any other questions?" he asked, pausing only a few seconds. "If not, then we will take a fifteen minute break. If you need to use the restroom, do so at this time. This will also be your last opportunity to leave before the start of the competition. During this break, please record your chip number with Lloyd here," he said, as he pointed to the guard at his side. "He will keep your chips if you leave this room, and return them to you when you return. Anyone who is not in this room by...let's see...it's 9:55...let's make it 10:15... will be replaced by someone from the foyer. Lloyd?" When the guard heard his name, he turned and took a notebook and pen that Mr. Huntley was holding out to him. Then a guard opened the door back to the foyer, and Mr. Huntley disappeared out a different door on the other side of the library.

It was an interesting twenty minutes. Everyone leaving the manor, even for a cigarette break was asked to leave their chip with the guard. It seems those left in the foyer had chips that determined what order they replaced those leaving the library. The people in the foyer were instructed in the rules of the game, so Mr. Huntley would not have to repeat himself. They were also told that once the game officially began, those who were left would all be allowed to see a DVD of Mr. Preston. Jack meandered back into the library a little early. The last dozen or so contestants were almost in a full sprint as they tried to beat the chiming Westminster clock in the foyer.

"Everyone, please?" said Mr. Huntley, to silence those who

didn't silence themselves when he walked into the room. "You can begin looking around at the books while Lloyd here counts heads and replaces any missing individuals. I will begin accepting book titles as soon as there is a full complement."

"And exactly what is a full complement?" asked the ever curious Bill White.

"To be precise, eighty one," said Mr. Huntley, as if he had been prepared for that question since the beginning. "The significance of that number will be explained to you on the DVD, or by Mr. Preston himself, if you are so fortunate."

"What DVD?" asked one of the new replacements.

"Upon completion of this contest," he said, ignoring the question, "those of you who have remained, but failed to win an audience with Mr. Preston will be able to view this DVD, and hopefully have your questions answered. This way your time with us today will not have been wasted." At that statement, Mr. Huntley glanced over at the guard, who was just letting two more people into the library. "Lloyd, if these new people have their correct chips, we will be starting."

"Yes sir, Mr. Huntley," Lloyd said, as he took their foyer chips and let them pick new ones out of the hat. He then walked out into the foyer and returned with an ornate throne looking chair, setting it in front of the door Mr. Huntley was always disappearing through. As Mr. Huntley sat down in the chair, he had a look on his face that surprised Jack. There was a seriousness to it that did not fit the game show atmosphere. As silly as all this seemed to everyone else, for some reason known only to Cliff and Mr. Huntley, it was not. Jack prayed in a way that he never felt was proper. He selfishly asked God to somehow help him win this interview.

5

"Let's play!" Mr. Huntley said, in a not-so-good game show voice. "I am now ready to take book titles. Just remember that if I have to call someone's number, you have a maximum of two minutes to give me a title. You must be prepared to produce the book to verify the author. Just to keep people from cheating, I suggest that when you give the title of a book, stand in front of it to block it's view from the rest of us. Anyone intentionally trying to see past that person will be asked to leave. Does that seem fair to everyone?"

There were a number of mumbled objections to having to play this game at all, but none to the rules, so Mr. Huntley continued. "Again, if no one raises their hand and offers a title in five minutes time, I will begin to call numbers. Should anyone need to leave for a while, we will continue without them. However, we will not award the interview until that person returns, or forfeits his chip permanently. I will answer any other questions after we begin. Do I have any titles?" he asked, as he sat down in the fancy chair. Jack could tell that Mr. Huntley wanted to get this over with just as much as the rest of them did.

The first hour eliminated about 40 people very quickly. Some were cocky, thinking they had found the perfect book, only to find someone had read it or already seen it in the library. Most of them though were playing the lottery. They would grab any book off the shelf, name the title, and take their chances. So far it hadn't paid off, except to get them out of the library quickly.

Jack wasn't taking any chances. He was determined to remove a huge weight from his shoulders and break it over Cliff's head, so he kept searching the shelves.

After another hour, about two dozen more people had been eliminated. Enthusiasm had stalled, however, and Mr. Huntley was beginning to call numbers. Those with numbers in the 40's knew they had plenty of time. That was still no relief for their necks that were getting stiff from reading book titles sideways. Jack was getting very fatigued, and was beginning to question if this was all worth it. If a news organization offered five figures for the live interview transcripts, as some had suggested, it probably was. So he decided to stick it out until he found a sure thing.

Then he saw it. A book that he was willing to gamble no one knew the author of. It was probably skipped over by everyone, and even if they saw it, they may not know the author, since his name was not on the cover. Jack raised his hand.

"Mr. Watchman," he heard Mr. Huntley say, with almost a surprised intonation. "Do you have a title for us?"

"Yes I do, Mr. Huntley," he said, with a familiarity that was obvious to all. "The Bible".

"The Book of Books," stated a man in a clerical collar. "The Bible?" asked another person. "No fair!" said another. Someone muttered "Well, that should take care of him." Then a man shot his arm up and said, "I know the author. It was King James!" to which someone added, "No, it wasn't King James, it was the scholars who translated it for him." Meanwhile Jack just stared at Mr. Huntley, slowly shaking his head no.

Wondering what he was up to, Mr. Huntley asked, "You do realize that the Bible is a collection of books, don't you Mr. Watchman?"

Not wanting to give away what he really *was* up to, he answered, "Mr. Huntley, that's the title I have chosen. I would like to proceed with the contest."

"Okay, Mr. Watchman, we will proceed. Does anyone know the author of the Bible? We will have to accept Mr. Watchman's judgment of when you have or have not produced the author. If he does not accept any of your suggestions, he will then be required to produce evidence of who the author is, in order to remain with us. Is that clear, Mr. Watchman?"

"I am ready, Mr. Huntley." Jack was hoping that most of the people in the room would consider this just a joke and that it was his way of getting out of the game. Maybe it was. It had become evident that naming a title was a do-or-die proposition. On the other hand, suggesting an author for the title cost a person nothing. You could guess all you wanted. Jack was just hoping that no one would guess correctly.

"Moses," came one guess. "Apostle Paul," guessed another. "King David," said a couple more people. Jack kept shaking his head no with each answer. One person started rattling off the name of every book in the Bible, and saying anyone of them could be considered the author of it. Finally someone made the suggestion he was hoping for, that he would have to state the author's name, and prove it.

"Does everyone give up?" Jack asked Mr. Huntley, just to be sure.

"Are there no more suggestions for an author?" asked Mr. Huntley, restating Jack's question.

"Is it fair to use a book with more than one author?" asked Bill White. "I mean, what if I chose the Readers Digest condensed book collection, or Encyclopedia Britannica, or something. What then? I thought we had to produce a book with a single author."

"You are required to produce the author, not the publisher," responded Mr. Huntley. "Readers Digest would be the publisher.

I cannot rule in Mr. Watchman's case until I have heard his response to the request that he produce an author. Does anyone object to him doing that, and if so, do you have a suggestion yourself?"

Although some of them thought Jack was pulling some sort of trick, most just wanted to get out of there, and decided that he did too. No matter what author he chose, they assumed he couldn't prove it, so he was soon to be relieved of his chip.

"Mr. Watchman, I hear no objections," said Mr. Huntley. "Would you now tell us who you believe to be the author of the Bible?"

Nervous but determined, Jack looked directly at Mr. Huntley and said "Jesus!"

"I challenge that!" said the man in the clerical collar so quickly that Jack assumed he was expecting what he was going to say. "The Bible is a collection of smaller books. Although many of these books were written about Jesus, there is no evidence whatsoever that he wrote any of them."

"I have to agree with Reverend Davis," said someone else that Jack did not recognize.

"I'm sorry," said Mr. Huntley. "I remember Reverend Davis as the chaplain at the hospital, but I don't recognize you."

"That's okay," said the man. "I'm really not sure why I was invited anyway. But I considered it an honor I couldn't pass up. I was fond of Mr. Montgomery's books and read a number of them when I was a missionary. My name is Rick Holstein. I'm the Pastor of a Lutheran church in Medford."

"Well, hello Pastor Holstein, glad you could make it. I cannot at this time divulge why we invited you, but rest assured it was intentional. Was there something you wanted to add to what the reverend was saying?"

"Oh, well, I probably won't be saying anything that Reverend

Davis wouldn't say. I just wanted to mention that it would be more appropriate to say that God wrote the Bible."

"Now wait a minute," said Reverend Davis. "I don't know that I agree with that either. I don't believe that Mr. Watchman can prove that either God or Jesus could be considered the sole author of the Bible. After all, Mr. Huntley, that is what you are after, is it not, the sole author of the book?"

"Wait a minute; I think you're wrong there," Pastor Holstein scolded. "How can you say God wasn't the author? Second Timothy three sixteen says that all scripture is given by God, so I believe that makes him the author."

At that statement Mr. Huntley held up his hand. Everyone in the room turned to look at him, unsure whether he was doing so as a referee or because he wanted to speak. At first he was just silent, staring down at the teak conference table. Then he turned to Jack and said, "I don't know for sure if either of these two have proved their point, or that you have proved yours either. Do you have something to say that can support your claim as well as answering your critics?"

"First of all, I need to clarify something," said Jack. "All I need to do officially, to win this so called contest that is, is to prove my claim that Jesus is the author of the Bible. Is that correct?"

"That, uh, that is correct," stammered Mr. Huntley.

"Whether I agree or disagree with these two?" Jack asked.

"I don't understand what you mean, but if you prove your point, it doesn't matter how that relates to what they are talking about. However, you do have to prove your point to the satisfaction of the judging committee."

Not wanting to give away his strategy, but trying to make sure his strategy would work, Jack responded, "Since I am playing this game for the chance to interview Mr. Preston, I would prefer that he be the final judge as to it's relevant worth."

Mr. Huntley gave a small tell-tale smile and said, "He *is* the judging committee." That was precisely what Jack was counting on.

"First of all, I will have to agree with Pastor Holstein." Jack said as he grabbed the Bible from the shelf. He found the verse that the pastor had quoted, and handed the open book to Mr. Huntley. "If you look at that verse in second Timothy," he added, as he pointed to the bottom of the farthest left column, "you will see that it does say in verse sixteen that all scripture is given by inspiration of God."

"Okay, I see that," said Mr. Huntley. "How does that support your statement?"

"That still doesn't prove that Jesus is the author, which is what Mr. Watchman claims," argued Reverend Davis.

"He's right," said Mr. Huntley.

"Just let me finish," said Jack. "I absolutely agree that God inspired everything written in the Bible. However, if you would, find the first chapter of the gospel of John." Jack waited a moment while Mr. Huntley thumbed through and found the chapter he mentioned. "If you have found that chapter, read the first part of verse 14."

Mr. Huntley searched for a second and then said, "And the word became flesh and dwelt among us."

"If I could, I would like to ask these two that are challenging me, who is it that the author is referring to here as 'the Word'?" Jack asked, looking toward the other end of the table where they stood.

"Jesus," answered Pastor Holstein. "I believe that's evident in the following verses." Reverend Davis agreed with a feeble nod of his head.

"Then I believe my statement still stands," said Jack "because I believe that God is the author of the Bible, and I believe that

Jesus is God, based on the first verse of this same chapter that states 'In the beginning was the Word, and the Word was with God, and the Word *was* God.' I believe it would follow then that all scripture is given by inspiration of Jesus."

"I still don't agree with that," said the Reverend so quickly that it appeared he knew what Jack would say. "We know the first five books of the Bible were written by Moses, the Psalms were written by King David, and much of the New Testament was written by the Apostle Paul. In Exodus it says the Ten Commandments were inscribed on stone by the finger of God. Beyond that, I don't believe that Mr. Watchman can prove that Jesus wrote the whole Bible himself."

As prepared as the Reverend was to challenge him, Jack was prepared to respond. "I did not say Jesus *wrote* the Bible, I said he was the *author*." This was Jack's chance to play his ace in the hole. The one advantage he had over everyone else in the room was his understanding of Cliff Montgomery. "Mr. Huntley, since I am playing for the chance to speak with Mr. Preston, I ask that only he be the judge of that. What I submit to you, and ask that you take to him to judge, is that the men that the fine Reverend here said wrote parts of the Bible, were not the authors of the Bible, nor authors of individual books within the Bible. They were merely Gods penmen, just as I was once Mr. Montgomery's penman. Just as Cliff was the author of his books, and I was merely a writer, so Jesus was the author of Genesis, and not Moses."

All eyes looked to Mr. Huntley for his response, while Jack looked at the Reverend. The blush in the Reverend's cheeks indicated he was moved by what Jack had just said, but to what, Jack didn't know. His grinding teeth indicated anger, his bowed head maybe shame. Jack had not intended to slam him personally. He had been in the Reverend's position once. He knew how it felt.

Mr. Huntley just stared at the Bible in his hand. After a few moments, he said, "I believe Mr. Preston will have to make this judgment call. I hope that all of you, especially you, Mr. Watchman, will willingly abide by his decision."

With that statement he motioned to the guard and pointed at his chair. "We will now take a recess of undetermined length. Once the guard has notified you of my return, you will have five minutes to return to this room. Please, do not stray too far without telling one of the guards of your whereabouts." Then he walked out of the room, and Lloyd put the chair back in front of the door, and sat in it himself.

Several people walked over and handed Lloyd their chips and left. Most of the others left the room just to take a walk or grab a cigarette. Jack on the other hand was lost in thought. He had just realized that he had admitted something to everyone that he formerly would not admit to himself. He had confessed that Cliff truly was the author of his books. Jack, as the writer, was just a tool. Anyone could have been the writer, though some may have been better at it than others. Cliff would only have had to deal with different people differently to get his desired results. It did mean something that Cliff had chosen him to be his main writer, but Jack honestly never deserved the title of author. Suddenly, Jack's primary fuse had fizzled, and his reason for exploding at the sight of Cliff was beginning to go dead. The only fire remaining in him came from all of the unanswered questions.

6

"Whattaya think'll happen?" said a voice behind Jack. "Don't really know," he replied. The woman he was speaking to appeared to be making more than just small talk. "Should I know you?" Jack asked.

"You probably don't remember me," she replied. "My name is Jennifer Lynn. I worked for Mr. Montgomery, uh, Preston, opening mail."

"Jenny?" Jack said, looking for the freckles he remembered. "Jenny Baker?"

"Use to be," she answered.

"Cliff sent you an invitation?"

"Believe me; I was more surprised than you. I didn't even think he ever noticed me. Then when he fired me I thought I'd done something wrong. I still don't know what to think."

"Well, don't feel bad. I didn't last much longer than you," he said, trying to console her.

"But, except for the Staff, I thought you were his main man."

"So you called Mr. Huntley that too, huh?"

"Well, yeah, but not to his face. I just did it 'cause everyone else did. I don't even know why everyone called him that."

"We all called him that because Cliff was always leaning on him. You know, like a shepherd leans on his staff? A staff is like a cane, or a big stick?" He could tell by the puzzled look on her face that she wasn't getting it, but her nodding head was trying to convince him she was. "So, you're married now?" he asked, trying to change the subject.

"Yes, to Robert Lynn. He worked at the publisher. I used to see him when I would pick up the mail for Mr. Montgomery. He was pretty mad when I got fired. He wrote to Mr. Montgomery quite a few times, but never got an answer."

"None of us ever got an answer," lamented Jack. "Not from Cliff or Mr. Huntley. I don't think the publisher ever heard anything either."

"No, they didn't. Robert said they sent his mail to some post office box, but they never would tell him anything else, and he didn't think they knew.

"I take it your husband didn't get an invitation?"

"No, and he wanted to throw away mine… Mr. Watchman, could you do me a favor? If you get to see Mr. Montgomery, could you ask him if he remembers me? He probably doesn't but….I'd still like to know….why he fired me that is….and what happened to him. I, uh, I can give you my phone number. Could you? Please?"

"Sure, Jenny, if I see him; after I ask him why he fired me." Jack thought it was good to see her somber face break a smile. In fact, with the smile she looked young enough for him to recognize the young woman he saw at the mail desk so many years ago.

Ralph walked in to the conservatory looking for Cliff and found Lloyd's son Steve staring out the window. When he located Cliff in the kitchen he asked him, "What's going on?"

"Steve saw someone sneaking through the trees out back."

"Don't worry," came a low voice from the conservatory. "I called front security. They found him. They're holding his camera till this is over."

Ralph said to Cliff, "That's probably a good idea." Then he

yelled toward the conservatory, "I'll take care of Mr. Preston for a few minutes."

Realizing they wanted some privacy, Steve walked toward the library door and said, "If you need me, just tell my dad. He'll know where I am."

"Sure, thanks Steve," Ralph said with a wave of his hand. He then pulled up a chair in the dining room as Cliff wheeled himself out of the kitchen.

"So, you have some news for me," Cliff asked?

"Yeah, but not what you expected."

"Someone found the book?"

"Nope."

"Then why are you in here?"

"Someone found a different one; and you won't believe who that someone is."

Tired and impatient, Cliff hung his head and asked, "Who is it, Ralph?"

"Jack Watchman."

Cliff didn't move for a second, then he lifted his head and stared at Ralph. "I don't remember that we invited him."

"We didn't. He must have used someone else's invitation. Maybe he's standing in for someone else. We did allow that you know."

"I don't believe it. Jack Watchman. How strange." Cliff seemed to drift into another place and time. Then he suddenly caught himself and asked, "What about the book?"

"Well, that's even stranger. The book is very familiar, but nobody could come up with the name of the author."

"If it was in my library, I should know it. In fact, so should you. What was the book?"

Ralph paused for effect, looked at Cliff over the top of his glasses and said, "The Bible."

"The Bible?" Cliff asked in amazement. "So who is supposed to be the author, King James?"

"No, that one was tried. He says Jesus was the author."

"The book was *about* Jesus. He wasn't the author. He wasn't even around when the first part was written. What's Jack thinking?"

"He says God was the author of the Bible and Jesus is God."

"Religious garbage," Cliff fumed.

"He showed me a verse in the Bible that he says confirms it, and a couple of clergymen out there agreed with it."

"So what? I may not have read the Bible, but you and I both know that it was written by a bunch of different people, and translated by a whole lot more."

"He told me to tell you that those men were just God's penmen, just like he was your penman; and you were the real author of your books, not him."

"Oh, that's tricky," Cliff said in disgust. "Okay, so you said he showed you a verse. Let's see it."

"Actually, he showed me two," Ralph said as he walked toward the library to get the Bible.

Jack and Jennifer both heard the door latch turn, and the door open 3 inches and into the chair holding Lloyd. As he was trying to move the chair out of the way, they heard Mr. Huntley say through the narrow door opening, "Please hand me that Bible there, will you?" Lloyd handed Mr. Huntley the Bible and then the door closed, without either of them ever seeing Mr. Huntley.

"I don't know if that's a good sign or a bad one," Jack said.

"If he wants to look at the Bible, it has to be good," said Jennifer. "Well, that's what I believe anyway."

"And I've met some people who can study the Bible for hours

and still mess it up." Jack saw Jennifer's countenance drop when he said that, so he added, "but let's hope that God can make them see it right."

"For your sake, I'll be praying that way," Jennifer said with a smile.

"Thanks Jenny, I appreciate that." And he certainly did.

Ralph walked briskly back into the dining room, thumbing through the Bible as he did. "Here's the verse he was talking about. It's in John chapter one, verse, uh, verse fourteen. Here, I'll let you read it. And if you don't mind, I really need to visit the boy's room."

"Sure, fine, go ahead. Wait—what was the other verse?"

"It was, uh, John three sixteen, uh, second Timothy three sixteen. It was second Timothy, chapter three, verse sixteen." Ralph's voice kept getting louder as he walked further down the hallway.

Cliff looked until he found the verse in John that Ralph mentioned. He read, 'the Word became flesh and dwelt among us'. *That can't be right*, he thought to himself. *It doesn't say anything about Jesus being the author.* He then started thumbing through the Bible looking for the other verse. Suddenly he stopped looking, and just stared at a particular verse. He was still staring at it when Ralph returned. "Go tell Watchman he won."

"What, just like that?" Ralph asked.

"Yes, just like that. Go tell him he won, get rid of everyone else, and bring him in here. We'll discuss why later."

"Okay sir, if you say so." Ralph knew the tone of voice. Cliff's mind was made up, end of story. He walked over to the library door again, banged it into the Lloyd-filled chair again, and told Lloyd to gather the people together. He then went back to see Cliff one more time to get an understanding of what to tell the other contestants.

"Tell them to watch the DVD and go home," Cliff responded to Ralph's questions. "That's what you told them would happen, isn't it?"

"Yes it is, but what should I tell them if they ask questions?"

"Just tell them I've seen what Jack wanted me to see and I accept what he claims, or something like that. Just go do it, you'll think of something."

Ralph sat quietly in the dining room for a few minutes, then nervously got up and went into the conservatory to think. He knew that for some reason Jack wanted to interview Cliff. How was Jack going to react when he found out *their* true motives. How would Cliff react if Jack was no help to them at all. Was it going to be as ugly trying to get these two together as it was to keep them apart so many years ago? And why was he the one in the middle again?

Jack and Jennifer were still talking when they heard Mr. Huntley tell the guard to bring everybody together. "Well Jenny, I guess this is goodbye, one way or another."

"It doesn't have to be for forever. I gave you my phone number, didn't I? Oh no, wait, I didn't. Here, let me write it down for you. I'll just use the back of this invitation. I don't need it anymore anyway. If you do get to talk with him, please call me if you get to ask him about…you know…all that stuff we talked about. And if you gotta leave, call me later and I'll tell you what happened after you left. Okay?"

"Sure. Tell you what. I'll call you first of next week regardless of what happens. Okay?"

"Okay big guy, it's a deal. I'm home all day Monday, call anytime."

"Okay, Monday it is."

"Good, Monday, now, if I can just find a pen."

It was almost ten minutes after they were all sealed into the library before Mr. Huntley returned. He had on his usual poker face, but he seemed like he was a little uncomfortable with what he was about to say. "The decision has been made by Mr. Preston regarding Mr. Watchman's claim that Jesus is the author of the Bible."

Jack didn't think this sounded good. He glanced at Jennifer, but she seemed focused on what Mr. Huntley was saying.

"The debate regarding the existence of God has been bantered around for centuries. However, the passage that Mr. Watchman made reference to can be considered the same as the authors name on the front of a book. Jack's arguments say that Jesus wrote the Bible, and for the sake of this contest, Mr. Preston accepts that." That statement brought a lot of angry comments and flying round "TO IT" chips. Mr. Huntley just raised his voice and continued. "Mr. Watchman, please wait here in the library until I return. The rest of you please follow me back into the foyer. Lloyd, make sure that Mr. Watchman is comfortable, and that everyone else finds their way out to the foyer."

Mr. Huntley ignored all of the protests as he walked into the foyer. A number of people stopped to shake Jack's hand before they left. Jenny shoved a piece of paper in his hand, which he in turn put in his wallet without reading. As she walked away through the foyer she gave Jack a thumb's up. All Jack saw in the crowd was the thumb, part of an arm, and the top of a strawberry blond head, but that was enough.

Through the door Jack could hear Mr. Huntley thanking everyone for coming, and to please stay long enough to watch the DVD of Mr. Preston, which he hoped would answer their concerns regarding him. Jack could still hear a few people protesting as Mr. Huntley returned to the library. As he came in, Jack got up out of the throne-chair that Lloyd had beckoned him into. This time Mr. Huntley's hand went out, not up.

"Jack, I'm glad to see you. How's Barbara?" It was almost as if he hadn't even seen Jack for the past six hours.

"She's doing well, Mr. Huntley..."

"Well, what about kids, did you two ever have any?"

"No, we never did. We..."

"That's too bad, you would have made great parents."

"Well, we never tried not to. But, then again, we never felt robbed by not having any. We always had each other and we were busy enough without having any little Watchman's."

"Yeah, well, I guess I was always too busy to get married. But I enjoyed watching my sister's kids grow up."

"I didn't know you had a sister."

"Yup. Younger. And cuter," he said, laughing and slapping Jack's shoulder. "Anyway, I don't think you came here to talk to me. We shouldn't keep Mr. Preston waiting." The thought came to Jack that he would probably be more comfortable talking to Mr. Huntley than to Cliff. "Lloyd, you may go help the others in the foyer. Please lock the library door as you leave."

The conservatory they walked into from the library was absolutely stunning. There was ornate wood trim around the windows that was almost completely hidden behind a jungle of plants, most of them tropical. Jack recognized huge banana trees, tree philodendrons, and palms of various types. There was a wall of orchids on one side and a collection of bonsai trees. "This place is really something," he finally had to say.

"Yes, Mr. Preston built me a wonderful place to put all my plants."

"You live here?"

"Oh, I've always lived with Mr. Preston. Ever since I was a kid."

"You have?"

"Yes, I have."

"But I'd been to your place before, you know, the apartment on Fourth St.?"

"Oh, yes, there. I kept that place for when I needed to get away from Mr. Preston for a while. But then sometimes Mr. Preston would use it to get away from me," he said, with another laugh.

"I never, none of us, I don't think, ever knew you lived with Cliff."

"Probably because I never socialized much with those of you I worked with. I'm sorry about that Jack. Nothing personal. I just had other interests."

"So how did you first get together with Cliff? I mean, you said you were a kid. Were you adopted, or what?"

"Oh no, I was never adopted. Not officially anyway. No, I was just a neighbor kid that, well, I suppose I should have Mr. Preston tell you what he would care to about that. Let's go see him. He'll meet you in the next room."

They walked from the conservatory through a sliding wood door into a smaller, but just as ornate, room, stacked high with bookshelves containing more of what looked like interesting artifacts than there were books. This was Cliff's trophy room. He wasn't a big game hunter, so his trophies were native head dresses, pottery, figurines, and other things he had collected from his travels. There were also a lot of pictures of him with people, probably important people in some other culture. Looking out through some tall slender windows, Jack was admiring the courtyard outside, when he heard a barely familiar voice say, "Jack, have a seat."

7

At the sound of the voice, Jack turned to see Cliff staring at him from a wheelchair. He didn't know quite how to approach him, or what to say, so he decided to just try and be himself.

Meeting Cliff after all these years filled him with kind of a nervous anger. Trying not to let it show he asked, "Hello, Cliff. How have you been?" He felt a little hypocritical asking it, but in some ways he *was* curious. A part of him was concerned for his well being, while another part hoped Cliff had suffered. He could tell the years had taken their toll, but sometimes the how and the why tell more than the appearance reveals.

"I have had my up and downs, how about you?"

"Same here. But all things considered, the ups have prevailed."

"When would you like to get started?" Cliff asked rather abruptly.

"I don't know," Jack responded. "Was there something you had *planned* to tell me, or do I get to ask a lot of my own questions?" Jack had determined that he was going to be as blunt and to the point as Cliff had always been with him. He could feel the anger, although calmed by 2 decades of time, still creeping to the surface. Cliff was going to get hit with the hard questions that Jack had never gotten an answer to way back when, regardless of his age or condition.

"Ask all the questions you want, Jack. I will answer all that I can. If you don't mind, though, Mr. Huntley will remain with us.

Any questions that he can answer, he will. That way I will save my strength for when it's required."

"That would be fine. In fact, the first question I will ask should be quite simple for you to answer," he said, looking over at Mr. Huntley. "Could you please finish telling me how you met Cliff, and why you've been so devoted to him all these years?" What Jack really wanted to ask was, 'How could you have been so devoted to Cliff as to treat the rest of us so badly?' He couldn't seem to phrase the question that way.

Mr. Huntley looked over at Cliff, and Cliff gave him an almost imperceptible nod, as if he was determined to allow Mr. Huntley to do something he himself had determined not to. "As I was starting to tell you," Mr. Huntley began, "I was just a teenager when I first met Mr. Preston. I actually met Mrs. Preston first. I was about fourteen when she called to me through the fence, 'cause I lived next door. She asked if I wouldn't mind helping her do a few things in the yard. I just went over to help her 'cause she needed it. I didn't expect to get paid. I'd never had a job before. Anyway, I worked for her all day; they had a big fancy yard. When I went to leave, she handed me a five dollar bill. That was a lot of money back then. After that I always hung out on their side of our yard, hoping she would call me over again. And she did, a lot."

"I don't think I ever remember you saying you were married, Cliff. What happened? Did she leave you or what?" As he asked that, Mr. Huntley looked at Cliff, but Cliff just turned his wheelchair a little and faced the conservatory. So Jack turned and looked to Mr. Huntley for the answer.

"Mrs. Preston would never have left him." said Mr. Huntley, obviously in defense of Cliff. "No, it was nothing like that, Jack. One day there was a terrible storm coming. Mrs. Preston called our house and asked me to come over and help her put the cushions from the patio furniture in the storage shed before it started raining. I was just taking in the last bunch when I heard an explosion. I ran out and saw branches and leaves all over the yard. I didn't know what had happened. Then I saw M-Mrs. ..." As his face contorted with emotion, Mr. Huntley turned to face the conservatory himself. After a few moments he continued, "Mrs. Preston was lying on the ground. Half of her clothes were blown off. Lightning had hit the big leaf maple tree that hung over one edge of the patio, and struck her too. I ran to her and... she was... moaning...and squirming. I got scared and ran home and told my mom what had happened. She had heard the noise, so she yelled at me to call an ambulance, while she ran to help Mrs. Preston."

Jack could tell that after all these years it was still difficult for Mr. Huntley to talk about it. "I take it she didn't survive," he said, trying to help him continue.

"She did, for a couple of weeks," he said, pausing. "That's what was so hard. She was so badly burned, and in so much pain." Mr. Huntley fell silent again. Then he reached over to Cliff, who now had his back to him, and put a hand on his shoulder. Cliff didn't move for a while, and then nodded again. "Mr. Preston was in Africa at the time, doing research for a book. He couldn't get home in time. We tried to reach him, but, well, she was in a coma by the time he returned, and died a couple days later."

Mr. Huntley went silent, and Cliff just stared at the conservatory. "What he didn't tell you," Cliff said, eventually breaking the silence, "is that this boy never left Gloria's side. For two weeks he was there, and I wasn't. I sort of fell apart after she died. This...young...seventeen year old man, took care of me. Me, Cliff Montgomery, world adventurer. For almost a year he kept up my yard, my house. He even brought me food his mother made. I never paid him. Never thought about it."

The room went silent again. Jack didn't know what to say. Finally Mr. Huntley spoke. "I really didn't mind helping. In fact, I was stalling. Mrs. Preston, before she went into the coma, had told me to tell Mr. Preston not to let this accident stop him from writing. She loved his writing long before the rest of the world did. She was afraid he would do exactly what he was doing. But I was afraid to talk to him. I had hardly ever talked to him. I was always hoping he would say something first, but he never did."

"Then the notice came from the publisher," Cliff added.

"Yes, the notice from the publisher finally forced the issue. Mr. Preston wasn't returning their calls or letters. They were waiting for the Africa book. They were pretty upset. They had given Mr. Preston a healthy advance..."

"Ah, it wasn't much at all," said Cliff.

"It would have been a lot to me," said Mr. Huntley. "Anyway, Mr. Preston said something that made me mad, and I guess I kinda snapped."

"I'll never write again!" said Cliff, as if recalling a shameful memory.

"When he said that, it was as if I saw Mrs. Preston again, in all her pain, struggling to tell me to stop him. I started screaming at him that he was a fool. He lost the best thing in his life, and now he was going to throw away the rest of it," said Mr. Huntley, the passion of the moment creeping into his voice. "And I told him Mrs. Preston would hate him for it."

"I kicked him out of my house," said Cliff. "But the kid had a lot of guts. He kept coming to my door until the reality of what he said sunk in. No one else did. He finally told me that he would take care of the house while I was writing. It was right then that I realized that he had already been doing that. I felt pretty embarrassed, and very grateful. I don't think I would be where I am, if Mr. Huntley hadn't verbally popped me upside the head back then."

"That brings up another question," Jack said. "Why, after all these years, don't you call each other by your first names? I mean, you always let *me* call you Cliff."

"When I finally did start writing again, I had this young man contact the publisher for me," said Cliff, pointing to his Staff. "A new publisher. I had somewhat burned my bridges with the other one. All I insisted on was that he always refer to me as Mr. Montgomery when he was doing book business. To help him remember to do that, I always called him Mr. Huntley, rather than Ralphy."

"*Ralphy?*" Jack said, looking at Mr. Huntley.

"I still prefer Mr. Huntley, if you don't mind."

"*Ralphy?*" he repeated.

"I have a question for you, Jack," said Cliff, running interference for Mr. Huntley.

"What is that, *Mr. Montgomery?*" Jack asked, in a kind of chiding way.

"What is it that you really came here to ask me?" This was typical direct-and-to-the-point Cliff-speak.

"I wanted to know what happened to cause you to drop out of the writing business. You hurt a lot of people when you did that, and didn't give any of us the satisfaction of knowing why." Jack was still surprised to hear his tongue speaking much more civilly than his mind really wanted it to.

"I got ALS, Lou Gehrig's disease. It put me in this wheelchair. Doctors don't know why it hasn't killed me. Within a few months I was having trouble walking, and I couldn't write. What good is a writer that can't write? They said pretty soon I would start to have trouble speaking. In fact, they only gave me two to five years to live. I tried to quickly finish the books I had started before that happened. For some reason it never did kill me. I even learned to walk again for a while. But I never could write very well. Finishing the books kept the publisher off my back. I returned the advance on a few.

"But Cliff, you still had us to help you," Jack protested. "You could have dictated the books to us. We could have found a way to make it work."

"You don't understand, Jack. I organized all my books with hand-written notes that you never saw. It just wouldn't have worked for me. I was a proud man. I wanted the world to remember the great Cliff Montgomery, not the crippled Heathcliff Preston. Mr. Huntley here protected me all that time as well. Besides, I never knew I'd live this long. No one did."

"We know what we did was wrong," said Mr. Huntley. "But once it was done, we couldn't come up with a clean way to reverse it."

"Until you came up with this contest, huh?" Jack asked.

"Well, no, we didn't think this little contest would heal past wounds."

"I'm dying Jack," confessed Cliff, rather abruptly. "Cancer. Doctors are more convinced this time. They guarantee me I won't reach my goal."

"And what is your goal?"

"Immortality."

Jack looked at Cliff to see if he was serious or not. Cliff kept his poker face, but Mr. Huntley couldn't. Out of the corner of his eye Jack saw a grin creeping across Mr. Huntley's face. He decided to call Cliff's bluff. "Don't expect me to help you with that," Jack chided. "Cause even if I could, you'd be the last person I'd want to share it with."

"Touché," Cliff conceded. "To be honest, I was hoping to live to be a hundred."

"So how old are you now?"

"Eighty one."

Recalling a bit of trivia, Jack asked, "Is that why there were 81 of us competing for an interview with you?"

Cliff and Ralph just looked at each other and laughed. "The only reason we did that was to limit it to *some* number," said Mr. Huntley. "We know the media. They want a story. If we don't give them a human interest angle, they will probably make one up that we don't like. Mr. Preston originally never wanted anyone to know about his aspirations to reach one hundred. He was afraid it would jinx his chances."

"So what changed your mind?" he asked, looking at Cliff.

"I don't believe in chance any more," said Cliff, with a penetrating stare.

"Just what exactly is that supposed to mean?" asked Jack.

"Why did you choose the Bible as your title?" he asked, with the same unnerving stare.

"I was taking a chance that no one else understood what I did."

"About what?" interjected Mr. Huntley.

"About the Bible, and about my relationship with Cliff," he answered.

"Is that why you appealed to Mr. Preston to be the judge?"

"Precisely. I figured Cliff was making up the rules, so he might be impressed by my submittal. Whatever the reason, it appears to have worked."

"So it has," responded Cliff. "But do you believe it was by chance?"

"Not entirely. But what are you driving at, Cliff?" he asked, trying to figure out why he was getting the stare down. Besides, Jack thought that he was supposed to be interviewing Cliff.

"Does it appear to you like I've lost some of my mental faculties?" asked Cliff.

"Well, no. But then I haven't seen you for quite a while. I

suppose Mr. Huntley here could answer that better."

"Well, I haven't, and Mr. Huntley here will agree, won't you?"

"Absolutely," said Mr. Huntley, in a very convincing manner.

"This cursed disease took the bounce out of my step and the words out of my hands," said Cliff, making motions in the air like he was writing. "But my mind and my speech have remained sound. I need to tell you a story that will make you think that I've taken total leave of my senses. I need you to look beyond the bizarre nature of what I am about to tell you, and to give me your best explanation of what happened."

Jack could tell by the fact that he was now also getting the stare from Mr. Huntley, that whatever it was that happened concerned him as well. "You have my word that I'll try," he responded honestly.

"Fine. Good enough," said Cliff. "Jack, all my life I have considered myself agnostic. I didn't know if there were gods or ghosts or any kind of spirits out there, and I didn't care. I was too busy to waste my time in a church or doing some strange ritual to appease some idol. In fact, I thought religious rituals were mostly harmful, if not a total waste of effort. Something happened a few months ago that made Mr. Huntley and I start to wonder whether we should consider becoming religious."

At that statement, Jack looked at Mr. Huntley and asked, "What might that be, a close brush with death or something?"

"No," said Mr. Huntley. "Don't laugh; it was a game of Monopoly."

8

"Monopoly?" Jack asked, kind of caught off guard. "You mean the board game? With the money and hotels and Boardwalk and stuff?"

"Exactly," said Mr. Huntley. "So you've played it?"

"Only probably a hundred times. Who hasn't?"

"How long does it take to play a game, usually?" he asked.

"Oh, you know, about two or three hours. One time a cousin and I played off and on for almost a week before we finished a game."

"Have you ever finished one in twenty minutes?" he asked, again with the stare.

"Not that I remember. I never paid much attention how long it took. But we usually wouldn't start a game unless we had all afternoon to play it. And it usually took all afternoon."

"Well, Mr. Preston and I did."

Somehow Jack just couldn't picture those two playing Monopoly. He hadn't played it much himself since he grew up. He didn't have the time. "Somebody must have had real bad luck, or the other person real good luck. Which was which?"

"I lost," said Cliff.

"In twenty minutes?"

"That's right, in twenty minutes," stated Mr. Huntley, somewhat triumphantly. "Every time Mr. Preston would roll the dice, he would land on a property that I just bought. If he didn't, he would land on luxury tax or something. Even when we landed on Chance, he always had to pay, and I always got money."

"That sounds strange," Jack said, kind of incredulously.

"It didn't seem strange to me," said Mr. Huntley. "I kind of liked it. I usually lost more often than I won anyway. Mr. Preston insisted on playing another game, since we still had the whole afternoon."

"So who won that one?" asked Jack.

"I did," said Mr. Huntley again, "in about twenty minutes."

"Closer to fifteen." muttered Cliff.

Mr. Huntley gave Cliff a glance and continued. "The same thing happened. Mr. Preston never got to buy any property because he always landed on one I owned. I was enjoying it."

"I wasn't," said Cliff. "I insisted we play another game. I think Mr. Huntley was a little hesitant; thinking two Monopoly games in one afternoon was plenty. But I just had to play another."

"So, what happened?"

"Same thing."

"You're kidding. You lost again? In twenty minutes?"

"Yes, he did," injected Mr. Huntley. "By this time I was as spooked by the whole thing as Mr. Preston was."

"I don't know if I was as spooked as I was angry," said Cliff. "I got mad and yelled at the air 'Whatever you are that's messing with this game, leave it alone and get out of this house!' I think I sort of scared poor Mr. Huntley here."

"So, then what happened?" Jack asked eagerly.

"We played another game. This one lasted over three hours."

"Who won?"

"Mr. Preston did," said Mr. Huntley

"But that doesn't matter," scolded Cliff. "It really wouldn't have mattered who won. What mattered is that this game seemed to happen by chance. I landed on his property, he landed on mine. It was a normal game. I'll be honest, Jack. It really shook me up."

"Did it ever happen again?"

"No, it never did. But that doesn't matter either. It shouldn't have happened to begin with. The probability of it ever happening is inconceivable. I might have ignored it if we had played one twenty minute game. But three in a row? And why did it change when I said what I said?"

"Are you asking *me?*" Jack asked.

"Yes, if you might have an answer."

"I don't know that I do."

"Do you know that you *don't?*" asked Cliff, rather pointedly.

"What makes you think I might?" asked Jack. He felt like he was being interrogated, but he didn't know why.

"Because you used the Bible to get here."

"But someone could have used a different book."

"By chance, they could have."

"And by rights they should have," Mr. Huntley added.

"What's that supposed to mean?" asked Jack.

Mr. Huntley looked to Cliff before he would continue. With a hand gesture Cliff reluctantly gave him the okay. "When we set this contest up, we planted a book in the library that we expected would be found by someone in particular."

"Who?"

"We didn't know. We hoped someone would be, uh, *guided* to find it."

"Oka-a-a-ay," Jack said unconvincingly. "I guess that may be understandable after the Monopoly game. But I still say that someone could have chosen that book by chance."

"And I told you, I no longer believe in chance," Cliff stated, again with a stare that unnerved Jack.

So Jack returned the stare and asked, "What is so important to you about the Bible? I thought you said you were agnostic."

"I was. I suppose I still am. Before all this happened I was sure God didn't exist, except maybe in the South or during a war. But now I'm beginning to question what I believe. I question what everybody believes. I'm even questioning what Gloria believed."

"And what would that be?" Jack asked. Somehow he knew that this was the key to understanding one of the strangest conversations he had ever been involved with. Cliff, however, was not responding to the question. It was just the two of them, staring at each other, and Mr. Huntley staring at the ground. This time he didn't seem willing to speak up on Cliff's behalf. Jack decided to take a stab at answering his own question. "Did Gloria believe in God? Was the Bible important to her?"

"It was more important to her than me!" Cliff snapped.

Jack saw Mr. Huntley's eyes get real big at that statement. This was clearly a remark that had never been made before. "Did you resent that?" Jack asked.

"It wasn't that I resented it. It was just... I didn't have a lot of time to spend with her. In the short amount of time that I was home, I needed her to be focused on me. She had plenty of time for her religious activities when I wasn't around. But she insisted on spending, quote, 'quiet time with her Lord' unquote. As far as I know, all she did was read the Bible. That was valuable time that I wanted -- I needed -- to spend with her. So I ask you again, why did you choose the Bible, and what do you know about Jesus being the author of it? Is that what you really believe?"

"Yes it is."

"Why?"

Jack was speechless. That was a question he had wrestled with many times before, and for many years. In parochial school he could have answered that question in less than two minutes. The words he had memorized then didn't seem adequate now. "I just do, that's all," was the only response he could come up with.

"You disappoint me, Jack," chided Cliff as he slumped back in his chair. "I thought you had aspirations of being a writer. You can't be a writer if you can't put into words what you feel in your heart. Why do you believe what you believe? Jack, please. I need to know." Now both Cliff and Mr. Huntley were staring intensely at Jack. This time their eyes were pleading.

Meanwhile, in his heart, Jack was pleading with God to give him the right words to say. He had never been in this situation before, even though he always thought he would like to be. Now that he was, he was petrified. "I still don't understand why you're so convinced that I can help you."

Mr. Huntley quickly stuck up his hand to get their attention. "Uh, Mr. Preston, I'd sort of like to know too what convinced you to let Jack win. You never told me."

Cliff pointed at the Bible that was now sitting on the dining room table. "Get that Bible will you, and open to the page I bookmarked." Mr. Huntley got it and leafed through it as he walked back to the trophy room. Meanwhile, Cliff asked Jack, "Why did you say Jesus was the author, and not God?"

"Well, by chance someone else could have said God was the author and I would have lost. Saying that Jesus was the author was safer. And like I said, I thought it would have more influence on you."

"To be honest, it didn't," Cliff said pointedly. "I thought it was a trick, and the verses you used were unconvincing."

"So what changed your mind?"

"Yeah," chimed in Mr. Huntley. "I still don't get it."

"Do you see something interesting on the left page, in the right column, about a third of the way down?" Cliff asked Mr. Huntley, who started scanning through the verses in that area.

As he continued to look, he said, "No…I don't see…oh, my!"

He stared at the verse for a minute and then handed it to Jack. "You might want to read verse two," he said.

"Verse two, huh? Of Hebrews twelve?" he asked as he put on his reading glasses. "Let's see, verse two, 'Looking unto Jesus the author and finisher'...oh, I see what you mean...Jesus the author...huh. How did you find this verse?

"I stumbled on it while I was trying to find the verses you were using."

"Just stumbled on it, huh?"

Cliff stared at Jack again and said, "Yup, just by chance."

"And you don't believe in chance?"

"That's right."

"And so you think God is messing with your Monopoly game, huh?"

"I think some kind of spirit spooks messed with it."

"So now it's some kind of spirits?"

"Spirits, gods, what's the difference?"

Suddenly Jack knew why he was at Preston Manor—he *knew* the difference. Knowing that fact didn't make him any more comfortable, but it convicted him to do what he could to help these two one time friends and enemies of his. "Okay, I will try to tell you what I know, and explain it as best I can. But when *I* come to some bizarre stories, just remember, you started it."

"Fair enough," said Cliff, with a chuckle.

9

After pausing a very long moment to collect his thoughts, Jack decided that he was thoroughly confused about what Cliff was asking for. "Cliff, what is it you're really needing to know? I mean, on one hand you got this weird Monopoly game; on the other you seem to be trying to find God. I'm assuming you're facing the end of your days and you want to make sure you're doing what's right, eternally speaking, that is."

"Sort of," answered Mr. Huntley, with a nod from Cliff. "Things seem to be pointing to the fact that there's something out there. Mr. Preston would like to know what that something is before..."

"Before he's out there," Jack continued?

"Exactly."

"Then why didn't you just go to some preacher and have him explain it to you? Why all of this hoopla? And why me? You know, you can pick up 24 hour a day religious stuff on your satellite dish out there."

"No offense, Jack," said Mr. Huntley, "but we didn't choose you. In fact, we probably never would've chosen you, if not for all of this hoopla. What we wanted to avoid was opinion. There are so many people out there sharing their opinions. We have no idea if any of these people are experts on anything. We don't care..."

Mr. Huntley was interrupted by a barely audible noise from Cliff. He and Jack both looked at Cliff and saw him holding up one hand to stop the conversation. They both knew what that meant. Cliff wanted a moment of silence to organize his thoughts before he spoke. When he spoke, he expected the silence to continue.

Cliff slowly raised his head and looked at Jack with a penetrating stare. "Jack, when I went to a foreign place to do a story, the politicians in that place tried to form my opinions, to use me to their political ends. This was true of dictators, presidents, or tribal leaders. I had to sneak past the rulers to get to the ruled. It was the lives lived that intrigued me. My first and most difficult task when I entered a new place was to find a guide, someone who lived in the foundation of society, not the pinnacle. Properly judging that person's motives and capabilities was paramount to my success.

"Pretty soon I will die, and I don't know what that means. Over the years hundreds of people have tried to convince me of what it means. I could go to heaven or hell or purgatory. I could come back here as a ghost, a guide, an angel, or a cow. I always believed that death was nothing more than a flat-line on a heart monitor. For most of my life I thought that would suit me just fine. But I've seen enough lately to think I'm wrong in believing that." Jack suddenly felt the stare from Cliff penetrate to his core as Cliff asked, "Do you have what it takes to help me know?"

Jack was surprised when Cliff quickly stuck his hand up again to keep him from speaking. Then he recalled that Cliff often would stop people from delivering an emotional response. Usually he would say 'Don't answer me until you think about it.' So Jack stared back at Cliff while his mind swam furiously with answers, doubts, experiences and stories. Then one quick thought pushed all the others out; *You got me into this, God; so I'll let you take over from here.*

"I don't think I'm going to be the type of guide you're thinking of," Jack finally stated. "But I know I can point you in the right direction."

"How will that be different than anyone else?"

"I'll give you a map."

"What do you mean?"

"I'll give you a way to double-check my directions, and check the directions others have given you. You do like to check everything out for yourself, right?"

"That's right."

"Then I think the first place to start is to make sure of the final destination. Intricately detailed directions don't do any good if you don't end up where you want. In the list you gave, where do you want to go?"

"What list?"

"Heaven, hell, purgatory, nowhere, or back here as who knows what?"

"Oh, that list." There was silence for a few minutes. At one point Cliff looked at Mr. Huntley, as if pleading for him to answer the question. But Mr. Huntley just turned away. "I guess I need to be straight with you," Cliff finally said. "I need to go wherever it is that Gloria went. I need to find her, be with her again."

"Oh…I see. Well then, if I was to speculate on where that would be, based on your description of her, and her religious habits, if I were you I would choose heaven."

"There can't be any speculation, and I don't want your opinions. I have to know, absolutely for sure."

"Then just choose heaven."

"What?"

"Make my life easy and choose heaven."

Cliff acted like he really didn't have time for games and said, "Okay, heaven."

"You need an invitation."

"Jack, you said you could point the way, make your point already."

"Okay I will. Heaven is where God dwells. He is the one who invites people to live with Him. Think about it. Why am I sitting in front of you right now? It was because I was invited. And why was I invited? I haven't a clue. But would I be here if I would've forged an invitation from you? No, because you only invited those you knew, or those who asked. From what you've said, Gloria probably asked God to go to heaven."

Ralph halted Jack with a hand gesture and asked, "By the way, where *did* you get an invitation?"

Jack was stunned. "Well, you sent me one."

Ralph cocked his head a bit and said, "I did all of the invitations, and I know I would have remembered if I'd have sent one to a Jack Watchman."

"You didn't."

"I know I didn't…what do you mean?"

"You sent it to J.W. Gilbert."

"Who's that?"

"That's my pen name."

Cliff suddenly came to life and asked, "*You're* J.W. Gilbert?"

"Yeah, I thought you knew that."

"J.W. Gilbert?" Ralph asked again.

"Dr. Paradox," said Cliff.

"Oh, yeah, right…Jack is Dr. Paradox? You're kidding."

Now Jack was confused. "Who's Dr. Paradox?"

A smile crept across Cliff's face as he said, "The author who says he knows God and hates religion."

"Oh…oh, I get it. But you didn't know J.W. was me?"

"Uh, no Jack," said Ralph. "There wasn't a picture of you on the book cover, or on the Internet."

"Yeah, I guess you're right. Did you read the book?"

"Nope," said Cliff and Ralph in unison. Then Cliff asked, "Were you finished making your point?"

"About what?"

"Getting invited."

"Uh, no, I didn't. What I was trying to say, was that you, Cliff, had control over who stood out in that library, and who stands in front of you now. God has control over who stands in front of Him, and it's only right that He does. It makes perfect sense to me that He invites only those who desire to stand before Him. On the other hand, I could have turned down your invitation, and then I wouldn't be here."

Cliff thought about that for a moment and said, "A lot of people wanted to get in to see me just to profit from my existence."

"It's that way with God too. But those people didn't get in to see you, did they?"

"No, you're right, they didn't."

"Do you want my opinion?" Jack then asked, starting to get a bit excited. "I think that the desire in your heart to know the truth about God is actually His invitation to *you*. Now, is that desire tempered by skepticism? So was my desire to meet with you, but I didn't let it stop me. Quite frankly, I think some of the strange things going on here could be a sort of invitation to you, to at least force you to consider the possibility. Even your curiosity about the Bible is involved. That is the map to finding both God and heaven, and probably Gloria."

Cliff quickly changed the subject. "You said you believed God himself was the author of the Bible."

"That's correct. I believe that the Bible was written for us by God as a map for finding Him. That's why it can be trusted. There are a few things about studying it, though, that you need to know if you are going to use it to try to find God. Simply put, you need to search the Bible to find out what it is that God's trying to say to *you*," Jack said, as he pointed at Cliff.

"To me, personally?" he asked.

"That's right. The reason for that is that everyone is approaching him from a different place. His instructions direct you from your particular location."

"How's that possible?"

"You wrote a lot of books, Cliff. In them you were trying to say something to anyone who would listen. You should be impressed to know that God wrote the Bible in such a way that he can say something to each individual who reads it and say things that are relevant to that individual, at that time, that place, that circumstance. Take for instance the book you wrote about the Pearl Harbor attack. Would you have written it differently if the only person to read it was the grandson of a Pearl Harbor survivor? How about if he was the grandson of a Hiroshima survivor? Or how about if he was part of a tribe in the Amazon jungle? Do you see my point?"

"That'd be impossible!" Cliff snapped.

"What's impossible for us is not impossible for God. The point I am trying to make is this; I can show you how I find things in the Bible, and how I communicate with God. But it's no good unless you want to develop a relationship with Him on your own."

"Jack, to be honest, I don't know that I have enough time to read the Bible or develop relationships."

"You probably have more time than the thief on the cross did," said Jack.

"You mean the one that died with Jesus?" asked Ralph.

"Exactly. He had enough time to ask Jesus to remember him. Cliff, you remembered me, well, sort of, and now I'm carrying on a conversation with you that I never in my wildest dreams thought I would. Right now, right here, you could ask God to speak to you, and to allow you to know Him.

"I'm not sure that I'm ready to do that right now," said Cliff.

"And I'm not saying you *have* to. The point I am trying to make is that you *can*. Somehow the world has gotten this impression that if you spend enough time celibate, poor, and on your knees, that you will eventually break through God's hard exterior. I guarantee you that's not the case."

"So, what is the case?" said Ralph. "I mean, why are we here? What does God want from us?"

"He wants ten percent of everything you have, one day a week of your time, and he wants you to die for his cause."

"*What?*" exclaimed Ralph. "You *are* kidding, right?"

"Of course I'm kidding," Jack responded. "But I am also trying to make a point. You see, that's what I was taught as a child. It somehow just didn't make sense to me. Why would a God that created everything I see need any of it *from* me? Couldn't he just make more for himself? And why would he need me to spend one day a week doing nothing? What difference would that make to Him? Now, the dying for his cause part I just made up. But there are a lot of religions out there that teach that. All of those questions caused me to become an agnostic for a lot of years."

"So what changed your mind?" asked Cliff.

"Well, desperation mostly. I got to a point in my life that I desperately needed to know the truth. Probably similar to what you're going through right now. You need to know the truth about where your wife went when she died, and where you're going."

"And I need to know that they are the same place," Cliff added sternly.

"Understood," Jack responded.

"So, did you find a religion that answered all of *your* questions?"

"No, actually, I never did."

"What do you mean, you never did? You're religious now, aren't you?"

"No, I'm not. Remember, I wrote a book about hating religion. Like I said, that's what turned me off to God in the first place..."

"If I might interrupt," said Ralph, "It's interesting you should say that. After the Monopoly game, Mr. Preston thought there might be something in this house that connected us to...out there. We sort of challenged whatever it was to help someone win the contest. If someone won using that kind of help, they might know the answer to our questions. To be honest, we assumed the person we were looking for would be some spiritually enlightened person; not you."

"Well, thanks a lot," joked Jack.

"But then, a guy that knows God and hates religion was a bit intriguing," Ralph added.

"So you did invite a few people who hadn't asked to see you, huh?"

"Yeah, but I don't think hardly any of them came," recalled Ralph. "Well, one of them was Reverend Davis. He came. He talked to Cliff about God when Cliff was in the hospital. He was the chaplain on duty. At the time he didn't know he was talking to Cliff Montgomery the author. He--"

"Back to the point, Ralph," snarled Cliff.

"Uh, yes, uh, where were we Jack?"

"I, um, you were saying that I didn't like religion. I still don't. Now, I do go to church now and then. Don't get me wrong, there's nothing wrong with a bunch of people getting together and praying, singing, and all that. I used to go three or four times a week. But to me, the term 'religion' means man's attempt to figure God out and try to appease Him. Religion eventually becomes polluted with mankind's ideas and opinions."

"Is that why there are so many of them?"

"That's one of the reasons. Did you ever hear the story about the ten blind men and the elephant?" Jack asked them. When all he got was a couple of blank stares, he continued. "Ten men blind from birth were led into a large room. In this room was an elephant. Each man was led to a different part of the elephant and was asked to describe what they felt. The one that was feeling the elephant's ear said it felt like a large piece of leather. The one feeling the toes said it felt like a small boulder. The one at the tusk said it felt similar to a large copper pipe. The one holding the trunk said it was like a large snake. None of them had ever seen an elephant before. All ten blind men described something different and argued over what it was."

"The point is?" grumbled Cliff.

"The point is," Jack continued, "none of the blind men were wrong in what they were describing. They just couldn't see the whole picture. I don't think the people in different religions are completely wrong in what they believe. I just wish they would determine in their hearts to see the whole picture, rather than argue their individual points so vehemently."

"So, the big picture is that there is a little bit of God in every religion?"

"No, not at all. That's right, you didn't read my book. I don't think God is in *any* religion. God is in heaven. Religion is in the mind of man. Religion is like the opinions that all of those blind men had. The observations were legitimate, but the reality was much bigger than any of them."

"Do you think you have the whole picture?" challenged Cliff.

"Well, no, just a broader one. I'm not afraid to study the Bible or talk about God with anyone in any religion. But I do have a few ground rules."

"Your own personal religion, so to speak?"

"No, just a few things I know to be true."

"Such as?"

"Just like the elephant, God is what He is, regardless of what we think about Him. Just because the blind man holding the trunk thought it was like a snake, that doesn't mean it's a snake.

"Jack!" Cliff said sternly. "Be concise and give me specific information."

"Yes sir," Jack said without really thinking about it. He suddenly felt like he was back in the old office. While he was busy adding verbiage to the book, Cliff was looking for where to remove it. He felt Barbara tapping him on the chest, saying, 'Listen more than you speak'. He looked at Cliff and asked, "What would you specifically like to know?"

"Religion alone can't explain some of the things I've seen."

"Such as?"

"I've walked on fire."

"With the right technique probably anybody could."

"Just what I thought. But it was what I felt when I did it that shocked me."

"What was that?"

"When I stepped onto the coals there was suddenly a cold sensation around my feet and calves."

"It felt cold and not hot?"

"Right, like opening a door on a wintry day."

"Well, quite often people who have dealt with evil spirit beings, like demons and ghosts and such, have experienced a chill in the room where those spirits were. My opinion is that some spirits protected you from the heat."

"Why?"

"Maybe to deceive you into worshipping them. The most common reason though is to get you to hate God for some reason, or at least ignore Him. Tell me, did somebody do some ritual before you did that? Some chanting or something?"

"There was chanting going on the whole time we were doing it. I didn't understand what they were saying."

"They were probably inviting the spirits to that place to do what they did. Did anything bad happen to you afterwards? Maybe nightmares or something? Usually when you participate in that sort of thing you have to pay the piper."

Jack and Ralph both watched the color drain from Cliff's face. "Are you okay Mr. Preston?" Ralph asked. "What's wrong?"

Cliff slowly turned to face Ralph. He was so gripped with emotion that he couldn't speak. Fear, anger, sadness, terror; all seemed to be having their way with him. When he could finally get a word out, it was only one, "*Africa!*"

Ralph stared at Cliff, trying to comprehend what he meant. "Mr. Preston, I don't understand," he said in frustration. Cliff's eyes only got bigger, begging with Ralph to know, and to help.

"Jack looked at the two of them and asked, "What happened in Africa?" He got no response from either of them. "Ralph, I didn't read the book. What happened in Africa?"

Suddenly it came like a sucker-punch. "NO!" Ralph yelled as he stuck his face right in front of Cliff's. "Is that what you were doing when Mrs. Preston…" He couldn't finish. He gave the wheelchair a quick shove and stormed off into the kitchen. "No, no, NO!" they could hear him yell, occasionally punctuated with the pound of a fist.

Jack moved to Ralph's chair so he could look Cliff in the eyes. Cliff looked as troubled as Jack felt; right now only Cliff knew why. "What is it you're not saying?"

Cliff looked toward the kitchen. With a hushed voice he said, "That's not the whole story."

"Can you tell me the rest? I think you need to."

Cliff hung his head and was silent for a minute. "Before we walked on the coals we had been drinking some native concoction. I assumed it was something to numb the pain I was going to experience walking on the coals, so I drank quite a bit. Soon after I crossed the coals I blacked out or something, I don't remember. I didn't come to until the next morning. When I woke up I found myself lying in bed with two of the native women."

Cliff went silent again, so Jack filled in with the obvious. "I suppose you were as naked as they normally were."

Cliff nodded in agreement.

"Did anything else go on?"

Cliff looked Jack squarely in the eyes as he said, "I never, ever, knowingly cheated on Gloria. Ever! I admit I enjoyed looking. Some of the native women, especially the young ones, were hard to keep your eyes off of. But that morning...I don't know what happened to me."

"So you think something might have happened that you don't remember?"

"I wish I didn't remember. Jack, I came to my senses in the midst of raping one of them!"

10

"Oh no Cliff, you're kidding!" Jack spoke loud enough for Cliff to make a quick nervous glance toward the kitchen. So he whispered, "Ralph doesn't know, does he?"

"No, he doesn't." As Cliff looked toward the kitchen, he seemed to be longing for someone to understand, and explain what caused him to do what he did. "And I don't think now is a good time to tell him."

"You don't really know either, do you; I mean, why you did what you did?"

"It wasn't like me at all! I abhorred that type of behavior. That sort of violation was common in that village, and it repulsed me."

"Was the other woman trying to stop you?"

"Stop me? She was helping me! The girl I was raping was her fourteen year old daughter! I just about went out of my mind when I realized what I was doing. What was worse, I watched myself doing it for a while before I could stop. I fled the village in shame. Days later when the villagers found me, I thought they were going to kill me, and I didn't care. But they weren't bothered by what I'd done. They were only trying to relay the news about Gloria's accident. Right when I heard about the accident, I knew some bad Karma had caught up with me."

Jack was about to disagree with him when the kitchen door opened. Ralph walked out a bit sheepishly but still wearing an angry scowl. "Sorry guys, I don't know what hit me. I guess it

irritated me to think there may have been some connection between what Mr. Preston was doing in Africa and what happened
to Mrs. Preston."

The statement he made seemed too stiff and rehearsed.
Ralph was hiding his true feelings, and probably for a good reason. Like a festering sore, Jack knew this horrific deed needed
to be opened up and exposed. And healed. The truth, all of it,
would need to be known. That truth seemed to be dumped out
in Jack's mind like a huge jigsaw puzzle. He was feverishly trying
to put pieces together, to get a clearer picture. He had experienced this piece himself, that piece was from a book he'd read,
these pieces were laid out in the Bible. It was all there. He suddenly realized he had been gathering pieces for twenty years, just
so he could put them together for Cliff. How could he possibly
get Cliff to understand?

"When will I know?"

Jack's thoughts were suddenly brought back to Preston
Manor. He looked at Cliff a bit dazed because the question only
barely registered. "When will you know what?"

"When will I know what it is that's been toying with me,
tricking me, maybe even destroying me? I'm convinced something's out there. Okay, fine. It got me this time, it got me last
time. How do I get free of this torture and fight back?"

"You'll know the truth, and the truth will set you free."

"Jack, I understand I may not know the truth. How will I
know for sure when I have discovered the truth?"

Jack looked at him sternly and answered, "When you *know*
that you know!"

Cliff stared right back at him and asked, "And exactly what is
that supposed to mean?"

"It says in the Bible that if you think you know, you do not
yet know like you ought to know."

"Where does it say *that* in the Bible?" asked Ralph.

Jack got a blank look on his face and after a few seconds said "I could find it for you, but I can't quote chapter and verse."

"That's not necessary," grumbled Cliff. "But explain to us what you mean."

"Sure. Oh, by the way, if you want to look it up, I remember that it's in Corinthians in the first couple verses of one of the chapters," he said to Ralph who was grabbing the Bible Jack had used to win the contest. Jack then proceeded quickly before he received another remark from Cliff. "The operative word in that verse is *think*. If you have only analyzed the information with your mind, you still have not learned it well enough. To know the truth completely, you need to be taught it by God himself."

"Are you saying you can't learn it from someone else?" asked Ralph.

"That's not the point I am trying to make."

"Then what is the point exactly?"

Jack was just starting to get real frustrated with the direction the conversation was going, when he remembered a story that he recently heard from a friend of his. "If I could, I would like to tell you two a quick story to kind of explain what I am talking about."

"A short story?" asked Cliff.

"I'll keep it as short as I can. A friend of mine is an HVAC technician in a high rise building…"

"H-V-A-C?" asked Ralph.

"Heating and air conditioning," responded Jack.

"Oh, okay."

"Anyway, this mans boss told him to get rid of an annoying squeak that was driving a secretary nuts. He was told that there was a damper in the ceiling near the secretary that needed to be lubricated. Since this technician worked nights he was able to fix it while she was gone and not disturb her. One night he got up in the ceiling by the secretary's desk, but there was no damper. He looked, but could find nothing near her desk that might squeak. Since he hadn't heard the squeak, he didn't know what to look for.

"He eventually had to talk to the secretary, try different tricks until he could recreate the squeak, and try different things to stop it. When he found something that squeaked, stopped the squeak, and then retested its operation and heard no squeak, he was satisfied he had fixed it. He then contacted the secretary a week later to confirm that the squeak had not returned."

"And the moral of the story is?" asked Cliff impatiently.

"There are a few, actually. First, even though his boss was an authority, and acted like he knew what the problem was, he was wrong. He could have been right, and surely had been in the past. But no one is perfect. Secondly, this man had to go to the source, in this case the one who heard the squeak. If I remember right, Cliff, you always insisted on getting to the source of information when you wrote your books. You said you didn't trust second hand information."

"That's right," affirmed Cliff. "It always seemed to be missing important information."

"Third," Jack continued, "he kept searching until he was certain he had found the real thing, in this case the squeak. And lastly, he tested what he found to make absolutely sure. In this case he confirmed the squeak was gone. In searching for God, first you need to understand that those in authority, who act like they know all about him, could be wrong. Second, you need to go to a reliable source of information, which would be the Bible. It is the first-hand source of information about God. Third, you search diligently until you know that you know you have found God. Lastly, you take the time to re-examine what you believe you know, just to make sure."

"And how does all that happen?" asked Cliff.

"I was afraid you were going to ask me that."

"Are you saying you don't know?"

"No, it's not that. It's just not easy to explain. Not briefly anyway. It would be simpler for me to go back to the beginning and explain it the way I understand it."

"Are you thinking that will take weeks, or hours, or minutes?" asked Cliff, which was a common question he had when Jack was writing for him.

"I could easily stretch it into weeks, but I could probably deliver it in a nutshell in less than an hour," he responded, not quite knowing how he would do it.

"Okay," said Cliff, "I can give you an hour. But try to keep it concise. Just give me an outline and a little informative filler."

"Okay, well, first of all, there was this big explosion. Then atomic particles shot out at the speed of light. Pretty soon the heavier particles collected together and turned into stars." Jack paused to look at them both. It took almost two whole seconds for Ralph to catch on, and when he did he just dropped his head and snorted.

"Jack, please," came a response from Cliff, "I don't have a billion years. Speed it up a bit."

"No problem," said Jack. "You've seen the movie *The Bible* anyway, right?"

"Yeah, sure," said Ralph.

"So you know how the earth was created, according to the Bible anyway?"

"I suppose"

"I would like to talk about what happened just before that."

"Before what?" asked Ralph, "The movie?"

"No, before the earth was created."

With a gesture of impatience, Cliff said, "We're listening."

"Okay," Jack began. "In the beginning, God created the heavens and the earth. Stated differently, before the earth was created, God created the heavens."

"I understand what you're trying to say," said Ralph, "but what does that have to do with finding God?"

Jack looked at the two of them. He realized that if he tried to feed them anymore religious rhetoric he would lose them. He wanted so badly for them to grasp the things that *he* was excited about. He suddenly remembered Barbara's words to him, '*Try to listen more than you talk*'. As he looked at them he pictured Ralph seeing Cliff off at an airport. He decided to ask Cliff, "Are you prepared to take off on this next adventure?"

Suddenly, Cliff perked up and looked at Jack quizzically. "What are you talking about?"

"Well, you told me you are going to die. So when you die you either cease to exist or you go someplace. I happen to believe that there is life after this one and a place to go to, what most people refer to as heaven. You said Gloria believed in heaven, and may have gone there. So my question is, are you ready to leave for a destination like heaven?"

Cliff felt that twinge of panic that he hated so much. He squirmed in his wheelchair and tried to make it look like it had nothing to do with Jack's questions. Ralph recognized the angst in Cliff's actions and to defend him asked again, "What does that have to do with finding God?"

I'll get to that in a minute," Jack said. "The point I am trying to make, is that there is a whole other place out there, and death is the one-way ticket to that destination. I'm trying to make sure you know where you're going, and what you'll find when you get there."

"Just continue," said Cliff anxiously.

"Okay, what I wanted to explain was the difference between

the heavens and the earth, and the way we were created. The very first verse in the Bible says God created the heavens and the earth. The heavens are the dwelling place for spirit beings such as God and the angels, and the earth is the dwelling place for physical beings like humans and animals. However, unlike animals, humans were also created with a spirit. That spirit, along with your soul, goes to heaven when the physical body ceases to function."

Cliff stuck his hand up and said, "Wait a minute. If the spirits go to heaven, how do you explain what's going on here."

"Are you talking about the Monopoly spook?"

"Yeah, or some of the strange things I've seen in India or Africa. Things that just aren't...physically possible."

"Like what?"

"Like people just floating around in the air."

"No strings attached?"

"We were sitting outside! There was nothing to attach strings to! I know it sounds strange, but I know what I saw. Ralph, you remember the story about the floating man. Tell it to Jack."

The Floating Man

Cliff watched as the crouching figure approached him. Somehow his travel guide, Padman Pradesh, had found him in the crowd of villagers. "Mr. Montgomery, you should very much not be sitting in this place!" he whispered.

"Padman, sit down before someone sees me," Cliff whispered back, as he tried to hide his white Anglo face. "What are they doing anyway? They look like they're in a trance or something."

"They are giving themselves over to the spirits of the

village. Many children in the village are sick because some-one did not offer proper sacrifices. Many children will die if the ruling deity is not appeased."

"And how will they appease this deity?"

"Please Mr. Montgomery, let us be leaving. The spirits will be angry if the ceremony is defiled."

"Padman, tell me, how will they appease him?"

"The witchdoctor will know. Maybe one of the healthy children will be sacrificed to save the others."

Cliff's eyes got wide as he exclaimed, "That's terrible!"

Mr. Pradesh could not grasp Cliff's horror. "Would it not be better to lose one child rather than a whole village of children?"

"What do you mean?" Cliff asked.

"If the children die, the village will die," Mr. Pradesh answered. "Who will do the work? Who will have more children? No, it is better for one than for many to die."

"Why does it have to be a healthy child?"

Amazed at Cliff's lack of understanding, Mr. Pradesh said, "Because a sick child will die anyway, it would not be a sacrifice." He then glanced at the men seated at the other side of the bonfire. He quickly put his hand in front of Cliff's face to keep him from speaking again. "No words now, the spirits have come." He then bowed his face to the ground and put a gentle hand on Cliff's shoulder to let him know to do the same.

Cliff decided to bow so he wouldn't look too obvious. As he was going down, he chanced a peek in the direction Padman had looked. He saw a man in a bright white robe, and then he saw something that almost made him gasp out loud. Next to the man in the robe was a man sitting in a lotus position, obviously in a trance, and floating a full two *feet off the ground. He continued to rise until he was clearly above the heads of the villagers. None of the villagers seemed as impressed as Cliff was; they were all either in a trance or bowing.*

Cliff kept his head low, but he couldn't take his eyes off of the man that was now floating around the bonfire. As he floated overhead, Cliff just had to look closer. "Jesus, that's weird," he whispered to Padman. When he said this, the man started to descend, and then dropped the last foot and a half to the ground. The noise brought everyone out of their trance, or up from their bowed position. Cliff kept his face hidden, but kept peeking at the no-longer-floating man who was visibly dazed.

He then noticed that the man in the white robe was looking around at the crowd. He suddenly trained his eyes in Cliff's direction, and then spoke something to someone standing near him. He watched as that man maneuvered his way through the crowd until he stood right in front of Cliff. He then spoke a few words to Cliff in a dialect that Cliff didn't recognize. "What did he say?" Cliff asked Padman.

"He thanked us for coming and asked us to leave," Padman answered.

After recalling the story, Ralph said, "At the time I remembered you saying it was probably some kind of parlor trick."

"I bet now you're not so sure," added Jack.

"To be honest, I knew it wasn't a parlor trick when I saw it," Cliff confessed. "The guy floated, or levitated, or whatever, right past me. There was nothing around him. There couldn't have been! It was just *spooky*. Somehow the ritual was disturbed because of my presence there. I guess because I was a westerner. I left gladly."

"That sort of thing is odd to us in the, quote, civilized world. But if your physical eyes were opened to see what was happening in the spirit realm, you probably would've seen that the man was being carried around by a bunch of demons." Jack looked over and saw Cliff with a look on his face like he had just figured out a card trick. He continued, "They probably dropped the guy when they heard the name of Jesus."

"What do you mean?"

"Well, if Ralph quoted you exactly, you said, 'Jesus that's weird.'"

"There's no way that guy could have heard me say that!"

"I'm sure he didn't, but I bet the spirits carrying him did."

"You really think so?"

"Cliff, honestly, it doesn't matter what I think. You know what you saw actually happened. I can tell you that I've seen similar things happen dozens of times in response to the name of Jesus. The Bible says he is God in the flesh and he came to destroy the works of the devil, such as deceiving people into thinking they can levitate."

Ralph jumped in to the conversation and said, "But you said the spirit beings lived up there, in heaven."

"I didn't say *up* there." To emphasize the point he was about to make, Jack stared them both down as he said, "It's not in a physical location; it's *spiritual*. It's an entirely different realm than the one we occupy.

"As far as the spirit beings you were talking about, the Bible calls them demons or unclean spirits. They are angels that rebelled against God so he banished them to earth. Satan is their leader and appears to be the only one allowed access to God. So now when we go to heaven we are away from demons. But here on earth they still hassle us. In a way, what happened with the floating man wasn't very different than walking on fire."

Cliff snorted as he said, "How are we supposed to understand all of this stuff?"

Jack hoped he would say that. He locked eyes with Cliff again and stated, "By entering the spiritual realm yourself."

Cliff held the stare and said, "I think I am about to do that."

"You are talking about after you die, but I'm talking about entering it now, before you die, not when it's too late to rebook your flight."

Cliff kept his eyes locked on Jack's while he tried to determine if Jack somehow knew what he was thinking or had just made a lucky guess. "Okay, keep going. But you're going to have some explaining to do."

"I expect I will," Jack said with a smile. He settled back in his chair and thought for a second. Then he said, "In the story Ralph just told, about the floating man, you said that the ruling deity would probably demand the life of a healthy child, in exchange for not killing the other children. Is that correct?"

"From what I was told later, the villagers knew the rules, and they knew the costs for not following what the ruling deity demanded," Cliff stated disgustedly. "Someone was supposed to have sacrificed a goat, but they just couldn't afford it. They took a chance that the deity wouldn't notice. Their child was the first to get sick and die. When others started to get sick, the local doctors thought they had an epidemic starting, but the illness defied all medical treatments. It seemed as if the life was being sucked out of these kids. It was terrible to witness."

"So who was the floating man?"

"He was the local witch doctor. The couple who had caused

the problem eventually told the village leader, who then contacted this witch doctor. I was told that this guy went into a trance in order to speak with the ruling deity and find out what he demanded in order to lift the curse on the village. I didn't stick around to find out what that was. They even kicked Padman out of the village for bringing me there."

"Did you ever find out what happened after that?"

"Not really. I never again got a street level contact. Official word was that the doctors were able to avoid an epidemic, so I am assuming the children stopped dying. The cause and cure were never explained." Cliff just shook his head and asked, "Can we move on?"

"Sure," Jack said, "but I would like to use that story to make a point first. You said that Padman assumed that a healthy child would be the required sacrifice, and that he was okay with that."

"He was, I wasn't," Cliff replied.

"I totally understand. I wouldn't have been either. But you do understand the desperation of the villagers?"

With an obvious storehouse of pent up anger, Cliff said, "The desperation I could understand. I couldn't understand how a deity could demand the sacrifice of a child, or even a goat for that matter. I mean, I can understand there being some ritual before an animal is killed to be eaten. But a child? Come on, that just doesn't make sense."

"Do you think it would have made sense to the family whose healthy child would have been chosen as the sacrifice?" Jack asked. Before Cliff could answer, he added, "Would it have made sense to the child?"

Cliff shook his head, but stayed silent. Eventually he said softly, "I suppose if you knew for a fact that your death would stop the suffering of others, someone might agree to it. I couldn't."

"You're not alone, Cliff. Most people can't comprehend why

Jesus had to die. But all the way back in the Garden of Eden, God warned Adam that certain actions would result in death."

"Right, eating an apple," Cliff said mockingly. " I saw the movie."

"It's much more than just that," replied Jack. "In his disobedience, Adam gave away dominion of the Earth. It's a complex issue, but God never wanted death to be a part of the human experience. Now it is, and no one can escape it. Not anyone born of human parents anyway. On the other hand, Jesus was born of a human mother, but not a human father. He was God in human form, the visible image of the invisible God, to quote Colossians something or other."

"But he was crucified," stated Ralph.

"Yes, and he died. At least, his physical body died. Then three days later he was resurrected from the dead."

"On Easter," added Ralph.

Cliff gave Ralph a look, and then Jack. "Resurrected," he asked? "Explain the term."

"He came back to life, only it's different than when the doctors thump you and your heart starts again. Being brought back to life like that you will eventually die again, permanently. When you're resurrected you never die again. And yet you still have a physical body, sort of. Jesus proved that by eating fish after he was resurrected."

Once again Cliff lifted his hand slightly to stop the conversation. With his chin resting in his other hand, he just stared at nothing in particular half way between Jack and Ralph. Jack started to speak, but Cliff held up his hand and barely shook his head no. "Jack, my goal is to get to Gloria. If all of this religious talk is important to doing that, then I will try to understand it. But please try not to feed me anything that's not important."

Jack started to speak again, and then remembered what his

wife had said about listening. He then took a moment to replay in his head what Cliff had just told him, and what he was asking for. "Okay, first of all, if you want to get to where Gloria is, you will probably have to go to heaven."

"Probably?"

"Cliff, I'm not the judge. That decision is for God to make. But do you think she was the type of person that God *wouldn't* want in heaven?"

"I believe she would be welcome anywhere," Cliff replied.

"Okay then, if she is in heaven, then she is in the spiritual realm, not the physical realm. What I've been trying to say, is that you *can* enter that realm before you die. That is the point of being created with both a physical body and a spiritual one. But having an eternal spiritual body does not guarantee that it will be eternally in heaven."

"Then what *will* guarantee that I will end up in heaven with Gloria?"

Jack stared at the two of them incredulously, wondering why they couldn't see the obvious. "That would be God."

Cliff returned Jack's incredulous stare with his own and said, "Which one?"

Jack suddenly remembered that he was not dealing with someone who had a church upbringing. This man had seen people worshipping all sorts of gods. No wonder he was getting frustrated and confused by Jack's view of it all. Jack decided to try a different approach. "Cliff, let me ask you a question. In all of your travels, meeting people from all over the world, how many different gods do you think you saw being worshipped?"

Cliff took a second to consider the question and replied, "None!"

"None?" Jack asked, as his entire conversation plan fell apart.

"Right. None. I didn't see any of the gods that all those

people worshipped. I don't think they saw them either."

"But I remember you used to…come on, you know what I'm talking about."

"Maybe I do," countered Cliff. "But that doesn't mean you phrased the question correctly."

"Okay, okay, criticism noted. How many gods do you think…"

"Thousands," interrupted Cliff. "Why else do you think I had trouble picking one to worship?"

"What made you think you should only worship one?"

"Honestly?"

"Of course," Jack answered.

"I just couldn't fathom this earth being created by a committee."

"Ha. Isn't that a great line?" Ralph said to Jack with a little recognition in his voice. "When he said that to me, I told him that I couldn't believe that the God that created Marilyn Monroe would have also made Marilyn Manson."

"Okay, you got me. Can I continue?" This time it was Jack that was trying to make sure the conversation stayed serious.

"Please do," Cliff stated.

Ralph suddenly got serious too and said, "Yes, Jack. Sorry. It just struck me funny."

"No problem. Anyway, there was an important point I wanted to make before I got sidetracked. The Bible says in one spot that there are many gods and many lords. In another place God states that there are no other gods besides Him. Those two statements are not contradictory. In the first statement He is pointing out that there are many gods that are worshipped by men. In the latter statement He points out the fact that in reality there is only one, Him. All the others either do not exist at all, or if they do exist they are not really gods."

Cliff propped his head up with his hand and with a sigh said, "So, do they, and if so, what are they?"

Seeing the fatigue so evident in Cliff's face, Jack hurried to make his point. "If you want to worship a spirit being, then you probably could worship angels or demons, or God, because the Bible says He is a spirit. But only one of them is the Creator. It is the Creator that I think you are seeking, and it is the Creator that I believe is calling you." Jack hoped to see a glimmer of understanding in Cliff's eyes, but he was just shaking his head in a confused manner. So Jack asked, "What's the problem?"

"I just have a hard time understanding it. If what you say is true, millions upon millions of peopled are deceived in their thinking. In fact, I'm afraid if I would have stayed in India much longer, I could be kneeling right there with them."

"Then let's look at what evidence you have. There are hundreds of verses in the Bible that make reference to angels and demons. Many of those verses talk about them interacting with humans. If that's the case, it would be pretty easy to see how someone who didn't know any better would want to worship one of these creatures."

Ralph interrupted and asked, "But if that's what they want to do, does it really hurt anything? I mean, they seem to have figured out how to operate their society with a multitude of gods."

"Afghanistan operated under the Taliban too. But let's say you had been born in Afghanistan. The Taliban had the ways and means to influence how you lived, and you were a captive in that societal structure. You may not have believed as they believed. But if you didn't, then you needed to be liberated from their control, or suffer the consequences of being under it. If they influenced you enough, they could make you believe that good is bad and death is life. Demons influence people the same way.

"The subject of the entire Bible is that God wants to set you free of that kind of oppression. I know you want to keep this short, so let me just say that Jesus is God, and he has the legal right, and the power, to set you free from the enemy's rule. Rightfully, he needs you to ask for it. And when he offers his help, understand, he wants the end result to be permanent. He wants the rule of the terrorists in your life to be eliminated completely. Don't expect him to be too happy if you willingly allow any of them to remain."

"I don't think either one of us has any desire to mess around with demons or any of that other stuff," Ralph remarked. "But you haven't given us a clue how to comprehend it."

Jack thought about that for a minute and said, "I haven't, have I?"

"No, you really haven't," said Ralph, as he got up out of his chair. He knew Cliff well enough to see that he was getting dangerously fatigued. "How much more do you think you have to explain to us to make your point?" Ralph's question was blunt and sort of stung.

11

Looking at Cliff, Jack saw a fighter on the ropes, someone who had been knocked down but refused to stay down, and was determined to finish the fight. He thought about Ralph's question and decided he needed more time. He decided to ring the bell and end this round. "Cliff, I should probably be going. With your permission I can come back some other day and finish. Hopefully I'll be a little more organized."

"Please don't go Jack. If you don't have someplace you have to be, I'd like you to stay. If I could just take a quick nap I'll be good to go again in an hour or so. It's a lot to ask, but could you find a way to organize your thoughts here for a while?"

Cliff was trying to hide the desperation in his voice, but Jack could hear it, and it complimented the desire he had in his heart to share what he could. "Sure," he replied, "I brought my laptop computer with me. I'll just go to the car and get it."

"Thanks, Jack, I appreciate it. If you would care to use the library, Ralph will come get you when I am ready." He said this over his shoulder as Ralph was wheeling him out of the room.

"Sure Cliff," Jack said to Ralph's backside as they went through the door. "I'll just let myself out."

As Jack went through the door into the library, he heard the scrape of a wooden chair leg on the marble floor in the foyer, and then saw a guard jump to his feet, with his mind obviously a few winks behind.

"Are you leaving, sir?" he asked, trying to look alert.

"No, Lloyd, I am just going out to my car to get my computer." He seemed surprised that Jack remembered his name.

"I'll join you," he said, as he opened the door.

"Oh, that's not necessary," Jack said, but the guard continued out and locked the door behind them.

"I'll just wait for you here," he said, as he pulled his cigarettes out of his pocket.

"So what are you thinking Ralph?" asked Cliff.

Ralph was thinking that this whole process may be harder on Cliff than it was worth. But he knew that wasn't what he should be thinking. Cliff would be expecting him to be working toward the goal at hand, information. Just to be certain, he asked, "About the meeting so far?"

"Of course."

"It's a lot to digest."

"I guess that's to be expected."

"It's interesting, in a strange way."

"And occasionally strange in an interesting way." Cliff countered. "Do you think Jack may be the one?"

"You mean to guide you on this adventure?" He lifted Cliff into bed as he waited for an answer. When he didn't get one, he added, "Let's hope so. You know, he can really only point out the path."

"Great. All he can do is point, and I can't walk."

Quickly dodging that subject, Ralph moved the wheelchair away and said, "Let's give him a chance."

Cliff nodded in agreement and said, "Feed him something, maybe one of those platter sized sandwiches you're famous for. Load it up. Besides, you know how grumpy he gets when he gets hungry."

"Boy, do I ever," Ralph said, laughing. "He called home and snapped at his wife once. She called me and told me to get some food in him. Sure enough, he hadn't eaten all day." As Ralph said that, he dimmed the light. "Don't worry Mr. Preston, when you're ready to talk to him, he'll be ready to talk to you."

"Good. Think about what we should ask him. Maybe we can go through the list of questions."

Recalling how extensive the list was, Ralph replied, "He may have covered a few already. Just rest, I'll take care of it."

"Good. Thanks Ralph. Keep checking on me. Wake me if I sleep too long."

"Sure Mr. Preston." Ralph spoke those last words to a mostly lifeless individual. He always worried that someday the life that he treasured most, Cliff's, would leave him. He knew that when it happened he'd learn how to cope, but it was one of the few life lessons Cliff had never taught him.

As he walked out to his car Jack was overwhelmed with how different he felt now, compared to when he arrived. When he drove in he was ready to lambaste Cliff for the way he treated all of his employees so many years ago. Now he almost wanted to hug the guy. He still didn't feel that Cliff was justified doing what he did, but Jack was no longer so consumed with anger about it.

As he grabbed his laptop, he decided that he just needed some time alone. Lloyd wouldn't care for at least five minutes. The situation that he had been put in was so overwhelming. Some people wouldn't think twice about trying to share with someone what they believed about God. But Jack didn't want to share what he believed. He wanted to tell them the truth about God. He wasn't convinced that he could do that one hundred percent accurately and firmly believed that anything less just wasn't right.

Right now he was concerned that he'd spent too much time discussing demons and the spirit world. On the other hand, he knew that Cliff had seen a lot of manifestations of demonic activity in his travels around the world. He knew none of the conversation shocked Cliff like it would a typical American. Somehow though, he wanted to steer the conversation back to God and His love. His mind reeled under the task. He finally just collapsed in the driver's seat.

Barbara sat in her favorite recliner--the one in the media room next to her husband's favorite recliner--and watched another re-run of Star Trek, Next Generation. Normally Jack would be accompanying her, offering free advice to the writers of the show, who of course heard none of it. She had considered the unsolic-ited wisdom a bit of an annoyance before. Now she realized she missed it.

This was always their time together, even if the focus of at-tention was a non-sentient device. Years ago they had decided to find something that they both liked to do together and commit themselves to doing it. The form of the activity didn't matter as much as the consistency of doing it. No matter what happened in their relationship, on a regular basis they had to make up just so they could do what they had committed to do. Their regular activity now was praying together in the morning, but watching Star Trek was still a bonding point. It reminded her of snow skiing down a steep slope. If you didn't dig into the slope once in a while the downhill slide could get out of control. The time together, even if it was trivial, reminded them of the direction they were going. It also caused them to check and make sure they were not off track.

Tonight she hoped Jack wasn't wandering off track. She had no concern for their marriage. It had been tested and tried numerous times and had always held up. What worried her was Jack's peace. Cliff had destroyed that peace--and almost their marriage--many years ago. She would have preferred that he had quietly succumbed before now. A dozen scenarios had played out in her mind about what this meeting would be like between Jack and Cliff. Each scenario had ended ugly. Worse yet, each one had ended ugly between her and Jack.

She knew she had to stop thinking about it, and staring at the tube wasn't working. She was already recording Star Trek so Jack could watch it later. She then curled up on the sofa with the afghan and decided to have a little talk with God about what she thought He should be doing with Jack. She also asked for a little insight about what He actually *was* doing.

"Lord, what are you trying to do here?" Jack said, as he was sitting by himself in the car. "You know I'm not prepared for this. I don't know what Cliff needs; I don't know what he's looking for. You know something in me wants to just put my keys in this ignition and drive off. Father, please, give me the desire to stay, and the words to say. Most of all, help Cliff and Ralph hear the truth, regardless of what I say. Speak to them Lord. I truly believe they want to know you. I ask you to forgive me for the anger that I came here with, and I thank you for removing so much of it. If I might make another request, I ask that you strengthen Cliff physically. I can tell that he has been struggling to stay strong, and I don't know if I can be as brief as he needs me to be. Please give him strength in his physical body to hold up, or teach me to be concise. If it is the enemy trying to wear him down, I ask that you bind up that enemy and not allow him to operate in this place. I ask you for warrior angels to do battle on our behalf here, so that I can share what I need to share in peace. Lord, I need the convicting power of your Holy Spirit, and ask for it in the name of Jesus. Thank you Father."

He sat in silence there for a few minutes, hoping to hear some great revelation that he could share that would instantly answer all of their questions. It never came. What he did experience was an inner peace that made him want to stay. He still didn't know what he was going to say, but it no longer mattered. Grabbing his briefcase he headed back to the Manor. Lloyd was anxious to see him return, because it was a bit chilly outside. He stepped in first and held the door for Jack. As he returned to his chair in the foyer, Jack went to the library.

As he sat in the library he went through his briefcase and programs on his laptop looking for something that might help him explain things to Cliff. He did have a Bible program on his laptop. It was a word processing program that allowed him to look up a Bible verse by searching for key words or phrases. It also had a concordance that allowed him to look up each word to find out what that word originally was in Hebrew or Greek, and a definition of that Hebrew or Greek word. This tool had helped him many times to understand what they were trying to convey at the time these books were written, rather than what they thought it meant when it was translated. He had found that sometimes the meaning was lost in the translation. He remembered too that Cliff struggled with that same problem both in his research, and later when his books were translated into a foreign language.

He was clicking through a number of verses, when the door to the rest of the house opened up. "Here Jack, we thought you could use something to eat," said Ralph, smiling. In his hands was a plate full of sandwich. It looked like he had just ordered out to a deli, but Jack knew there were none anywhere near this remote location.

"Thanks Ralph, did you make this?" asked Jack, as he took the plate and drooled.

"Yeah. Sorry it's not a hot meal. I think you'll find something from almost every food group in that thing though."

"No kidding. The toothpicks are a nice touch."

"I had to hold it together somehow. You don't have to eat them if you don't want to. They do provide fiber, but they will probably stick to your ribs in a most unpleasant fashion," said Ralph laughing. He then pulled a small bag of potato chips and a can of Pepsi from under his arm. "Here are some leftovers of what everyone else got that watched the DVD."

"That reminds me; I never got to watch the DVD. Did I miss anything?"

"No, not really. Just a lot of Mr. Preston telling stories, and me saying the stories are over and to go home and leave us alone. What I wish we would've had was a bunch of out-takes from making the DVD. Mr. Preston had never been in front of a camera before, at least not of his own control. He kept trying to edit the DVD like he would a book. It was frustrating for him, but I had fun."

"Speaking of stories, could you tell me a little bit more about the early days?" asked Jack. "What was Cliff like then? And what was his wife like?"

"Well, in the real early days I didn't know Mr. Preston that well. What I knew about him came from Mrs. Preston. I am sure what she told me was a bit sugar-coated, and that's why I was able to ignore his attitude when I finally had to spend time with him," said Ralph, rolling his eyes.

"So, he's always had an attitude, huh?"

"Yeah, but it's a very misunderstood attitude. He is really

a good man, Jack. Mrs. Preston knew that and got me to see it before I ever really met him. Once I did meet him it took me a few months to find the good part, but it's there," Ralph said, chuckling. "For instance, some people would think he was stingy because he would never give a pan-handler even a nickel. But you wanna know what he did? He went and lived with them."

"He lived with them?" asked Jack. "You mean, on the street? In the gutter?"

"Yup. He spent two weeks sleeping on the sidewalks or in shelters. He ate at the missions and got to meet quite a few of the indigent. Oh, here's an interesting bit of trivia. Do you remember Pastor Holstein?"

"Yeah, the one who was arguing with Reverend Davis."

"That's right," said Ralph. "Well he was one of the people serving food at the rescue mission. He was a young kid that was training to be a missionary. I still don't think he knows that he fed Cliff."

"Is that why you invited him?"

"Yeah, mostly," Ralph responded. "Even though Cliff was an agnostic-atheist, he had a fondness for missionaries. He said he could relate to them. Well, some of them anyway, like the Aid missionaries that were living with the people and trying to help them. He despised the proselytizing ones that only seemed to want to give the natives a whole 'nother set of rituals. Anyway, regarding the homeless, he said many of them liked living on the street. Oh, sure, they would prefer more comfortable sur-roundings. The way he put it, they liked the freedom from responsibility. There was one guy there that didn't want to be there though. He was a real nice guy that just sort of fell on hard times."

"How was that?"

"Well, this guy's wife went a little dingy. She started hearing a voice in her head, thought it was God. She killed their only child, a three year old daughter, and then botched her own suicide. This guy--his name is Miguel--went off the deep end. He loved the little girl and now she was gone, and he lost his wife to life in prison. He started drinking and lost his business and then his home. He had so many lawsuits against him that if he would have gotten a job he couldn't have lived on what wasn't garnished. He finally just left society."

"Did Cliff keep in touch with the guy?"

"Oh, more than that. First, he checked on Miguel's story and found out it was legit. Then he contacted his former attorney, through our attorney of course. It seems the guy was either a bit shady or just plain incompetent. Anyway, Mr. Preston got some of the companies Miguel owed money to, to drop their claims completely. Others he bought off, sometimes for pennies on the dollar. Then he gave Miguel a job. Now he has his own business again and is doing pretty well." Looking at his watch, Ralph said, "Just a minute, Jack, I'll be right back. I want to see how Mr. Preston is doing."

Jack used the time alone to devour the sandwich less politely. The mayonnaise, avocado, mustard, tomato, and his moustache made the napkins quite necessary, and colorful. He hadn't realized how hungry he was getting. He was trying to get a picture in his mind of Cliff in rags when Ralph returned. "Is he doing okay?" he asked.

"Yeah, still asleep."

"What can you tell me about his wife?" asked Jack, as he ripped open the bag of potato chips. "She sounds like she was a wonderful person."

"She sure was. After all these years I still like her better than Mr. Preston," he joked. "But seriously, I probably spent more time with her those last years than he did. I was working over at their place all the time, even though she never did formally hire me. Sometimes at the end of the day she would pay me something, sometimes she wouldn't. Sometimes we would just sit and talk for hours, and sometimes I would even get paid for that. I never kept track of what she paid me. I would just stuff it away and when I needed some I would get it out. I had to get out a lot of it after she died and I was working for *Mr.* Preston," he said in a condescending but joking tone of voice.

"How did you ever learn to live with him," said Jack, trying to sound like he was kidding too, but in reality he was quite serious.

"When I would sit and talk with Mrs. Preston, she would usually talk about him. She would talk about his most recent travels, or who he met. She used to joke that he would talk for five minutes about meeting the leader of some country, and then he would talk for hours about meeting some local character. Mr. Preston was more impressed with some local artisan that could make a beautiful ornate bed than with some rich guy that could afford to sleep in it. It took a few years, but I eventually learned to appreciate conversation with him as well. I guess you kind of get used to trying to meet his demands because it will some day get you more interesting conversation. I know that doesn't make sense."

"No. I think I can sort of understand what you're saying. Just because I love talking with Barbara, I've learned to live with a lot of her little quirks."

"And you don't have any?" chided Ralph.

"Nope, not a one," joked Jack.

"Oh!" said Ralph, jumping to his feet. "I should check on Mr. Preston. I'll be right back."

Jack sat there and quietly finished the rest of his Pepsi. He could see how Cliff would be interesting to talk with. He had been to so many places and met so many different people. What he couldn't seem to get a grasp on was Cliff ever settling down enough to carry on a conversation. All he ever saw Cliff do was push, push, push. When he first saw Cliff in his wheelchair he thought it was justly deserved punishment. Now he was beginning to see Cliff, and the wheelchair, in a new light.

"Mr. Preston is ready to resume," said Ralph as he walked back into the library. Typical time-to-get-back-to-what-Mr.-Montgomery-wants speech from Mr. Huntley. This time, however, Jack understood better why he had it.

"That was quick," Jack said looking at his watch. It had only been about an hour or so.

"Yes, sometimes he revives very fast," Ralph replied. Jack personally hoped it had been an answer to his prayer, but he didn't say anything.

12

As they sat down again, this time in the conservatory, Jack asked, "Where did we leave off? Did you have any questions about what we've talked about so far? Anything else you want to know?" He was trying to give them some options as to which direction to take the conversation, because he didn't have a clue.

"Mr. Preston and I talked briefly while you were gone," said Ralph. "If I might summarize what you've told us so far, using the Afghanistan model, I would say that we are in the middle of a war, and we were born on the wrong side. I would assume then, that there must be something we have to do to get free of this bondage we are under; if that's what you call it."

"There sure is," said Jack. "You would have to be born again, only this time on the right side." He couldn't quite interpret the looks on their faces after that statement. It was sort of a puzzled, irritated, inquisitive, angry type of look. It was a look that lasted uncomfortably long. "What are you thinking?" he finally had to ask to break the silence.

"To be honest, ever since Jimmy Carter said he was born again, I've been uncomfortable with the term," said Cliff. "I just don't understand it. It seems to be used a lot, both by Christians and by others to mock Christians. What exactly does it mean to be born again?"

"Funny you should ask," said Jack.

"I knew you were setting us up," said Ralph. "Well, go ahead;

hit us with the religious stuff."

"Oh, do I sense some pent up animosity to ministers or something, Ralphy?" he said sarcastically. "Run into some street preachers downtown or something?"

"No," Ralph snapped. "Well, sort of. I guess I just hate it when religious people use terms that make sense only to someone in their own group."

"So do I. In fact, in normal conversation you would probably never hear me use the term born again, just because I dislike the way it has been misused. Did you know that Jesus said it first?" He said this as he grabbed the Bible again.

"No I didn't, but I'm sure you're going to show me."

"You bet I am," he said, and handed Ralph the Bible. "Read John, chapter three."

As Ralph read to himself, Cliff said to Jack, "I'll assume you're correct. Go ahead and tell me what you know about this born again stuff."

Remember how I was telling you that you will need to enter the spiritual realm if you want to find Gloria? Well, being born again is how you do it. A lot of believers think that the moment of death is the time that you cross over to the other side. But that moment of rebirth, being born again, can happen sooner, and it really should." Then Jack remembered that there was something he forgot to mention. "There is a reason you need to be born again. Did I say something earlier about corruption?"

"Not that I remember," said Cliff.

"Well, anyway, the Bible says that when we're born again we are born of incorruptible seed. What that refers to is the fact that God created his living things to reproduce, by seed, after their own kind. To corrupt means to make something bad that is supposed to be good."

"Like a judge or a government official?"

"Exactly. I bet you've encountered that a few times."

"Oh yeah."

"God did not originally create us to slowly deteriorate. That was a result of Adam's rebellious act in the Garden of Eden. It is the corruptible flesh that eventually gives up on you." Jack had not meant that last statement to be in reference to Cliff's health, and now he felt a twinge of regret for saying it. Cliff, on the other hand, was not showing any emotion one way or the other, so Jack continued.

"Have you ever looked at your horoscope?" asked Jack. "Have you read under your sign what type of a person you are supposed to be? You know, if you are a Libra you are supposed to be, I don't know, aggressive or something?"

"I've seen what you're talking about in the paper. Never paid much attention to it. Why?"

"I just wanted to make a point. A lot of people think that if you are born in a certain time period that you will be a particular type of individual. The sad thing is, a lot of people actually seem confined to be that type of a person. It is almost as if when you're born, you're put under the jurisdiction of some demon that manipulates your life and turns you into his kind of a drone. But when you are reborn into God's kingdom, you are set free to be whatever kind of individual you want to be. I believe God even sets you free to live a life totally contrary to Him, if that is what you choose. You'll probably reap the rewards that ignorance and rebellion are guaranteed to deliver. But you are still free to pursue them. Of course, people with that type of attitude almost never ask to be set free from it.

"When you're born again, you're born in a spiritual way. I believe that when this happens, we are again given the ability to communicate with God like Adam could in the Garden of Eden, before the fall. Once we can communicate with God, we can receive instruction from Him as to how to live our everyday lives."

"Is that where these TV preachers get the 'God told me this' and 'God told me that' stuff?" asked Ralph, not even trying to hide the sarcasm in his voice.

"I suppose." Jack had to respond, honestly. "But then again, I'm not them. I don't know what is going on in their heads. I question what they say probably more than you do. The difference is, I'm supposed to."

"What do you mean?" Cliff asked.

"When God gives you a message that is meant for someone else, it's called prophecy. Some people think prophecy is talking about end-of-the-world type stuff. In reality, it's anything told to you by God that is meant to be relayed to someone else, whether it's an individual, a group, or a nation. In the book of First Corinthians, chapter fourteen, it says that whenever a prophecy is given, what is said should be weighed carefully and the spirit should be tested. What was spoken *should* have come from God, but it could also have come from a demon, or even the mind of the person who spoke it. Unfortunately, I have seen very few instances of the message being challenged or tested, even though God says in His Word that we should."

"What if God speaks to you, and it's not for someone else, it's just for you?"

"Then you should still test what you heard. Whatever it was that you thought you heard should not be contrary in any way with God's written word, the Bible. Do you remember that time when you were doing research down on the Amazon? You told us the story once about receiving an invitation to visit a tribe of head hunters that supposedly came from the chief of the tribe. Did you have a particular reason for turning down the invitation? I mean, you'd been trying to get in to see this tribe for years, if I recall correctly."

"Yes, I do remember the tribe you're talking about. They were one of the lost tribes that were discovered in the early 1800's and then not seen again until the 1950's. A neighboring tribe delivered the message to me."

"So why did you turn down the invitation?" Jack asked again.

"Because the message read that I was supposed to meet the chief of the tribe at a neutral location upriver from their village."

"So?"

"So, I knew enough about this tribe to know that the chief would never meet *anyone* outside his village. He never *traveled* outside his village. It was taboo. Once he stepped out of the village, he was no longer the chief. It was that simple. What was the point you were trying to make?"

"The point I was trying to make was that you didn't let the zeal you had to reach this tribe blind you from what you knew about the tribe. Some people have such a desire to be touched by God that if they ever have a spiritual experience of any sort, they don't want to question it for fear of making God angry. In reality, God would rather we sought the truth, even if it means questioning *Him*."

"Have you ever had God speak to you something that was meant for someone else?"

"Yes I have, although I haven't always followed through like I should. There have been times that I said something when I thought I shouldn't have. There have been times when I knew what to say, when, how, and who to say it to, and did. Then I was told I was nuts, or the message was wrong, or I was of the devil or something. I would seriously question whether what I said was actually from God. Then I would find out, sometimes years later, that what I said was correct. The person it was for just didn't want to believe it. Most of the time what God shares with me doesn't mean anything to me. But to the person it is intended for it is precisely what they need to hear, or it's confirming something they already heard from God themselves."

"Has God told you anything about me?" asked Cliff.

That question caught Jack off guard. He hadn't even been trying to listen along those lines. The question humbled him almost as much as it humbled Cliff to ask it. The question seemed like a bit of a challenge and a lot of a plea. He just stared at Cliff for a moment, while he silently apologized to God for not even asking Him if there was something He wanted to tell Cliff, and then asked Him exactly that. As usual he heard no voice in his head, and didn't think he knew some deep dark secret that only Cliff would know. He just had a feeling Cliff had something he wanted to tell him or ask him, but hadn't.

"No Cliff, God hasn't told me anything, and to be honest, I haven't asked. But I would like to ask you something. Is there something you want to say to me, but haven't?" When he asked the question, Cliff turned away from him. Jack thought maybe he had offended him somehow, but he didn't say anything. He just waited for Cliff to respond.

When he did turn back around, he said, "Jack, I have been struggling with what you've been telling me. So much of it seems so foreign, so strange. When I try to analyze it, it sort of makes sense, and it sort of seems weird. So when you talked about testing what you hear, I decided to test you."

Panic washed over Jack. He felt he must have said something wrong and lost all of Cliff's trust. Now he was going to get the royal Preston boot.

13

"You've probably been wondering why I've listened to you so earnestly," Cliff commented. "To be honest, in times past I wouldn't have given you the time of day unless I thought it was in my best interest." Now Jack felt like God was allowing Cliff to know what *he* was thinking.

"A few months ago I had a dream," Cliff continued. "In this dream I was sitting on the front porch of a house out in the old west, having a casual conversation with another man. Somehow, I knew this man was an enlightened one, a being of light, a seer of the ages. He told me of wondrous things and explained all the mysteries of life to me. It's hard to explain, but it was as if the man spoke for days at a time and explained everything in minute detail. He seemed to know that this is what I'd been seeking for most of my life. For some reason, even though I'd been seeking this understanding for years, what he spoke didn't interest me. I found my mind wandering and I had a desire to end it all."

"By end it all do you mean all of his talking?" Jack asked.

"No, I mean end it *all*, the talking, the dream, even my very life. I was so exhausted and worn out from seeking, and now I was worn out from knowing. I was definitely tired of hearing. Anyway, in this dream as I was thinking about how much I wanted this to end, this man started slowly fading away. In the middle of saying something, he just vaporized. At the same time I saw an intense glow forming behind me on the right. I turned to see a bright light taking up most of the dirt street that this house sat on. There seemed to be a person in the midst of this light, but I couldn't make him out because my eyes just couldn't handle the brightness of the light.

"As I blocked the light with my hand, trying to see this being, I heard a voice that came sort of from this being, but, actually, it came from all of this light. It said to me, *"You have seen and heard many things, and filled your mind to over flowing, and yet you still know nothing. I am what you desire to know. I am sending someone who desires to help you know. Make room to receive him."* I then woke up so suddenly from this dream that my eyes still hurt from squinting."

"You never told me about that dream," said Ralph.

"I never told anyone," Cliff confessed. "I never knew quite what to think about the dream. I've never forgotten a single detail of it, except of course the massive amount of verbiage that the man spoke. That has never happened with one of my dreams before. It's as if I can replay the dream in my mind at any moment. It was actually that dream that caused me to push forward with this whole...hoopla thing." Cliff looked over at Ralph, who was staring at the floor. "I'm sorry, Ralph, I couldn't say anything to you. I couldn't tell anyone. For all I knew the dream could have just been a crazy dream, nothing more. Or it could have been a message from God. The person he was referring to could even have been you. It was just something I had to keep to myself."

All three of them sat there quietly, staring at their own unique patch of the marble tiled floor. Jack was not sure if the weight of the moment was on the other two as much as it was on him. Cliff finally broke the silence. "You seem to be lost in thought," he said in Jack's direction.

He was. As Cliff had been sharing that dream, Jack could see it as clearly as if he was day-dreaming it himself. He could almost feel his eyes squinting at the light. As if having just heard those words spoken again, he asked Cliff, "When the voice said *'Make room to receive him'* what do you think he meant?"

"At first I thought I should make up a room here in the manor to take in some holy man as a guest, maybe the guy in the bright clothes in the dream. To be honest, I was kind of repulsed by the idea. The more I thought about it, the more I kept getting thoughts about all of the things I believed and had formulated from all of the various cultures I had come into contact with. The conclusion I eventually came to, was that I was going to have to make room in my mind. I was going to have to discard some of what I believed to be true, to make room for the real truth."

"Such as the fact that Monopoly games take at least two hours?" Jack asked.

"I would say that's a good place to start," said Cliff, smiling.

"Are you thinking that I might possibly be that one that you are supposed to make room for?"

"That's what I'm beginning to wonder," he answered.

"Are you repulsed by *that* idea?"

"I wouldn't say that. Surprised, maybe."

"What if I told you I wasn't?"

"What?"

"What if I told you I wasn't the one you were to make room for?"

"But...how could you be sure? How could you have known that I was keeping something from you?" Anguish was becoming evident in his voice. He sounded like a man who was trying to find his way out of the wilderness, and just found out he had another whole mountain range to cross.

"Do you remember that time you crossed the Sahara?" Jack asked him.

"You're going to give me another example from my travels?"

"It worked last time, didn't it?"

"Yeah, I suppose."

"Well, do you? You told us that your water ran out two days before the desert did."

"Yes, what about it?"

"Let's say that I would've been the one to have greeted you when you finally arrived at that outpost on the edge of the Sahara desert."

"You probably would have *sold* me the water," said Cliff, in as mean of a voice as he could muster.

"Now, now, be nice," Jack chided, knowing he was kidding. "Suppose the water I gave you was murky, foul water. Would you have drunk it anyway?"

"At that point, probably," he said, "but just enough to get me to the next outpost."

"Fair enough. What if it was Perrier out of my boot? Would you still drink it?"

"Yes, but it would have been borderline. It would have broken my heart to see Perrier ruined like that though." That statement got Ralph laughing. He knew as well as Jack did that Cliff loved his Perrier.

"That was a little unfair, but I'll accept it as being honest. What if it was Perrier water in a Perrier bottle, but it had been laced with cyanide? Would you have been thirsty enough to drink it anyway?"

"Did I know it?" Cliff asked.

"Did I tell you it had cyanide in it? No. Could you have known? You tell me."

"Well, if I would have suspected something, I could have sniffed the bottle. If there was cyanide in it, I would have smelled it. Then I would have fired you on the spot."

With that, Ralph again did one of his spitting guffaws and

blurted out, "and probably not because you were trying to kill him, but because you ruined the Perrier!" They all had a good laugh at that one.

"I probably would have trusted you enough, or been thirsty enough, that I wouldn't have thought to check it." Cliff added.

"I appreciate the trust, Cliff, but you never know." Jack said, only partially kidding. He then continued, "What if I gave you the Perrier..."

"Another one?" Cliff asked. "How many more of these have you got? You're making me thirsty."

"Last one, I swear, I think. Anyway, suppose I gave you a Perrier, but you were too weak to drink it. Would you have been humble enough to let me feed it to you?"

"Well of course I would! I'm dying of thirst! I would have let you feed me Jersey marsh water. Ralph, uh...Mr. Huntley, get me a Perrier."

As Ralph jumped up, half sat, got up again, not knowing if Cliff was joking or serious, Jack continued. "The point I am trying to make Cliff, and I'd like you to hear this too," he said, looking at Ralph, who sat back down at Cliff's beckoning. "Too many desperate people grasp at the first thing they come across that offers them hope and quenches their thirst for enlightenment. What they receive could grant them life or it may take it from them. In their desperation they don't think to test it.

"I know who that person is that the dream referred to. In the dream, the voice you heard--who I truly believe was God trying to speak to you--this voice said there was someone who wants to help you know. Cliff, and Ralph, I want you to know about God, really. I want you to *know* Him too, not just about Him. But to be honest with you, really honest, with myself and you, I don't want to be the one to help you."

As he spoke this to them, it was as if he could see the

confusion in their minds, like he could feel the frustration in their hearts. At the same time, he felt the panic and the peace of knowing that he just told them something that he never would have told them if he could have chosen not to. Even if it *was* the truth, and he knew it was.

"Who is it then?" Cliff finally asked. The sound in his voice was like he had reconciled with himself that he had somehow burned his bridges with Jack, who now wanted out of this conversation. In his way, he was trying to give Jack the opportunity to end it. How little he understood about Jack, and the fact that he was having one of the best days of his life.

"Cliff, and you too, Ralph, that person who wants to help you know God, is God himself."

"What are you talking about? I don't understand," said Cliff.

"Neither do I," said Ralph. "And just where do *you* fit into this? How could you have known that Cliff was holding something back from you, and me?"

"The best way I can describe it, is to go back to the Perrier thing. Cliff, you can try to find fame, fortune, the Taj Mahal, or a lost tribe in Brazil. But one of the easiest things to find in this world is water. It's everywhere. It's in rain and snow, in rivers, in the ocean. It's in every breath you breathe in or breathe out."

"But it's not Perrier," said Cliff.

"No, it's not Perrier. But on the other hand, Perrier is just water."

"Now *you're* getting nasty," said Cliff.

"The point I'm making," Jack continued, "is that water is common, Perrier is special, especially to you. We have a tendency to give the word 'holy' the meaning of being super good or righteous. A holy man is someone who walks softly and doesn't carry a stick, if you know what I mean. In the context of the Bible, it not only means that, it also means unique, set apart, special, sort of one-of-a-kind. Like Perrier is to common water. To be unholy is to be common.

"I do know the person who wants to help you know God. He is God's Holy Spirit. He is a spirit, but He is unique, one-of-a-kind. There is only one God, and He has only one Spirit. In your travels you recall how the people in Africa, or South America, or Asia, or Japan for that matter, tried to appease numerous spirits. They had rituals, or sacrifices, or something to try to win the favor of these spirits so they could have health, or good fortune."

"Yes, I do remember all those ridiculous rituals," said Cliff. "I'm sure you remember how much I disliked them. Some seemed to defy common sense, like bathing in the horribly polluted Ganges River, or dedicating a temple to rats."

"It is difficult to understand," Jack went on, "but if you're thirsty for a relationship with God, His Holy Spirit is the Perrier. What am I, you ask? I am like the boot, or the bottle, or maybe a fancy glass. I am just the vessel that carries the Perrier, and, regarding the murkiness, I can contaminate it. If you are dying of thirst, you won't pour out the water and cherish the cup. I guess what I am trying to say is, drink the water, and forget the cup."

"What about the cyanide?" asked Ralph.

"I'm sorry to say that there are people out there who will offer you spiritual enlightenment that contains enough truth to whet your appetite but will contain enough lies to kill your relationship with God. Like you said, you can't tell if the talk-show experts are telling the truth, or if they are experts on anything. God never lies and he actually does know everything. So no matter how thirsty you are, you should still test what you are drinking, and not trust anyone, no matter who they are. Don't worry about offending God; he loves those who seek the truth. And certainly don't give any thought to offending the cup."

Ralph looked over at Cliff, who seemed to be lost in thought. Jack expected Cliff to be drifting off with fatigue by this point, but he appeared to still be quite alert. Finally Ralph, as if speaking for both of them, asked, "How *do* we test the water, or the spirit, or whatever?"

"Yes, Jack," said Cliff. "I understand the need for simile, metaphor, and analogy. Let me have it once in plain English."

There again was the voice of Cliff let-me-have-it-straight Montgomery. It was strange how now it seemed so refreshing to Jack. It used to annoy him. "Am I to understand that you believe God exists, at least enough to seek some kind of a relationship with Him?" he asked back, point-blank.

"Yes," said Cliff, so quickly that he must have anticipated Jack was going to ask it. Jack looked over at Ralph, who just nodded. He sensed, he hoped, there was eagerness in the nod.

"Then you have already done part of what it takes to know Him. In the Bible, in the book of Hebrews, chapter 11, it says that without faith it is impossible to please God, and that he who comes to God, must believe that he exists, and that he rewards those who diligently seek him. Any questions so far? I would suggest that if you have any, you'd better ask. Since I had a religious background, I have a tendency to gloss over important points that I take for granted everyone understands."

"Plus, you repeat yourself," said Cliff. "You already told us about God rewarding us for seeking him."

"Oh, yeah, sorry. It's an important verse."

"And you remembered where it was found," chimed in Ralph.

"I looked it up. Anyway, any questions?"

"What are the rewards?" asked Ralph.

"Finding him," snapped Cliff. "Pay attention Mr. Huntley. Jack, how can I get faith to please God? What exactly is your concept of faith?"

"In the Bible it says it is..."

"It is the substance of things hoped for and the evidence of things not seen," said Ralph, with a smug look on his face. When Cliff shot him a glare he said, "Well, it was right there in chapter 11. I was looking up what Jack said earlier."

"I suppose you know what that means?" asked Cliff.

"No. I was going to ask."

"If you read all of chapter 11, you will see stories of people that God considered to have a lot of faith," said Jack, to answer Ralph's question, and to get the conversation back on track. "In every case, I think you will see someone who looked past his particular physical predicament and believed that somehow God could change the situation. As an example, suppose you need to cross a deep canyon..."

"Another analogy?" asked Cliff impatiently.

"Yup. You'll get over it. You need to cross this canyon," Jack continued. "The only way across it is over a foot bridge. Faith isn't simply believing that the foot bridge has been built by the world's greatest foot bridge builder. Faith is crossing the bridge. You could have all the doubts in the world that you will survive. Doubting alone is not lacking faith. Pushing past your fears and walking across that bridge, even if you scream the entire distance, is real faith. What you can *see* is rocks two hundred feet below you. What is unseen is the strength of the bridge, and the skill that went into making it. Faith is putting your trust in the unseen part, and ignoring what you see.

"If you think back to what I was saying about all the angels and demons and stuff, you could consider them as what is unseen, where the physical world is what is seen. An example of this...Wait!" Jack snapped, holding up his hand to stop another Cliff rebuke. "This isn't an analogy. Ralph, look up Luke seven, verse...something or other."

"Oh, thanks," said Ralph.

"I am looking for the story about the faith of a centurion. Luke is the third book in the new testament."

"I know, I know," snapped Ralph, chidingly. "I used to be Catholic. I had to memorize the books in order. There were a few more in our Bible."

Somewhat surprised, Jack commented, "I didn't know you were Catholic."

"Yeah, well... here it is. Chapter seven actually starts with the title of 'The Faith of the Centurion.'"

"Hey, I actually remembered. He had a sick servant, and had sent someone to ask Jesus to heal him. Jesus then started out towards the Centurions house, but before he got there, the Centurion sent some people to stop him. Can you find that part, Ralph, and read the rest?"

"Uh, yeah. Let's see, *Luke 7:6-10 ...the Centurion sent friends to him, saying unto him, Lord, trouble not thyself, for I am not worthy that thou shouldest enter under my roof. Wherefore neither thought I myself worthy to come unto thee. But say in a word and my servant shall be healed. For I also am a man set under authority, having under me soldiers, and I say unto one go, and he goeth, and to another come and he cometh. and to my servant do this, and he doeth it. When Jesus heard these things, he marveled him, and turned him about, and said unto the people that followed him, I say unto you, I have not found so great faith, no, not in Israel. And they that were sent, returning to the house, found the servant whole that had been sick.*"

"Let me see that." said Cliff, grabbing the Bible from Ralph.

"It's about halfway down on the left."

"I'll find it." snapped Cliff. "Chapter seven."

Jack let Cliff read the verses for a while. Most people would think Cliff was being a bit rude, but Jack understood him. When he was interested in something, Cliff didn't let anyone come between him and the source of the information. When he grabbed that Bible, Jack knew he wasn't challenging his interpretation, or Ralph's ability to read. No, Cliff wanted as close to first-hand information as he could get. Jack was sure that some of that attitude eventually burned into his own conscience. He was reminded of something else he wanted to share with them. "Cliff, can I interrupt?"

There was silence for a moment. "Yes, go ahead," he finally said.

Jack knew what Cliff had just done. He had a unique way of creating a mental bookmark so he could go back to where he was thinking after he was through dealing with the current interruption. Most people would just yell, "Can't you see I'm busy?" Cliff could actually give you his full attention, if you gave him a minute to bookmark his thoughts. Jack never figured out how he did that.

"I would like you to read the first 3 verses of Hebrews, chapter one." Jack decided not to tell him where the book of Hebrews was located in the Bible. In fact, both he and Ralph knew the look on Cliff's face. At this moment he was not Mr. Preston, the cripple. He had just become Mr. Montgomery, the writer. There was something going on in Cliff's mind. He was shuffling information, categorizing, sorting, filing, outlining, all in his head. After all these years Jack was still ready to go fetch the tape recorder. His fingers were itching to start typing. Mr. Huntley was ready to schedule a flight to somewhere so Cliff could do research to fill a hole in his understanding.

Cliff eventually found the verses that Jack referred to, read them to himself, and then set the Bible down on the marble topped stand next to him. He then turned away from the other two and wheeled himself to the picture windows looking out onto his estate. Ralph picked up the Bible to find the verses Jack had just suggested that Cliff read.

"Could you read the first two verses please, Mr. Huntley?" said Cliff, as if he knew Ralph was looking at them.

"Sure Mr. Preston....*Hebrews 1:1-2 God, who at sundry times and in divers manners spake in the past unto the fathers by the prophets, hath in these last days spoken unto us by his Son, whom he hath appointed heir of all things, by whom also he made the worlds.*"

Cliff thought about what he had just heard, and then asked Jack, "Did you have something you wanted to tell me about these verses?"

Jack wondered if he was reading Cliff correctly. If he was, something about these verses had caused Cliff to see something, but the picture he had seen wasn't quite in focus. "I just wanted to point out that the writer of this book, some think the Apostle Paul, maybe never met Jesus before he was crucified. Most of those he is writing to, which I believe includes us, also did not know Jesus before he died. Yet Paul says that God now speaks to them, and to us, through Jesus. That tells me Jesus is alive, and He speaks to us now."

Cliff spun his wheelchair around again and looked intently at Jack. "Does he expect us to speak back to him?"

Jack tried to think of a quick way to answer yes to that question. "Let's say you're walking south down a street in New York City." As he said this, he pointed his finger down to illustrate it. "Three blocks north of you and a block and a half to the east another man is walking north. Does it make you angry that the other man does not acknowledge your presence?"

"What? He probably doesn't even know I exist!" exclaimed Cliff.

"So then it doesn't bother you?"

"Of course not."

"Let's say another man is walking north up the street you are on, coming right toward you. Does it bother you if he looks right at you and doesn't even say hello?"

"In New York City? No, not at all."

"What if he was your son?"

The look on Cliff's face spoke volumes. Even though he never had a son, Jack knew Cliff must have looked on Ralph as one. He also knew that Cliff understood New York City. It wasn't an unfriendly place. Living there you would say hello to many people you didn't know, and would never see again. But there are times that you're so busy that you hope you won't meet anyone who demands your attention. You won't even acknowledge people you do know, because you don't have time to engage in conversation with anyone.

"What's your point Jack?" Cliff said with a voice that spoke reluctance and eagerness at the same time.

"In the Bible, God doesn't say that we are to be a stranger to Him five blocks away walking a different direction. He calls us His children. We shouldn't be surprised if He gets a bit upset if we ignore Him, or keep ourselves so busy that we don't feel we have time to stop what we're doing and at least acknowledge His presence."

Cliff was silent as he thought about that for a minute. Then he said, "Would you mind if I asked a few questions, just to clarify things?"

"Not at all," Jack replied. "It'd probably be better if you did."

"First of all, why is it important that we develop a relationship with your god?"

"Let me clarify something first. He's not my god."

"You know what I mean." snorted Cliff.

"Maybe I do. But I need to be sure you know what I mean. He is not my god, or Billy Graham's god, or the Popes god. He's just God. He's not the god of any one person, or any one church, or any one religion, or any one country. It seems like mere semantics, but it's an important point. Until you understand that you can approach God the same as any other human in existence can approach him, you'll have a hard time developing a true relationship with him.

"As far as understanding why it's important, think about it. The Bible says in a number of places that God wants to give us treasures in heaven, that he's building mansions, and that he wants to give us eternal life. Why would he want to do that for someone who ignores him, despises him, or doesn't believe that he even exists? Would you, Cliff, want to give all of this away to a total stranger?" Jack asked as he pointed at the beautiful surroundings.

That last question caused Cliff to spin his wheelchair around and stare out the conservatory windows again. Jack could no longer even speculate as to what was going on in Cliff's mind. A hand on Jack's arm and a glance from Ralph told him that he didn't know either, but that they both needed to give Cliff some space.

14

It seemed to take forever, about ten minutes actually, before anyone spoke. "Mr. Huntley?" said Cliff. "Could I speak with Jack?"

"Well, yeah, but...Mr. Preston...I...are you sure?" stammered Ralph.

"Mr....Ralph, please. Just for a few minutes," pleaded Cliff apologetically.

"Yes sir, sure, Mr. Preston." Ralph said as he slowly got up from his chair. "Do you need me to get you anything? Some ice water, or tea?"

"Make me some of that cinnamon spice tea," Cliff replied. "I'll come get it when I'm through."

"Okay, well, I'll see you in a few minutes then."

"Sure, Ralph, in a few minutes," said Cliff, not too convincingly. They both watched as Cliff's staff of one walked out of sight. When he was convinced Ralph was out of ear shot, he said to Jack, somewhat quietly, "I would prefer you didn't repeat what I am about to say to Ralph. I would prefer to talk to him myself, in my own time."

"Of course, whatever you say," Jack half whispered. "What's up?"

"Oh, nothings up, Jack," Cliff said, in his normal tone of voice. "I just needed to understand a few things. You'll see what I mean, just let me proceed."

"Sure, go ahead."

"When you were talking about the story of the centurion--you remember, the one with the sick servant?"

"Yeah, in Luke seven?"

"I think so. Anyway, he was saying that he was a man under authority, with men under him. He would tell one person to go, and he would go, another to do this or that, and he would do it."

"That's right."

"That got me to remembering the time on safari in Africa. We had these tribesmen that were basically servants. Whatever we told them to do was done. Then I thought about Ralph. For literally his entire adult life he has been going where I tell him to go, and doing what I want him to do. He has sacrificed his own life to serve me...."

"I don't think he feels like he's sacrificed so much," Jack interjected, knowing Cliff was having a hard time continuing. "He's probably living a grander life style than he ever could have on his own."

"Then there were the other verses," Cliff continued, as if Jack hadn't spoken.

"Uh...in Hebrews?"

"I suppose. It said something about God speaking to us through his son, who was made heir of everything."

"Yes, that would be Hebrews, the first verses of the book."

"When Ralph was reading those verses, I was thinking of him again. Jack, you know I never had children. But I do consider Ralph to be the son I never had. I intend to make him the heir to my entire fortune. He deserves it for the sacrifice he's made. In fact, if he wouldn't have made that sacrifice, I'm sure I wouldn't have all of this."

"But that isn't what you wanted to talk to me about, is it?" asked Jack.

"No, not exactly. You said that God considers us his children.

Well, I consider Ralph as my child, even though he's far beyond childhood. As you were speaking, I probably should have been listening to what you were trying to explain to me about God. Instead I was...I was...". Cliff could not seem to finish his sentence. It appeared to Jack that he was locked in some kind of a struggle, probably to contain his emotions and maintain his tough guy image.

Then, in literally a split second, Jack himself was filled with emotion. It was an incredibly strong love combined with deep regret. Strangely, it was directed at Ralph. Then, just as suddenly, he was filled with an even stronger love. It reminded him of when his sister-in-laws sick baby was laying in an isolation ward in the hospital. He longed to hold his sister-in-law to comfort her, but restrained himself because it might appear inappropriate. He also longed to hold that little baby and stop its crying and screaming. All he could do was watch it through the glass and scream at God to heal that little child. This time, all of that love and desperation was directed at Cliff. "You were overwhelmed with love for your adopted son Ralph," he said, finishing the sentence that Cliff was struggling with.

"Yes. But how could you..."

"How could I know what you were thinking? I didn't. But I know how God works. When he needs to get a point across, he doesn't give you just the knowledge, he gives you the understanding. As I was trying to get my point across, that God really does exist, he was trying to get *his* point across. That point is that he loves you. You can't fully understand that love unless you understand what it means to love your own child that much. He gave you a love for Ralph that was beyond what you were capable of creating in yourself. Am I right?"

"Yes, Jack. In fact, it's overwhelming. Almost to the point of being embarrassing. Or painful. Are you saying that is how

God loves me?"

"I believe so."

"Why?"

"Why does he love you? I can't even answer that about myself. But I do know this. Somewhere in the past few hours he has given me a love for you like that. I guarantee you I didn't walk into this place with it."

"What must I do?"

"What must you do about what? Telling Ralph you love him?"

"No, Jack. Please. What do I do now to know God?"

"Cliff, I think you have already done what you need to do. You have changed your mind."

"I did what?"

"You've changed your mind. The Bible says you need to repent. To repent means to make a 180 degree turn. To change the direction of your thinking from selfish personal ambition to determining that you will spend the rest of your life seeking him, God. Instead of always looking inward to what Cliff needs, you start looking outward, to God, and to the needs of others. It is also important that you confess to others about the change in your thinking, like you just did with me. God will make changes in your life as you begin to seek Him and his guidance. Right now there's something you would really like to say to Ralph, but you find it too hard. In fact, you've always found it too hard. What is it?"

Jack heard nothing but stunned silence from Cliff. Jack wasn't sure why he said what he said. He certainly didn't know that Cliff had something to say to Ralph. In fact, as he thought about it, he assumed that with as much time as those two spent together, they would have said everything there was to say. Still, he felt a peace deep within that he had asked the right question.

He just hoped Cliff had the answer.

As the silence continued he could see that Cliff was wrestling with something in his mind. He knew Cliff needed help on the inside, where only God could know what it was. He decided that Cliff needed prayer. In the quiet of his mind, he cried out to God. *'Father, I know you're doing a work in Cliff. That's a work I don't wish to interrupt. But I feel that Cliff needs help. So if there are spirits of the enemy that are keeping him from speaking, I ask that he be released now in the name of your Son Jesus. I ask, in fact, that those spirits would be bound and not allowed to operate in Cliff. Help Cliff's mind to be free from doubt and fear, and give him the trust and boldness he needs to confess what he needs to confess in order to be set free. Thank you for your faithfulness Father, and your love for us.'*

As he spoke those words silently in his mind, Cliff turned and looked at him. He had the angriest scowl on his face that Jack had ever seen, and he had seen plenty over the years. At the same moment the love that Jack had experienced for Cliff was replaced with an intense hatred for what he now saw in Cliff's eyes. "Leave this place now!" Jack commanded, looking right into Cliff's eyes.

"I am not leaving, this is my home!" responded Cliff, in a voice that sounded different than the man Jack had been speaking with for the past hour. Fortunately Jack had dealt with this kind of a problem before. Cliff was harboring something. Something evil. Something Jack knew the real Cliff now wanted nothing to do with.

"Cliff's sins are covered by the blood of Jesus," he said, still looking right into Cliff's eyes, "and in the name of Jesus I command you to leave!"

The tormented look on Cliff's face suddenly left, and he began sobbing and crying as if it was coming from deep down inside of him. It was as if sixty years of anger, sadness, and pain were all churning out of him at once. As the sobbing started to subside, Jack laid his hand on Cliff's shoulder, and it erupted all over again. He knew exactly what Cliff was going through. It had been two decades since he had gone through something similar, but he remembered it like it was yesterday. And he still remembered the profound healing it brought to his soul. He would never forget it. Not for all eternity.

"Thank you, Jack," Cliff said when he could finally speak. Then the tears erupted again. This was a vulnerability he had never seen in Cliff. He knew that for the first time in his adult life, Cliff wasn't ashamed to be seen crying. Some people say that it's not good to crush a man's pride. Sometimes though, it's the pride that crushes the man. Cliff just had a huge weight lifted off of him. Without the heaviness of that pride, he could finally face his sorrow and anger, and be done with it.

"Jack, I need you to take me in to see Ralph. There's something I need to say to him." As Cliff said this, the tears erupted again. Jack decided to wait until they subsided. When Cliff felt he could face Ralph, he just pointed at the door that left the conservatory, and Jack guided his wheelchair through the house. As they approached the kitchen, Ralph heard them coming and met them in the dining room with the tea. Jack sat down at the dining room table as Ralph quickly set the tea service down and took Jack's place at the wheelchair.

After Ralph had positioned Cliff at the table and poured everyone some tea, Cliff said to him, "Could you please sit down, Ralph?"

For the first time since they had entered the room, Ralph looked at Cliff. He suddenly realized that this wasn't exactly the man that he had left in the conservatory, though he couldn't put his finger on what was different. Ralph slowly sat down as he asked, "What's wrong Mr. Preston? Are you okay?"

"I'm fine...I just need...to say something to you." Cliff spoke slowly and haltingly, like a long distance runner trying to catch his breath. "Ralph... everything I have?...It's yours."

"What? What are you talking about? You've already allowed me to use almost everything you own. Do you mean you're going to will everything to me? Jack, what is he talking about?"

"Ralph!" Cliff snapped, holding up a hand in Jack's direction. "Listen to what I said...Everything I own...is yours...Do you understand me?...I didn't say...it's going to be yours...or it's yours to use...It's yours...period."

"Quite frankly, I don't understand."

"I didn't think you would. That's why I said it."

"You're not making sense. Jack, did something happen to Mr. Preston?"

"I can't answer that," Jack said honestly. But he hoped it had.

"Ralph, be quiet for a minute and listen to me." It sounded to them as if Cliff was starting to revive. "I experienced something out there in the conservatory. It was something I hope to never experience again the rest of my life."

"Jack, what did you do to Mr. Preston?"

"Nothing!" exclaimed Jack, not knowing if he was lying or not. He was as confused about what Cliff was saying as Ralph was.

"Ralph, I said be quiet, please. Leave Jack out of this. Something strange happened to me. As I was talking with the two of you, in a brief moment of time, it was as if I relived every selfish moment in my life. I saw all of the times that I did whatever I did in whatever way would accomplish what I needed, with no concern for other people involved. The strange part was that instead of feeling the satisfaction of accomplishment that I usually did, I felt the crushing weight of slavery to the task. I assume that is what those individuals felt that I used for my own advancement."

At this point Cliff began to sob again, uncontrollably. Ralph, feeling confused and embarrassed for Cliff, tried to carry the conversation. "That does sound strange. What do you think it was?" he asked, looking at Jack. "You don't think it might have been a light stroke or something do you?"

That line of thinking seemed to snap Cliff out of it. Looking right at Ralph, Cliff said, "Ralph, I understand something now that I've never understood before. It wasn't the Pharaohs that built the pyramids. It was the slaves."

Confusion was still a large part of Ralph's thinking. He was, however, starting to understand that Cliff was being very serious about something. This wasn't twenty years of senility catching up to the old man. And for some reason, he felt like he was in the hot seat. He decided to keep quiet until Cliff was through.

"As I was witnessing myself being the selfish, driven man that I was, I also noticed something else. Ralph, you were the one I was usually leaning on. You were the slave...that...built my pyramid." Cliff could hardly get out those last words before going into another session of deep sobs and gushing tears. Jack could tell Ralph was only barely successful holding back the emotion himself, even if he wasn't sure why. Jack, on the other hand, knew why his composure had a hair trigger. It was joy for Cliff. He knew how hard it was, and how healing it was, for him to face that sin in his life and confess it. They both just sat there staring at something else in the room and waited for Cliff to compose himself.

"Ralph?" Cliff started again, getting their attention. "Do you understand what I am trying to say? I have--we have--what we have because of your due diligence. When I gave up writing, you brought back my pen. When the publisher dropped me, you found another. When I refused to see them, you faced them like the man that I never recognized you were." By this time Cliff's face was fully into a sob, but he kept going. "When I would snap at my employees, I now know it was you that kept them loyal to me. And when I fled from society, it was you that sacrificed your life to protect me. For many years I have been so proud of my accomplishments, and for some reason you were proud of me. Ralph, I have to say that your accomplishments overshadow mine, and I'm proud of you."

At that point they all lost it. All of these years Ralph had forced himself to just assume that Cliff appreciated his efforts. This was probably the first time Cliff ever acknowledged what so many of the rest of those in his office knew for years. It was uncanny the way Cliff's rebukes would roll off of Mr. Huntley. Jack felt quite ashamed now for the way all of them had talked about these two. Cliff actually did have a heart, and his Staff had strength. At the moment, he couldn't remember how he justified his past judgments of them.

"You know what?" asked Cliff, when he could finally speak. "There are headhunters who would eat men that cried like us." Through the laughing tears they all agreed they looked pretty silly.

After a couple more difficult-to-contain laughing sessions, Cliff said to Ralph, "Tomorrow I would like you--I would like us--to try to make contact with certain people on the list and talk to them personally, if they would care to. There are a lot of people I am indebted to that I've ignored. I don't have a lot of time left, but at least maybe I can make peace with some of them. There's one person that comes to mind right away. She was very efficient in her job and I didn't have to pay her much because she was so young. Remember her Ralph? The cute little freckle-faced gal that screened my mail? She had a real knack for knowing what was important to me, and saved me a lot of time. Did you ever locate her?"

"Yes, I remember her. She was one of the brighter spots in the office. I sent an invitation to her parents. I believe she RSVP'd but I don't remember seeing her here."

Jack suddenly remembered something and grabbed a piece of paper out of his wallet. "Here, you're probably going to need this," he said, handing it to Cliff.

"What's this?" asked Cliff, as he opened it up. "Who is this?...Is this?...Where did you get this?...Is this that girls phone number?"

"Yes, it's the phone number for the formerly young and freckled Jenny Baker. She was here, right there in the library. She really wanted to see you. I think she wanted a piece of your hide for firing her. Honestly, she is still a very pleasant young woman. She married Robert Lynn, one of the guys down at the publisher. He definitely wants a piece of your hide. If you're going to meet with them, you better send Ralphy in first," Jack said with a chuckle.

"I can see you still like to rub salt in my wounds," said Cliff. "Okay, I deserved it." After he said that, a somber look came over him. "Did you read this?" he asked.

"No. Why? Was there something there besides her phone number?"

"Yes, there is. It says...'Tell him I forgive him.'"

They all sat there in an emotional silence for a while. Then Cliff asked, "God knew I was going to need this phone number, didn't he?"

"I can't speak for him," Jack replied, "but that would be my guess."

"I don't believe you ever finished telling me what I needed to do to know God. He obviously seems to know me."

Jack thought about that for a few seconds, until he could recall where he had left off, and what he thought was the most necessary things for Cliff to understand. "The first thing to do is to confess your belief in God. Do you really now believe that God exists?" Jack asked him point blank.

"I do." Cliff said, with a bit of difficulty. "I can't explain why I do, but I know I do. It is as if I can feel him looking over my shoulder, watching me...and loving me." Cliff started to sob again, and Ralph just got a puzzled look on his face.

Jack felt compelled to continue, and said, "In your Africa book, you talked about blood covenants between rival tribes. You said that in order for the covenant to be sealed, someone from each tribe needed to shed blood."

Cliff stopped sobbing and looked at Jack. "That's right. One person from each side would represent their entire tribe. They would cut their arms and bleed into a bowl. Then they would mix the blood and each of them would drink some. The mingling of the blood meant that their two tribes were now one, they were all brothers from that point on, no more rivalries."

"And so all of the fighting between the tribes ended, just like that?"

"Officially, yes. But all of the tribe members had to accept the covenant and drop their claims against their rivals."

"Well, God established a blood covenant with us humans, and Jesus was the one who shed his blood on our behalf. We need to accept that covenant, and submit to the authority that has been established by that covenant, that Jesus is now the Lord of all. Are you ready to confess that Jesus is Lord of *your* life, and drop your claims against him?"

Cliff seemed to be caught off guard by that last statement. Jack wasn't sure why he said it that way, but now it was too late to take it back. He gave Cliff a few moments to respond, but didn't have the patience to let it turn into minutes. He finally had to ask, "What's going through your head Cliff?"

Cliff had an angry look on his face, and he was struggling with something. He finally said bitterly, "He took Gloria from me."

Jack was surprised at the grudge Cliff was holding. "Can you honestly tell me you know that for a fact?" Jack asked. "Gloria was killed by a bolt of lightning. Are you saying that you know for a fact that God directed that bolt of lightning right at her?"

Cliff hung his head and said, "No, I really can't"

"But you assume that because that is what you want to believe," Jack said angrily. "I'm sorry Cliff, but accidents happen. I can give you a lot of other scenarios that could have happened, based on what I have learned about God's character over the years. God could have altered the physical laws of the universe and kept the lightning from striking, but He rarely does that. He could have taken her home to be with Him, rather than suffer the pain from the lightning strike. Or maybe if He hadn't taken her home, you would have taken her from Him."

When Jack said that, Cliff started weeping. When he could finally speak he said, "I *was* trying to steal her away from God. Oh, please God, forgive me for doing that. I didn't understand. Now I do, and as Jack says, I do accept the terms of the covenant. Jesus, I still don't know why you did it, but thank you for shedding your blood for me. I do accept you as Lord in my life. And thank you for letting me live until this moment. I gave you a lot of reasons not to. And thank you for doing what you did to Jack. I don't know who else could have explained this all to me."

As if struck by another regret, Cliff said to him, "Jack, I do need to apologize to you, and to thank you. Again I can see my selfishness in this whole meeting that happened. But I was desperate. Please forgive me."

"Someday, Cliff, you'll understand that the pleasure was mine." Jack could tell that this whole process had taken a toll on Cliff, and that now he needed time to gain some strength physically. "Since I stayed far longer than I told my wife I would, I should be going. If I might get your phone number, I'd like to keep in touch. And let me write my number under Jenny's."

"Yes, please. Ralph, get him our number."

"Sure Mr. Preston," said Ralph, as he was already moving to find something to write with. While he was doing that, Jack shook Cliff's hand to leave. It may have been his imagination, but Cliff's grip seemed stronger than when he arrived. He then swapped phone numbers with Ralph, including a copy of Jenny's, said his goodbyes, and left.

As he was leaving, he realized that he had just seen what he had come there to see. He saw a mighty man fallen, an overthrown dictator. But he also saw something he had never expected. He saw that same man set in a new seat of honor. He knew the day would eventually come when Cliff would again have his name publicized before all men, when the God of all creation reads the name of Heathcliff Montgomery Preston from the Book of Life.

15

Jack tried to sneak quietly into the bedroom where his wife was already in bed. He was dying to tell her all that had happened that night. There were so many aspects of it that he knew only she would understand. He decided though that he wanted her wide awake when he told her. The news could wait until their morning coffee.

"Jack, you're home!" came a not-so-asleep sounding voice from the darkness.

"Sorry, I didn't mean to wake you," Jack replied.

"You didn't," she responded. "I heard you drive in. So how did it go?"

"It's a long story," he said. "Are you sure you want to hear it now?"

"Might as well. I probably won't go to sleep until I do," she said.

That was all Jack needed to hear. He proceeded to tell her about the news crews and the crowds. He told her about the contest and how he won it. He told her about all of the questions they had and how he tried to answer them. Most of all, he told her how God had prepared Cliff's heart, and how God had changed his own. Cliff was no longer Jack's enemy, he was his brother. When he told her the part about the blood covenant, they both started weeping. The wound Jack had received from Cliff was no longer a topic of conversation for them. They were both thankful for that.

"How about Mr. Huntley?" Barbara asked. "Did he confess a belief in Christ as well?"

"He never confessed anything, and quite frankly I don't know where he stands," Jack answered. "I was so concerned about what was happening with Cliff that I didn't pursue it. I got their phone number though. I'm going to try to get together with them again. I can do a little follow up on how Cliff is doing, and maybe talk with Ralph a bit."

"It seems so strange to hear you call him Ralph," Barbara commented. "I don't know if I ever heard you use his first name before."

"I never knew it," lamented Jack. "All these years and I never knew Mr. Huntley's first name. It's embarrassing."

"And what about calling him the Staff?"

"Actually, I think that was justified. Even Cliff admitted to constantly leaning on the guy. I still don't know if I can confess to him that we all called him that."

"You don't think he probably already knows?"

"I hadn't thought about it. Maybe he does. Maybe I should tell him. I mean, after all, it wasn't as much a slam on him as it was on Cliff. We were all really impressed at how much he could put up with. You know, Ralph is truly an amazing person. It would be hard to imagine God not allowing somebody like Ralph into the Kingdom, somebody who is so sacrificially giving."

"But you know that He could?" Barbara asked.

"Yeah, I know. I explained that to them. I sort of told them they needed to respond to His invitation. Cliff definitely understood, and confessed faith in God, and in Jesus dying for him. I should probably make sure Ralph understood it though, huh?"

"I would say so," Barbara chided. "I'm sure God can work with what you've told them so far, and His grace is pretty far-reaching.

But if you get the chance, definitely be more to the point."

"Yeah, I think you're right," Jack agreed. Already his mind was churning out scenarios of explaining to Ralph the need to make a firm commitment. A loving couple can verbalize their love, get physical, even get engaged. Marriage, however, was a covenant, even though some didn't treat it as such. Or maybe he could refer to signing the deed on a house, or getting the title to a car. As hard as he would try not to, Jack always seemed to have to help God explain things to people. In the end, none of his ideas really did much good. He knew he needed the teaching and convicting power of the Holy Spirit for Gods love to be understood properly. It certainly seemed to happen that way with Cliff.

For the next few weeks Jack and Barbara prayed for the men of Preston Manor. Jack called them a number of times to encourage them and give them a few pointers about developing a relationship with God.

One of the most enjoyable times he had though was showing them his Bible search software. He set up a meeting with them on the Internet, like he had learned to do with his clients. He then walked them through downloading the Bible software and taught them how to use it.

When they had a question about hearing God's voice, he showed them how to do a search in the Bible for 'God's voice'. When they discovered it to be like a shepherd calling his sheep, Cliff told them a story about witnessing true shepherds in action in the Middle East.

When Ralph started insisting that Cliff be baptized, Jack helped them look up every single verse there was on baptism. Together, the three of them discovered there was only one baptism, and that was repentance. They discovered that the ways to be baptized -- by water, by the spirit, and by fire – all had to do with repentance.

Being an author, Cliff found it fascinating, and intimidating, that anyone would scrutinize a manuscript to that extent. He especially loved the concordance, where he could look up what the original words were, and interpret them himself. And although he still had trouble comprehending it, he was awestruck at the thought that the author of this book could be looking over his shoulder, and working with him to understand it.

Jack knew that Cliff's time was short, and that he seemed to be doing a lot of his studying with the goal of positioning himself to land in his wife's arms when he died. That understanding, whether theologically correct or not, made Jack want to fall into Barbara's arms while she was still alive.

A loud noise in a strange dream was suddenly interrupted by Barbara's voice saying, "Jack, it's the phone!"

"Whhuuu…" Jack said, as he struggled for consciousness. The clock radio next to the phone said 4:34 AM. He struggled to reach the phone and sit up in bed. "Hullo?"

"Hi, is this Jack?"

"Yyeeess," said Jack hesitantly, not recognizing the voice.

"Hi Jack, this is Ralph…Huntley."

"Ralph? Hi. I didn't recognize you. How are you doing? How's Cliff?" Jack worriedly asked, knowing that a call at this time of the morning was not good, no matter how you looked at it.

"Sorry to wake you Jack, but something is just not right."

"Not right? Is Cliff getting worse?"

"Well, physically there hasn't been much change. But I'm worried about his mind. He's becoming agitated at times, sometimes fearful for no reason. And then there are other strange things going on."

"Like what?"

"Well, the dogs just take off. I mean, there is a fence, so they can't go too far. But they won't come near the house. I've finally started keeping them inside."

"Hmmm. Anything else?"

"Well, I don't know if it means anything, but I was walking past the den the other day, and a glass candle holder just exploded."

"The glass exploded? Did the flame get too close to the glass?' Jack asked.

Ralph was silent for a moment and then said, "The candle wasn't lit."

"Okay then," Jack exclaimed. "Would you like Barbara and I to pay you a visit? I think we need to."

"I would appreciate it Jack. Sorry to bother you."

"Oh, no bother. I'll talk to Barb about it and make sure we don't have other plans. Unless you hear otherwise, expect us about ten o'clock."

"Thanks Jack, I'll do that. See you then. I gotta go, Cliff's calling for me. Thanks. Say hi to Barb."

"So what's up, hon'?" Barbara said, as she propped herself up in bed. "It didn't sound good. Something about flames and glass."

"Ralph is worried about Cliff. He seems to be having sudden mood swings. On top of that, the dogs are freaking out about something."

"What about the flames?"

"Uh, yeah, that was kind of strange. He said he was just walking by the den and a glass candlestick just blew up, without the candle being lit." Jack scooted across the bed until he was practically sitting on Barbara. He put his arms around her and said, "I told him we would head up there, and try to be there by ten."

"It won't take us that long to get there will it?"

"I think we need to prepare for this one. I don't like the sounds of it. I have kind of an idea of what's going on. The den is Cliff's trophy room, where he keeps a lot of the things he has collected on his travels. He has a lot of real spooky things in there."

"Oh, I see. We better pray."

For the next two hours, Jack and Barbara prayed, and showered, and prayed, and ate, and prayed again. Then they drove to Preston Manor, and prayed again before they got to the property. They both had a peace and agreed that they were doing the right thing, that it would be a good thing, and that it would in no way be an easy thing.

16

Jack turned the volume down on his CD player as he slowly
pulled his car up to the guard shack. They had been listening
to praise music all the way up there, and they would leave it on
low until they were parked at the Manor.

The last time he was here, the driveway was lined with vans
and cars, and the shack held its full complement of two guards.
Now there wasn't a soul in sight, and the gates were shut. He
could see the keypad for entering a code, but he couldn't recall
Ralph telling him what the code was. He decided to push the
button that read "CALL" to see what happened.

"Yes, may I help you?" boomed a voice from somewhere by
the guard shack.

"I'm here to see Mr. Preston and Mr. Huntley." Jack replied
back, not knowing which direction to project his voice.

"Your name?"

"Jack Watchman."

"What company are you with?"

"I'm not with a company," he answered. "Just check. I should
have an appointment. I have my wife Barbara with me."

"I don't see you two in the book. I have a listing for a tall guy
with a mustache. Would that be you?"

"It could be."

"Turn and face the camera."

Jack looked all around the shack and finally said, "I don't see
a camera."

"That doesn't surprise me."

"Why?"

"We don't have one."

"What?"

"I suppose I can let you in. Do you have any fruits or vegetables to declare?"

"Ralph, is that you?"

"You mean you couldn't tell?"

"No. You sound like someone at a fast food drive-through window."

"Well, on my end you sound like Clint Eastwood."

"That bad, huh? Then why don't you just open the gate so we can talk face to face?"

"Sure, as soon as I can figure out which of these buttons opens the gate....oops."

"What do you mean, 'oops'?"

"Oh, nothing. But if the cops show up, just remain calm, and keep your hands in plain sight. And you better let Barbara do the talking. You sound threatening."

"Ralph!"

"Just kidding...here it goes."

"Thanks," said Jack, as he saw the gate start to open. "See you in a minute, Ralphy." When he said that, he saw the gate stop, then slowly close again. "Very funny...Okay, I'm sorry about the Ralphy thing...I promise, it will never happen again...Are you satisfied, Mr. Huntley?" The gate started to open, then started to close again, stopped, and then opened. The Staff always had to be in control.

As they headed toward the Manor, Barbara asked, "He didn't sound like someone in trouble, did he?"

"Well, no, but then he sort of was kind of a nervous jokester. I have this feeling that Cliff is looking over his shoulder, and he didn't tell him why we're here."

Jack drove past the gate and onto the narrow one-way road that wound through the trees. He enjoyed this meandering road to the manor. It was not in any hurry to get you there. Its purpose seemed more to allow you to enjoy the stately sequoia trees and huge rhododendrons. The entire length of the road was landscaped, with the predominant plant variety changing every so often, as if the design was done in themes. Even though this was fall, it was still a pretty drive. He could only imagine what it was like in the spring.

There was another road to exit the estate that joined this one at the entrance gate. It took a fairly straight route around the hill that blocked your view of the manor from the entrance. Jack figured it was designed for quick egress in case of an emergency. It was a lot wider too, probably designed for emergency vehicles. It was more than likely used by delivery vehicles also, because there was no way a truck would fit down the road they were on. It was far too winding and barely wider than a compact car. '*It would be a blast on a motorcycle though,*' Jack thought.

As he approached the manor, he noticed that his vehicle had been discovered by two Dobermans, one of which was huge. Surprisingly, they didn't bark as they followed him to the manor. He was pleased to see Ralph waiting for him at the carriage house. He hoped these dogs remembered him from his first visit, although they were never formally introduced. But having grown up with Dobies, Jack wasn't too afraid of them.

Barb, on the other hand, never fully trusted someone else's dogs. She knew they had a different way of responding to strangers than they did to their masters. "I'll just stay in the car," she told Jack. Jack determined to just hop out of the car like he owned the place, but to be wary around that really big one. As he stopped the car, he was glad to see that both of the dogs went straight to Ralph, flanking him on either side.

"Hi Ralph," Jack said as he got out of the car. "Obedient dogs you've got there!"

"Yes, I'm pretty proud of them," he said, with an obviously swelled chest.

"Do they do any other tricks?" Jack asked.

He just laughed. "No, they're not your circus type dogs. They only know three commands, but they do those pretty good."

"What would those commands be, chase cars, sit at your side, and eat?" Jack asked, pointing at the big one on Ralph's right.

"Oh, you're talking about Bruno?" he said, patting the dog on the head, as it jumped to its feet at the sound of its name. "Yeah, he's pretty big. He tips the scales at a hundred and sixty pounds."

"A hundred and sixty? Are you kidding?" Jack asked, remembering back to his own dogs who weighed less than a hundred.

"No, I'm not. Do you want to feel something real impressive? Come here and pat him on the back."

"It won't be impressively painful, will it?"

"Oh no," said Ralph, laughing. "No one has ever lost a hand with this dog." he said, as Jack reached down to pet the dog. Then he added "a couple of fingers, maybe," just as Jack's hand hit Bruno's back.

Too late to stop the momentum, Jack ran his hand across Bruno's shoulders. "That's unbelievable," he exclaimed. "That dog is as solid as a rock. What do you feed him?"

"Fruit!"

"You're kidding?"

"No, he loves fruit. I dropped an apple core once and he gobbled it right up. So then I gave him a whole apple and he devoured it. The vet told me that fruit is actually good for dogs but they usually won't eat it. Bruno does. He'll go out into the orchard and eat apples, cherries, and plums right off the ground. He just loves fruit." Then looking at Jack a bit askance, he asked "You're not a fruit, are you?"

Jack laughed and said, "No, Ralph, I'm not a fruit. Sometimes I feel like a nut, but not a fruit." He squatted down to pet Bruno real good. Bruno got excited, took one step sideways into Jack's leg, and about knocked him over. As he swung his arm in a circle to keep his balance, Jack asked, "What are the three commands, by the way?"

"Well, that's a bit complicated. The first one, which you saw, is 'Watch'. When I give that command, they'll run out and pace around any stranger on the property. They'll circle you and keep their eyes on you, but they're not supposed to bark or growl at you. When you get close to me, they'll move to my side and be prepared for one of the other two commands.

"So that's what they were doing when we drove in?"

"You got it. The second command is 'Guard'. In guard mode they will wander around the property looking for intruders. If they find one, they will circle him, barking and snapping. If the intruder is smart, he will leave the property. More than likely, after having Bruno snapping at him, he will freeze with panic and uncontrollably relieve himself," he said, laughing at the thought of it. "They're not supposed to bite anyone, but I wouldn't guarantee that they won't. They get snapping pretty close."

"No problem with door-to-door salesmen, I take it."

"Nope," he said, laughing. "The last command they were taught is 'Defend'. I have to give that command in a different language so I don't say it by accident in casual conversation, like I just did."

"Pretty dangerous command then?"

"Oh, yeah. It's a command to kill. They get pretty frenzied.

I would be afraid that I couldn't stop them once they pounced on someone. It's like having a loaded gun next to your bed. The security is comforting, but the responsibility is frightening."

"So, did you train them?" Jack asked.

"No, I sent them to someone who used to train dogs for the military. I'm supposed to run them through all three commands every so often, so they don't forget. I quit giving the defend command a couple of years ago. I don't know for sure what would happen now if I did."

"Have you ever had to use that command?"

"Not really," he said, kind of hanging his head.

"What's the matter?" Jack asked.

"Oh, killed a coyote once. It was pretty ugly."

"Is that when you quit?"

"Yeah, pretty much," he said, kind of quietly. "The dogs never caught the squirrels, and the snakes were no big deal. But cleaning up the remains of the coyote was, well…can we change the subject?"

"Sure. Oh, I have Barbara in the car. Barb, come on out. It's okay, they don't bite."

"You shouldn't lie, Jack" said Ralph softly.

"I didn't lie, I just didn't finish the sentence, they don't bite everybody."

"Hi Barbara," Ralph yelled, "Long time no see!"

"Mr. Huntley, it's been a long time all right."

"You can call me Ralph."

"But not Ralphy, correct?" Barbara said with a big grin.

"Jack, I can't believe you… then I'm going to tell her that you lied about the dogs." Ralph threatened, jokingly.

"What about the dogs Jack?" Barbara said, as she stopped in her tracks.

"Ralph, don't you think we should be getting in to see Cliff?"

Jack said, trying to change the subject.

"You can call me Mr. Huntley," Ralph snorted. "Mr. Preston is probably wondering what happened to us anyway." After he said that he did a quick whistle, pointed at the woods, and said "Guard!" The two dogs kicked up grass as they raced off into the woods, occasionally barking just for fun. Jack was quite impressed. Barbara was just happy for them to be elsewhere.

As they walked from the carriage house to the manor, Jack asked, "Who does all your landscaping?"

"Yeah, the flowers are beautiful," added Barbara.

"I have a guy come in and do the maintenance on a regular schedule, you know, mowing, weeding, that sort of stuff," he said, as he knocked a few fallen leaves off of an azalea by the back door. "Well, come to think of it, we've talked about him once before."

"We have?"

"Yeah, his name is Miguel."

"The homeless guy? He takes care of all this?"

"Yeah, him or his men. He also does all of the spraying so I don't have to bother with the chemicals. But I designed it all and did a lot of the hardscape myself, back when I was younger. I couldn't imagine doing that much work now. I am not sure how I did it then," he said, with a chuckle that indicated remembered pain. "But I still get my fingers dirty."

"Knowing you, you probably get them dirty a lot."

"Well, actually, yeah. I get carried away once in a while and get these bones a bit achin'. I guess it's just the Mexican in me wanting to keep working."

"You're Mexican?" Jack asked, somewhat surprised.

"Yes I am," Ralph said as he opened the back door to the house. "Well, half Mexican anyway."

"That explains why you tan so easily."

"Yeah," he said, laughing, "The Huntley side of me doesn't contribute much in that respect."

"Isn't the name Huntley British?" Jack commented as he wiped his feet on the welcome mat in front of the huge doggy door that was cut into the back door.

"Right, my father was from England and my mother was from Cancun, Mexico. They met while he was on a cruise there. She worked in a little tourist shop. From what I was told, it took three more cruises before he asked her to marry him."

"He must have had some money," he stated.

"Not after that!" he said with a laugh.

"So whose idea was it to name you Ralph?" Jack asked.

"Neither, actually."

"What do you mean?"

"My mother wanted to name me Raphael, after her grandfather. My father wanted to name me Raymond, because he thought it sounded good with Huntley. The name Ralph was as English as my mother would compromise."

Just then a somewhat raspy voiced interrupted them. "Are you going to explain why I called you Ralphy?" interjected Cliff, who was sitting in the dining room as the three of them walked in.

Ralph just shook his head and muttered to one of the dogs, "Just can't drop it, can they?"

17

"Hi Cliff!" Jack said to him, as he reached out to shake his hand. "How are you doing?"

"The doctors say I should be pushing up daisies by now," he responded. "So I shouldn't complain. If I could, I'd probably re-write the last chapter though. Or maybe edit it out completely," he said, as he slapped Jack's leg with the back of his hand. Then he looked at Jack real serious and said, "Either way, I'm sure it will have a happy ending!" Jack knew that was Cliff's way of let-ting him know that the Cliff on the inside was still doing well.

"That's what really matters," Jack responded, and he meant it.

"Cliff and Jack," interrupted Ralph, "If you could wait a few minutes, it's going to get sunny today, and I really need to put the covers on the greenhouse."

"Sure, go ahead. Cliff and I will just wait in the den."

"Thanks, it'll only take a few minutes. Barb, would you like to join me? There are a few orchids out there that you just have to see. They are blooming perfectly right now."

"I love orchids. I never had a good place for them. Except poor mans orchids. I have them all over the place, mostly in the paths."

"I don't think I've seen poor mans orchids. What do they......."

As the voices of Ralph and Barbara trailed off around the house, Jack walked into the house with Cliff. He jumped when the doggie door banged behind him. "Uhh, hi there Bruno, it's okay, I'm with him," Jack said nervously as he pointed to Cliff.

"Oh, don't worry about them," said Cliff. "They won't eat you unless I tell them to. Remember that."

"Let me make a note of it," Jack said as he pulled out his iPhone and started tapping it's surface. "Don't...let...Cliff... say...'to.'"

"What?"

"Oh, nothing. So, how have things been going since I saw you last? Have you been having any struggles with anything?" Jack didn't want to tip his hand with what Ralph had told him, but he felt he needed to get the conversation serious somehow.

"Why do you ask?"

"Well, I've seen it happen all too often where a new believer starts to waver when the struggles come, so the enemy makes sure they come."

"I still believe in God, if that's what you're asking," snapped Cliff. "Did Ralph call you up here to psycho-analyze me?"

"Why, is there a reason he should have?"

"Probably."

Jack didn't know if that last statement was an attempt at humor or a confession. But he knew he was beginning to see the agitation that Ralph was talking about. And possibly the fear. He wished that Barbara and Ralph would get back. He was not comfortable getting into anything too heavy without Barbs insight and wisdom. And he didn't want Cliff getting too agitated without Ralph there. As Cliff continued into the den, Jack wandered into the conservatory to see if he could see the greenhouse out the windows.

As he looked toward the south, he could see one end of a glass building, and through the steamy windows he could see a shape moving around. He figured that must be Barb looking at flowers. He could see Ralph cranking on something at the end of the building, and mesh type material working its way down the glass roof. *'Hurry up Ralph, I need my support group,'* he said to himself.

As Barbara rounded the corner of the greenhouse, her eyes were accosted by the variety of shapes and colors that the orchids displayed. She had been to flower shows, so she knew what to expect, but she had never seen so much variety in a private collection. "Did you propagate all of these?" she asked.

"Let's just say the propagation was under my control. I hired some people to help me. In fact, they would have been the ones to put this cover down, but I wanted to make sure we didn't have any interruptions, so I didn't call them in today."

"That was probably wise," she replied. "I'm sure you understand that what's going on is quite serious. We probably shouldn't be gone for too long. But while you're doing that, I'm going to soak up some more of this beauty. Do you sell any of these?"

"If I ever have some I want to part with, my landscaper, Miguel, finds a home for them. I split with him whatever he can sell them for. It's a pretty good arrangement. Why, would you like one? Go ahead and pick out a couple and take them home. I can tell you how to keep them alive."

"You're kidding, any two I want?"

"Well, there are a few I need for propagation reasons, but… tell you what, pick out three, and I'll retain veto rights."

"That would be great Ralph, thanks."

"No problem. You've got until I finish cranking this cover in place."

"Just take your time. Well, no, maybe we better hurry. Jack is probably waiting for us."

Ralph suddenly stopped cranking on the cover mechanism. "Did you hear something?" he asked Barbara.

"Nothing really, except that fan up there. What did you hear?"

"I don't know exactly. It sounded sort of like a dog, but it was faint. It didn't sound good, whatever it was. Maybe we better get back inside." As he said that he started cranking real fast, and Barbara made a quick decision on two plants and called it good.

Bruno lay sleeping near the library door, as Jack started walking out of the conservatory. The other dog was staring intently at Jack. When they made eye contact, the other dog started wagging his tail hard enough to shake his whole body. Not knowing the dog's name, Jack said to him, "Hello, puppy dog!" The dog excitedly started walking toward Jack. When he'd made it about three steps, the dog suddenly slammed to the floor with a horrifyingly loud yelp. Bruno jumped to attention, while Jack stopped dead in his tracks.

"What just happened to Buck?" yelled Cliff.

"I don't know," answered Jack. "All of a sudden all four legs went out from under him and he slammed to the ground. It looked like somebody dropped an invisible rock on his back. He seems okay now, just scared," he said as Buck came over to him and almost crawled in his lap. Jack nervously watched Bruno as Bruno nervously watched Buck.

Jack looked over at Cliff and was about to say something when he saw the look on Cliff's face. His eyes were as big as saucers as he looked back and forth between the window and Buck. "What's wrong, Cliff?"

"It was the strangest thing. I was looking out toward the east and saw a tiny black cloud in the distance. I was wondering if it was going to get as sunny today as Ralph thought it was. Suddenly the cloud started moving toward this direction. It was slow at first, and then all of a sudden it came right at me. Right when I thought it was going to hit the window, Buck yelped. Jack, I think the spooks are back. Let's do something about it right now! I'm tired of putting up with this."

Jack had to agree, to a certain extent, but he was not comfortable jumping into that kind of a battle without his armor-bearer, Barbara. Just as he was about to tell Cliff they should wait, the back door opened.

"What was that noise?" said Ralph, as he tossed his gloves in the corner of the entry. "It sounded like one of the dogs." As he said that, Buck came up to him kind of sheepishly. "Was that Buck? Jack, what happened?"

Jack told them what he saw happen to Buck, and what Cliff saw with the cloud. "Cliff is convinced the two are related," he told them, "and I agree with him. Whatever it is that's going on, it's serious. We need to pray."

Barbara looked at Cliff, and then glanced around the den. "Uhh, can we pray someplace other than in the den?" she asked, as she looked at Jack with pleading eyes.

Jack understood the look and took the lead. "I think the conservatory would be a good place. We can just drag another chair in there." He headed quickly to the kitchen to grab a chair before Ralph or Cliff could respond. Just as quickly Barbara grabbed their Bible off of the table in the library and headed to one of the two chairs already in the conservatory.

Ralph waited for Cliff to wheel himself to the conservatory before going in himself. As they entered, he asked Jack, "Is there a reason you didn't want to be in the den?"

As he sat down in the kitchen chair, Jack responded, "Tell me, where was it the two of you played that Monopoly game?"

"We played it right there in the... den. Jack, are you saying you think there is a problem in the den? With spooks?"

Jack looked at Barbara, and the look in her eyes let him know that she was thinking the same thing he was. "Before we get into that, I think we need to pray. Are you okay with that?"

"Sure, go ahead," said Ralph.

When Jack got a nod from Cliff, and a bowed head from Barbara, he proceeded. "Father, right now we need your help in this place. We need your warrior angels to surround this home and we need them present in these rooms. We need your Holy Spirit to guide our discussion and fill our minds with your wisdom and discernment. Lord, you know the enemy is harassing the people in this home, and now even the animals. Cliff has asked for this to stop, and we all agree with him. Please help us to put an end to this, and for your peace to again fill this home."

Barbara then added, "Lord, we need you to provide us with the armor necessary to face this battle. We need your righteousness as a breastplate, our feet shod, our helmets of salvation on, and your truth as a belt binding it all together. Please give us the faith we need as a shield, and your words as a sword in order to fight back. We also ask that the enemy not be allowed to retaliate against us or our loved ones for the ground we will take back today. We ask that the blood of Jesus cover us, and in his name we ask for the victory today. Amen."

"When you said it was a battle," Ralph said, "I didn't realize you meant it in such a military fashion."

"It is very much like a military operation." Jack said to Ralph. "It is also very legal, in its own way. When I refer to them as 'the enemy', I mean it literally. There is nothing good that they intend to do for you. Even if they give you temporary wealth, health, or power, it is for the purpose of winning your trust so they can destroy you more completely." Turning to Cliff, Jack said, "It's wise that you want to rid your life of them, and it is your right."

"So what do we do first?" Cliff asked.

"It is very possible that there is some legal trick that is giving the enemy access to this place."

"I would say 'probable," added Barbara.

"What Barbara is referring to is something we saw in the den that very often provides an opening into a persons life for demons to infiltrate. Sort of like leaving a door open to a house."

"So, what would that be, and how do we close the door? Cliff asked.

"Well, to start with, I would say the idols on the shelves in your den."

"They aren't idols to me," Cliff countered. "They were just gifts from various people I met, mostly tribesmen."

"Were any of them witchdoctors?"

Cliff went silent when that question was asked, and started getting the agitated look on his face again. When Jack saw it, he glanced over at Barbara, and realized that she was praying silently, evident by her lips just barely moving. Jack turned to Cliff and said, "Cliff, in the name of Jesus, look at me!"

Cliff slowly turned his head and looked at Jack. He still had a scowl on his face, so Jack said to him, "Cliff, do you want to be rid of these?"

Cliff started to look away, and then turned back toward Jack and said, "Yes... I do."

Jack then said, "Father, Cliff says he wants to be rid of these spirits that are tormenting him. By the blood of Jesus, I..."

"NO!" yelled Cliff.

But Jack just continued, "By the blood of Jesus I ask that they be driven out of Cliff. We take the sword of your Spirit and sever any ties that Cliff has to these objects in his den, and any connection that evil spirits have to these objects. In the name of

Jesus we ask that any spirits removed from Cliff or these objects would be escorted off of this property by your warrior angels, and sent where you determine they should go, and not allowed to return. We thank you for your grace in that, Father."

The three of them watched as Cliff's head dropped almost to his chest, and then slowly raised up to look at them. "Thank you, Jack," he finally said after a few moments. "I knew something wasn't right, but I couldn't seem to tell you. I just couldn't… Sorry Ralph. I'm sorry for…"

"It's okay Cliff," interrupted Jack. "Been there, done that. The enemy likes to get back in if it can."

"What are you talking about?" asked Ralph.

"Well, when I was up here the first time, I cast an evil spirit out of Cliff. In Hollywood speak you'd call it an exorcism, in a lot of religious circles it's called deliverance. Whatever you call it, it is simply Jesus setting a person free from the influence of an evil spirit. It's hard for me to say if that particular spirit came back, or there was just another one that needed to be dealt with. Either is possible. It doesn't matter, because Cliff just wanted to be rid of it. Isn't that right Cliff?"

"Yeah," Cliff said, as he straightened up again to look at him. "It's hard to explain how that feels. It's like a weight was lifted off of me, but I didn't realize it was on me until it happened. I feel exhausted, but lighter. Does that make sense?"

"It'll feel different to everyone," Jack answered. "Some people don't feel anything at all, and some will get knocked unconscious for a while. This is actually going pretty easy compared to most. I think that's a testament to your determination to be rid of it, and probably God just being gracious to us."

"I don't think we're done yet," added Barbara.

"You're talking about the idols in there?" asked Jack.

"And other stuff," said Barbara.

Jack turned to Cliff and asked, "Are you attached to any of those things in there?"

"Most of those things I wasn't attached to when I got them. I just didn't want to offend the person giving them to me. I'll never see them again, anyway. I'm assuming you think I should get rid of them."

Barbara piped up and said, "I'd burn them rather quickly if I were you. Even if they're worth some money, just destroy them. Don't send that curse to someone else."

Ralph got up and walked into the den, glancing up and down the shelves at the African masks, small dolls from South America, Buddha statues, coconut monkey heads, and other figurines. "Are you saying these things attract spooks, or what exactly?"

"These things in particular?" Jack asked. "I don't know. Sometimes these things are mass produced in a factory and pawned off to tourists. Often they are handmade by local artisans. And sometimes they are prayed over by a shaman or a witchdoctor or something in order to curse the person receiving them. Barb and I have a philosophy; if in doubt, throw it out."

"Or better yet, burn it," added Barbara. "It's just a thing anyway, it's no great eternal loss. But keeping something around that has been cursed can be very bad. Even deadly."

"Well let's not waste any time," said Cliff, as he started wheeling himself to the den. "Ralph, go fire up the burn barrel."

Ralph hesitated, looking at some of the ornate decorations on some of the items. "Are you sure you want to just burn all of these? I think some of them are encrusted with jewels."

"Ralph, you can get those on the jewelry show for ten bucks. I can afford to do this right. What do you think Barbara?"

"To be honest, I would appreciate you burning them more than I would appreciate you giving them to me, even if they were encrusted with diamonds. I've felt the effects of those curses. I even came close to dying once. It's just not worth it."

When Jack heard those words from Barbara, he headed for the den himself. "I'll grab a few of these and follow you out to the burn barrel," he said to Ralph. "Barb, would you pray with Cliff?"

"Sure." As she watched Jack gather up a few idols, she told Cliff, "As far as the legal aspect of why these spirits were able to invade this home, it was because you unknowingly invited them in when you accepted these gifts and brought them home. You might say they were like a Trojan horse. In order to reverse that invitation, you need to ask God to forgive you for doing it. Then you need to say that the evil things that came with these objects are no longer welcome in this home, and ask God to have them removed. Does that make sense to you?"

Cliff thought about it, and said, "It sounds like when you have an unruly tenant."

"Right, and you're the landlord. You have to do things legal like, and then the sheriff has the power to remove the tenant. But it's *your* house, *you* have the authority, and *you* have to file the complaint. Otherwise the tenant can't be forced out."

"So then what do I do, just talk to God about it like he was a judge?"

"That would be it exactly," Barbara answered. Then she was very moved when Cliff started talking as if he was a landlord pleading a case about all of the troubles some tenant was causing him. And he had a lot of tenants that he was upset with, all sitting on a shelf, or coffee table, or end table. He seemed to remember what each one was supposed to have been given to him for, who gave it to him, and why he thought it may be causing some issue in his home. With each petition, the room felt a bit lighter. She could only imagine what it was doing for Cliff.

18

As the smoke billowed up out of the barrel, Jack and Ralph stared into the flames. The coconut monkey head was the latest object to meet its demise. "Whoa, look at that one!" Ralph exclaimed. "Is that grotesque or what?"

"Boy, yeah, you talk about spooky. I don't think he's grinning any more now." Jack understood this was serious business, but he did take joy in seeing these things destroyed. There had been too many times that he had seen marriages fall apart, people driven out of their homes, and horrible illnesses afflict people, just because they had inadvertently accepted these things into their lives. "Father, again I ask that nothing be allowed to retaliate against us for destroying this voodoo doll," he said, as he slammed the doll into the barrel.

"If I might make a personal observation," Ralph said. "You seemed especially motivated to toast that little doll."

"We had a bad encounter with a doll that was even cuter than that one," Jack answered. "Barbara and I had sacrificed a vacation one year to join our church doing some missionary work in Mexico. A dozen of us couples helped rebuild some homes that had been damaged in a storm. One of the local women offered Barbara a gift of a homemade doll for helping them. Barbara didn't realize that the woman was the daughter of a Shaman. She thought it was 'soooo cute' and brought it home.

"After a few weeks she started getting fatigued and lethargic. We didn't think anything about it at first, but it eventually got very serious, and she was literally wasting away. The doctors couldn't find a cause, but they confirmed that the symptoms were killing her. In particular her blood count showed that her liver was starting to fail." The memories caused Jack to go silent for a while.

"I'm assuming you eventually tied the illness to the Shaman?"

"I didn't, but someone else did," Jack said, as that memory seemed to revive him. "I had a lot of people praying for her, but nothing seemed to help. I mean, a few times she revived for a while, but then she would lose ground again. Then a man from the church asked if he and his wife could come to the house and pray for Barb. No one had done that before. I told him yes, even though Barb was not really wanting any company at that time. She didn't have the strength to, well, look her best. And I wasn't any good at helping her with that."

"I can't imagine Barbara in any shape not looking attractive," Ralph noted.

"She'd appreciate you saying that, but honestly, she looked twenty years older than me at that time. She was very self conscious. But I was desperate. I couldn't have handled losing her, and I'm afraid I would have been bitter at God if I would have."

"So what happened?"

"Well, this couple had had experiences that I had never heard of," Jack continued. "As soon as they walked in the house, one of them said to me, 'Your wife has been cursed!' For the life of me, I couldn't think of who would have done such a thing. To be honest, I didn't even know why a curse could hurt someone like Barb. But like I said, I was desperate, so I listened."

"What did Barbara think?"

"We hadn't gone in to see her yet. In fact, the couple just started slowly walking around the house, and didn't even ask to see Barb. So I left them to do whatever they were doing, and I told Barb they were there. She was upset with me at first, until I told her they wanted to pray for her. Then she just started weeping, so I held her for a while, and then went back to the couple.

"When I got back to them, they were in the family room, holding this doll. They asked me where it had come from, and I told them about the trip to Mexico. Then they told me that God had showed them that Barb had a death curse on her. There was a demon of death and destruction that was organizing the attack, and there was an object in our house that was opening a door to this creature." Jack got angry all over again as he thought about it.

"That sounds a lot worse than the Monopoly game," Ralph said, trying to lighten the mood a bit.

"Yes it was, and it was a lot to take in. If I would've heard that sort of thing a few weeks earlier, I probably would have chased them out of the house as lunatics. But I was desperate, and they explained it to me using a story from the Bible, about when the Israelites had brought an evil object into the camp, and people started dying. Anyway, to make a long story short, this couple prayed for the curse to be lifted, then we asked forgiveness for bringing the doll into our house, and we burned it. Barb revived a lot almost instantly. Some of the damage took over a year to heal. But God restored her, as you can see."

"So that's where you learned to do what we're doing today?"

"Eventually. It took a few years to learn to hear God's voice well enough for us to understand these things. But we were motivated, although I'm still reluctant to blurt things out like that couple did."

"But Barbara isn't."

"You noticed that, huh?"

"How did you tie it to the Shaman?"

"Well, the couple had said something interesting while they

were praying. They asked that the head of the ones who had caused this, would be covered with the trouble that their lips had caused. They said that statement was from the Psalms. They said they were usually reluctant to pray that way, but they felt that whoever had done this was a sort of serial curser and needed to be stopped.

"A couple years later, we revisited that same Mexican village. The villagers were shocked to see us. They knew that Barb had taken the doll, and they knew about the curse that went with it. They were afraid to say anything to us, because the Shaman was very powerful. They said that this Shaman and his daughter suddenly got ill. Some of them offered to pray for the two of them, but the Shaman refused. But on his death bed he asked for prayer for his daughter. He died, but she lived. She also gave her life to Christ, along with a number of other villagers. Even more got saved after we showed up. They then truly believed that the God of the missionaries was stronger than the god of the Shaman."

Jack and Ralph went back to hauling things out of the den, as Cliff and Barbara kept pointing out things they had prayed about. All four of them then looked through the whole house searching for anything they felt might be offensive to God. Quite a number of books got burned, and even an old wicker chair that had belonged to one of Ralph's relatives that had committed suicide.

"Is there anything else we need to do?" asked Cliff.

Barbara looked at him and asked, "Do you have any tattoos?"

"No I don't, but why do you ask?"

"There have been times that we have prayed for people, and we were not having any success with our requests," answered Barbara. "I mean, it's not like we expect God to give us everything we ask for, but at some point we need to know if we need to pray differently, or we need to stop praying. When we reach that point, we ask God to somehow show us why a person is afflicted the way they are. There have been times where God showed us that the person had tattoos that were making them a target."

"I understand exactly," said Cliff.

Ralph remarked, "'You do?"

"Yes. That's why I never got tattoos. Some of the tribes I spent time with ritualistically tattooed and scarred their bodies. They offered to tattoo me, but I refused."

"Why?" asked Jack.

"If a rival tribe would have seen that tattoo on me, they would have killed me. Even if the Chief of their tribe had given me permission to be there, that tattoo would have marked me for destruction by someone who had a beef against the tribe that had tattooed me."

Then Ralph said, "So it would be like the voodoo doll?" Then Ralph confessed to Barbara that he had heard about her illness, and was sorry she had to go through it. Then Cliff had to hear the story, which was a bit different after Barbara injected her perspective of it.

"How do you get to know God well enough to recognize His voice, and not be fooled?" asked Cliff, after he heard how Jack and Barbara had prayed about the doll.

"I consider reading the Bible to be the only sure way," he said. "It also helps a lot to hang around other believers and hear their stories. We used to like Bible study groups, where you got a bit of both. Plus, we got the opportunity to pray for each other, and quite often got to see God work."

"How do you mean?" asked Ralph.

"Well for example, if someone had a physical problem, we would ask God to show us what the real problem was that was causing the physical symptoms that the person was experiencing, and let us know how to pray effectively."

"And He would tell you?"

"Not always, but He did quite often. He might give us words to pray, or a mental picture that explained the problem, or sometimes--I can't explain how—we would just know."

"So He didn't just speak to you?" Ralph questioned.

"Well, in our Christian lingo we would say He spoke to us. In reality He just communicated the information to us in any manner that He could get it through our thick skulls. He spoke to different people differently, and we would each share what we thought we heard, or saw, or whatever."

"It's hard for me to understand what that's like," confessed Ralph, "but it sounds intriguing."

"I gotta to tell you, those of us that were praying got blessed as much as those that got healed. I mean, you know in your heart that God exists. You know he is out there watching you and that he cares for you. But seeing a miracle happen before your very eyes is still quite inspiring."

"You've actually seen a miracle happen?" asked Ralph. "What sort of a miracle?"

Cliff interrupted and said, "Yes, Jack, and how do you define a miracle? Some people consider birth to be a miracle."

"I don't consider giving birth to be a miracle," answered Jack. "Well, if I gave birth it would be. But I do consider creating a life to be one. But that's not what I'm talking about. I consider a miracle to be something happening that only God could have caused to happen, like when Barb was healed. Let me give you another example. In one of our Bible studies a gal had a toothache. She had been to the dental school and had a tooth pulled. You know how the molars have multiple roots? Well, they missed one of them. She could still feel the sharp edge of one in the hole where her tooth had been. She was going in the next day to get the last piece pulled out, but until then she was in agony.

"We could have just offered her a pain reliever, but someone asked her if she would like us to pray for her. She said yes, so we did. We all laid our hands on her--which is what the Bible says to do--and prayed for her. I happened to have my hands on her shoulders when I felt what I could best describe as a current go through my hands and into her shoulders. Right away she said the pain was gone. As we were going back to our seats, I asked her about the piece of tooth. She said it was gone also. That did not surprise me because I assumed the broken piece was the source of the pain. It didn't make sense to me that God would remove the pain and not remove the cause of it. I would classify a piece of tooth suddenly vanishing as a miracle."

"I think I would too," said Ralph. "Especially if I was that girl."

"Yeah, she was happy to not have to go back to the dental school."

"Have you seen very many miracles like that?" asked Cliff, with an unexplainable look of a reporter on his face.

"What, teeth disappearing? No, I would have to say that was the only one," he joked. Cliff just stared, unwilling to recognize it. "Just kidding," Jack said. "Yes, I've seen hundreds of miracles, some minor, some major, some seemingly coincidental. In every case, though, I could see God's hand changing a situation to make life a little easier for someone. Oftentimes it would happen without us even making a formal request for it."

"What do you mean?" asked Ralph.

"Well, as religious people, we tend to come up with a lot of rituals for getting God to grant us our wishes. You know, folding our hands, kneeling, fasting, face-in-the-rug, things like that. Often, miraculous things have happened to me and I hadn't done any of those things. I just had a need, and God knew it." A tear started to roll down one of his cheeks as his memory recalled some of those instances. "Sometimes I get real formal asking God for something, and I don't get it. Then He gives me something else that I just wanted, but didn't feel right asking Him for."

"It sounds like he wants to make sure you understand that you're not the one in control." said Cliff.

"I think that's precisely it. Here is another story that you might find interesting, if you don't mind."

"No, go right ahead." said Ralph.

"Again, it took place at our Bible study," he said. "The daughter of one of the ladies in our group came along with her for a visit. At some point in the study, God spoke to the man whose home we were meeting in and told him He wanted to heal this girls hearing. When he asked her about it, she said she didn't have a problem with her hearing. That sort of confused us."

"I would imagine," said Ralph. "Did that kind of embarrass the guy? Was he hearing wrong himself?"

"Well, what he did was ask the girl to cover one ear, and then the other, while he kept talking. She said that his voice did sound different from one ear to the other. So he told her that God must have known it and wanted to heal it. Again, we all laid hands on her and prayed for her. Pretty soon she could hear the same out of both ears."

"That must have surprised her," said Ralph.

"It probably did. It didn't surprise the rest of us though. We had seen that sort of thing happen a number of times by then. But that's not the end of the story."

"It's not?" asked Ralph.

"No. A number of us had noticed that this girl had a bad eye.

When she looked one direction, both eyes would move. When she looked the other way, one of them stopped in the middle, causing her to look cross-eyed. This same man asked her if she would like us to pray about that, and she agreed."

"So God healed her eye too?" asked Ralph.

"No, He never did, at least not that night. And boy, I'll tell you, we prayed and prayed and prayed. I guess we were a little over-confident, and certainly presumptuous. While we were praying for the eye, though, God showed one of the other women that this girl had a problem with the muscle structure on one side of her face. Since it was on the same side as the bad eye, we assumed it referred to the muscle controlling that eye. So we prayed that God would heal the muscle structure on that side of the face, just as the lady had been shown. You know what happened?" Jack asked.

"God healed her eye?" asked Ralph.

"Wrong!" said Cliff. "Jack just said that her eye wasn't healed then, am I right?" he asked, looking at Jack.

"You're right, Ralph's wrong," he said. "This girl was kind of a pretty girl, but one side of her face was just a little pooched up." As he said this he pushed one of his cheeks up to illustrate it. "When we prayed for her, her cheek dropped down to normal. I think she left there a little prettier."

"And God never healed her eye, huh?" said Ralph. "That sure seems strange. I wonder why."

"Believe me, so did we!" he exclaimed. "Three of us couples sat around and discussed that for quite a while after the others left. We finally realized that God had never told us that He wanted to heal her eye. That was our request. He told us what He wanted to do, and He did it. Let me explain how I understood it."

"Another analogy?" asked Cliff.

"No, it's actually more of an illustration. Let's say you are walking down a street..."

"In New York?" asked Ralph.

"It doesn't matter where it is, that's not the point," he said, as he looked at Ralph, who was grinning. "Very funny Ralph. You're walking down this street, and you see a man walking toward you that is all hunched over. You take pity on the man, and in your heart you say to God 'See that man over there? I'm going to lay hands on him, and I would like you to heal him.' What do you think will happen?" he asked them, and received a full complement of shrugged shoulders. "That's my point exactly. You don't know. Maybe nothing.

"Now let's say you are walking down the street, and you see the man that is all hunched over. This time you hear God's voice in your heart saying, 'See that man? Tell him I want to heal him.' Now what do you think will happen?" he asked again, and got the same response. "I guarantee you," he continued, "that the man will stand up straight and be healed. God said He wanted to do it. All He required was obedience from us. I like to say that obedience is better than presumption."

"So you would say that's why faith healers can't just walk in and empty a hospital?" asked Ralph.

"Right. I believe that without the power of God, we ourselves are powerless to do any more than assist in the natural healing processes that God built into us. So in every way God still deserves the glory for any healing. To use an earlier illustration, suppose God filled you with His healing power, like filling a cup with Perrier. He then pours that power out of you into someone thirsty for His healing touch. If He wouldn't have filled you, you would have had nothing to offer the thirsty person."

Ralph's countenance turned real somber and he asked, "So

there is probably no way that God is going to heal Mr. Preston?'"

"I certainly wouldn't say that!" exclaimed Jack, once he realized what Ralph had said. "God does what he wants, and I've found no way to twist his arm otherwise. What I have found, is that I need to ask, and then listen, and then obey if He instructs me in some manner. But I must admit, I have seen him heal someone once He's been asked, more often than I've seen nothing happen at all."

"Well, I've been asking God a lot for that," said Ralph, "and I haven't seen him healed, and I haven't heard any reason why not."

"Again Ralph, I can't speak for God, unless of course He tells me to. That hasn't happened very often. But I can ask you this, what does Cliff want?"

"What do you mean? Of course he would want to be healed. No one would want to die of cancer. You don't, do you Cliff?"

They all looked at Cliff, but he didn't respond right away. He eventually said, "Of course I wouldn't want to die of cancer. But, I'm ready to go, if that's what is planned for me."

Jack understood, because he had been through this same scenario with his father. "So you don't want to live forever?" he asked Cliff.

Cliff laughed nervously and said, "No, not in this body anyway. And not without Gloria." With that statement they all understood, in a lot of different ways, that his heart was no longer anchored to Preston Manor.

Barbara remembered how hard it was for Jack to let go of his father. He agonized for hours, fasting and praying for him. He begged others to pray for him. Although he saw some tremendous changes in his father, he never saw the miraculous healing that he so desperately sought. She now saw that same desperation in Ralph's eyes, and knew this was all very difficult for him. "Ralph, you need to pray according to God's will, and Cliff's will," she finally stated. "And from what I have heard, in both cases that will is to bring him and Gloria together again. I think you can also pray that, however that happens, it is peaceful."

Cliff looked at her and said, "Well put Barbara, thanks."

"I can do that," said Ralph, "and I will."

"And we will agree with you on that," said Barbara.

19

"Was there some other big question you had?" Jack asked. He decided by the look on Cliffs face that he needed to move this meeting along.

"Yes there is," said Cliff, "but I'm not sure how appropriate it is."

"What is it?"

"How does someone become more important in God's eyes?"

"Just so I understand the meaning of the question, what exactly is your definition of important?" Jack asked. "In other words, are you talking about being important to operations, or high in social status?"

"I'm not sure how to explain it. When I would visit some native tribes, I would need to get permission from the chief, in order to live with the natives. The problem was, I had to be someone important in the eyes of the chief, or I couldn't get an audience with him."

Jack had to think about that for a minute. "So what you're saying is, you want to be with Gloria, but you feel you are going to need permission from God, and you're not important enough to him?"

"Not as important as her," Cliff said. "Gloria was a naturally good person, and she loved God, I know she did. But I probably did more to destroy people's faith in God than anyone. I probably damaged her faith. For her to see me in heaven, she'll probably need to drop way down the goodness ladder, if you know what I mean."

Jack might have thought that statement was comical, had he not seen the serious look on Cliff's face. Suddenly a Bible story came to mind that he thought fit the situation quite well. "You may not be as unimportant to God as you think. If you want, I can give you an example from the gospels.

"You've got one?" asked Cliff.

"I think I have a quick one," said Jack, "In Matthew it talks about a rich man that came to see Jesus, asking him what he should do to inherit eternal life. He says he has kept all the commandments, so Jesus tells him to sell all he has and give it to the poor, and then he will have treasure in heaven. Unfortunately, the guy couldn't bring himself to do it." Jack was aware that he was talking to a very rich man. He looked over and saw Cliff staring at the ground. Jack was sure he understood that the shoe fit well.

Jack then made the comment, "Cliff, you've already done it."

"What? I've already done what?" Cliff asked.

"You've already given everything away. Remember? You gave it to Ralph. It's his responsibility now."

A daydreaming Ralph suddenly snapped to attention. "What are you two talking about?" he asked.

Cliff just grinned and said to Jack, "Why yes, I have, haven't I?"

"Come on guys, what are you talking about?" Ralph protested.

"We'll discuss it later Ralph," said Cliff.

Jack looked seriously at Cliff and said, "So you see, you've already done something that someone who actually met Jesus couldn't do. Don't you think you'll get recognition for that?"

"Recognition for what?" Ralph moaned. "I hate it when you guys do that."

"What about worship?" asked Cliff, ignoring Ralph.

"What about it?" asked Jack, in mock annoyance.

"God must require some form of worship," he said. "It seems to be universal among most of the world's religions."

"Oh it's big among Christian religions as well," remarked Jack. "But remember, you're asking someone who's not real hot on religion. I thought you really disliked worship rituals. I remember you coming back from trips ranting and raving about some group of people wasting their lives worshipping...oh... whatever."

"Yeah, well, I still think it was a bit stupid. That's why I want to know if it's required, and what's required, and why. It's hard for me not to believe something's wrong about it."

As they were talking, Ralph got up and started for the kitchen. "Is there anything any of you would like? I can get you a snack if you're hungry."

They all shook their head no, without really considering the question. Then Ralph's question finally penetrated Cliff's consciousness. "How about some cheese and crackers?" Cliff said it so quietly that Jack thought he was talking to him.

Before Jack could respond, Ralph stuck his head through the pass-through and asked, "Would you like a little summer sausage too?"

"Just a little," responded Cliff.

"I'll bring some for Jack and Barb too," he said as he ducked back into the kitchen.

The conversation touched something in Jack, but instead of remarking about it, he grabbed his Bible and started searching for something. He then turned to Cliff and asked, "When you hear the word worship, what comes to mind?"

"Oh...a million people in Mecca," he responded. "Hindus kissing a rug, Polynesian human sacrifices, maybe a church full of people singing, hands in the air, eyes closed, and swaying... That's quite a varied interpretation, isn't it?"

"Yes it is, but they're probably all valid, historically anyway," Jack said. He was trying to formulate in his mind how he was going to explain his next example. It was not going to be easy to talk about. "Thanks Ralph," he said as he got handed a tray of sausage, cheese, and Ritz crackers. "You know what I like."

"Actually, I know what Mr. Preston likes," he said. "It seems to settle well with him for some reason."

"Not much else does," piped in Cliff.

"If you two are ready," said Jack, "I think I'm prepared to explain a few things about proper worship of God." He said that because after he heard what Ralph said, he truly was ready. "What I have to say will probably make the both of you uneasy, but please hear me out."

"I hate it when someone says something like that," said Ralph. "If it gets too uncomfortable, can I leave?"

"If it gets too uncomfortable," said Barbara, "I'll join you."

"No," said Jack with a joking sternness.

"Oh...okay," conceded Ralph, acting like a schoolboy.

The light hearted banter was making it more difficult for Jack to get serious, so he decided he had better get to the point before it went too far. "The examples you gave, Cliff, are all very common in the world. I don't think any of them is exactly what God is looking for. We see here in John, chapter four, that it says 'Those who worship God, must worship him in spirit and in truth.' What do you think is missing in that statement?" He got the usual blank stares one receives when he asks a leading question.

Jack quickly answered the question himself. "Think about our three-part nature; our spirit, soul, and body. If we worship God in spirit, we would use our spirit. When we worship him in truth, we have to use the part of us that would seek and discern the truth, our soul, the thinking, reasoning part. What it does not tell us to do is to worship God in our flesh, or physical body.

"I don't think it's wrong to worship God in our flesh. I just don't think it's what He's seeking. In a lot of ways, we humans think the fleshly side of things is most important. We have to see it, hear it, or touch it, before it means anything to us. The beginning of the verse that I read, verse 24, said that God is spirit. I think it's understandable why he would prefer to be worshipped in the spirit."

"I guess what you're saying makes sense," said Ralph.

"It would make more sense to me if I knew what worship meant," said Cliff in a frustrated tone of voice.

"Well I think I have a couple good examples," said Jack, hoping he didn't look as nervous as he felt. "First, when you look up the meaning of the Greek word for worship, it does mean to lie prostrate in reverence, like you'd expect. But it also says to kiss, like a dog licking its masters hand. Since you have dogs, I suppose you can understand what that means as far as attitude."

Ralph glanced over in the direction of the back door. "I believe so," he said. "From their point of view, everything comes from their master."

"Exactly. A good example of unconditional love." Jack hoped the next thing he would say would come out right. "Cliff, don't take this wrong, but Ralph here worships you."

"What?" exclaimed Ralph. "What are you talking about?" Jack wasn't sure if Ralph's face was turning red from embarrassment or anger.

"Just so I don't take it wrong," said Cliff. "I assume you're going to explain yourself?"

Jack took a quick breath and let it out. "Yes I am," he said. "First of all, try to eliminate that mental picture in your head of a South American native worshipping a sun god. Obviously Ralph doesn't drop to his knees and prostrate himself before you. That's what we consider as worship, and I think it's partially incorrect. What he does do, though, is wait on you. Sure, maybe now your physical condition requires it. But I remember that he treated you that way when you were healthy.

"Are you sure I can't leave?" asked Ralph.

"I'd like you to stay," said Jack. "I'm sorry to put you on the spot, but you should be honored. You are exhibiting some very godly traits. I feel bad that I never really noticed it until now." Ralph's face was about as red as was humanly possible.

"Anyway, I have noticed that Ralph is his own man. He's not a slave in this home, so I'm not referring to a slave-to-master type of worship. He has his dogs and his landscaping and his conservatory."

"And his greenhouse," added Barbara.

"And his greenhouse," conceded Jack. "But I believe that even when he's working elsewhere, he has one ear cocked, listening for your voice. He anticipates your desires because he knows you. He enjoys working with you on projects, and supports you in everything you do. He truly enjoys your company."

"So how do you equate that with worshipping God?" asked Cliff.

"In the spirit is how God communicates with us. To worship him in spirit would be to always keep the lines of that communication open. One spiritual ear cocked so to speak. If you were merely Ralph's employer, he would have his own house, you'd see him five days a week, and he would quit when he felt like it. Ralph sincerely would never leave you. You will have to leave him. I don't care if you want to call it love, or respect, or admiration. To a certain extent, worship is all of those and more. But you need to add the permanency to it in order to understand what I mean by true worship. Does he worship the ground you walk on? I doubt it. But I don't think God wants that from us either. That wouldn't be consistent with the desire he states for fellowship with us, or when he says he wants to set us free. Jack looked over and saw Ralph staring at the floor. "What are you thinking, Ralph?"

"Oh, well...I don't know...I guess..."

"What about worshipping God in truth?" interrupted Cliff.

"Yeah, what about that?" piped in Ralph, hoping to get out of the spotlight.

"I guess a good example of not worshipping in truth is if Ralph here did what he does for you solely for the inheritance. Even though the day-to-day actions may be the same, the attitude would be totally different. God can see right through that. People who worship God in truth will continue to worship him after they die. They truly mean it.

"Because they truly love him." Ralph said so softly that the others barely heard it. But Jack had heard it, and he knew something was going on in Ralph's heart. He had been watching him out of the corner of his eye for a while. This topic of conversation was having a dramatic effect on him.

"Would you like to talk about it?" Jack said, hoping to break through the bubble of introspection that Ralph was in.

"Jack, I do what I do for Mr. Preston because I love him, okay?" snapped Ralph. "I don't do it for the money, or the house, or the conservatory. And I am not his servant!"

The three of them were surprised by this sudden burst of emotion from Ralph. "I don't think Jack meant you were..." Barbara started to say, but Jack motioned to her that it was okay. He was again beginning to feel sudden emotion in his spirit, like he had with Cliff at their last meeting. This time it was different. This time he felt a deep love for a woman he never knew, and an ungodly anger.

"You didn't always take care of him because you loved him

though, did you?" Jack asked gently.

"What are you talking about?" Ralph snapped back.

"When you first helped Cliff after his wife died, you didn't do it because you loved him, did you?"

"What would you know about it?"

"You did it because you loved his wife."

"Jack!" shouted Cliff. "That's enough!" But Jack knew it wasn't enough, so he ignored the rebuke.

"It was just a teen-age infatuation!" shouted Ralph. "Nothing more."

"I'm not saying anything happened between you two. But you can't deny the fact that Gloria was the only woman that either one of you ever loved."

"Jack, you…" Cliff was about to do whatever he could to get Jack to stop, but was interrupted by Ralph, who burst into uncontrollable sobbing. Truth had just set a captive free, but only in one area. There was still something Ralph had to face up to. Jack wasn't sure what that thing was, but he knew the Holy Spirit was prompting him to keep pushing. Looking at Ralph he was reluctant to do it, because he felt like he would be kicking someone while they were down. But with the burden he felt in his heart, he had no choice but to continue.

"If you didn't help him because you loved him, then why did you do it?" Jack asked, but he got no response. "Ralph, I don't know what it is you need to get off your chest, but I know you need to do it."

But he couldn't do it. Every time Ralph would try to speak, the emotion of what he had to say would come out, but the words wouldn't.

Just when Jack was going to question him again, he realized he didn't need to. He suddenly knew what Ralph was hiding. In an instant, a story from the Bible had come to mind. He remembered King David hoping Bathsheba's husband would die in battle so he could take her as his own wife. That desire had destroyed King David, and it had backfired on Ralph as well. He hated to have to confront Ralph with it, especially in front of Cliff. He silently prayed to be released from this duty, but the burden didn't leave him. So he asked for God's grace to cover them all. They were going to need it.

"Ralph, listen to me," came a voice from a wheelchair. "Would you have preferred that it was me that died that day, rather than Gloria?" Jack felt relieved that he hadn't had to ask that question. Ralph looked like he had seen a ghost. "It's okay if you did," Cliff continued, "because I did."

When Cliff said that, Jack felt a huge burden lift off of his shoulders. He was able to maintain his composure, but inside he was weeping as hard as the other two now were. God's truth--and the power of the Holy Spirit to deliver it--had set two captives free at once. God uses whoever He desires to use, and Jack sure appreciated the fact that he chose Cliff to deliver that blow. It seemed to have worked best that way.

Cliff and Ralph spent a long time discussing past feelings. Ralph had thought that God was punishing him for wishing Cliff would never come home. Cliff was just bitter at life and didn't know whom to blame. Cliff had felt that, if there was a God, he hated him. Jack just listened and marveled at what he saw and heard. This was true freedom. Two friends for life finally free to be totally honest with each other. It was amazing what God could do. It didn't matter that their theology wasn't perfect. God could work on that, now that their hearts could receive it.

"Jack?"

"Yes...Ralph...what is it?" Jack stammered as he was torn from his thoughts.

"We have a question."

"So, what's the question?"

"You mean you haven't been listening?"

"Well yeah, sort of. I just missed the last part. What was the question?"

"It's one that gets asked a lot in the media, and neither one of us has ever heard a good answer. Why do bad things happen to good people? If God is in control, why is there so much suffering in the world?"

"That's two questions. Are you asking me why we aren't in heaven?"

"What do you mean?" asked Ralph.

"Well that's the place where no bad things ever happen. This isn't heaven that we are living in now, so it's not going to be a perfect place. There are evil people out there with a completely free will. There are evil spirits out there bent on destroying God's creation. Shoot, there are God worshipping people out there ready to blow people up in the name of their religion. I believe it's only by the grace of God that this planet is populated at all."

"So you're saying God is not in control?"

"It really doesn't matter what I think," protested Jack. "What does the Bible say? In Genesis it says that God told Adam to take dominion over the earth. In second Corinthians four it calls Satan the god of this world. In a number of places it says Jesus is Lord. I think mankind should use the wisdom that is offered to him by God and care for this world properly. The problem is we don't do it. I wish God was in total control, but that would be paradise, and that will happen in the future. From what I see, Satan is in control of a lot more than he should be, and God's people are for the most part dropping the ball."

"Sounds like we're in a transition period."

"We are definitely in a transition period. I think we're in a time of testing as well. Most importantly though, I think our protection is on an individual basis. God calls us his children, and spiritually we seem to grow like children. When you're a newborn you are highly protected and nurtured. You grow to where you're given more responsibility and are exposed to more danger. But God's protection is always available if you ask for it. A lot of people fail to ask. That sounds like a mixed answer to your question, but it's a pretty complex subject. One thing that gives me comfort is this verse in Jeremiah twenty-nine."

As Jack said this he pushed the Bible over so they could both see it. "In verse eleven God says he knows the plans he has for our lives, a plan to prosper us and not harm us. I have found that to be very true."

"It sounds like you need to know God to have his protection," asked Ralph.

"He seems to protect a lot of people without them asking for it. But if you think about it, the police mainly protect those who ask for it, even though they're hired to protect everyone."

"That's true. I suppose it would be somewhat similar."

"Ralph, if you're satisfied with that answer, can I ask you a couple of questions?" asked Jack rather seriously.

"Uh, sure, what do you need to know?"

"Have you heard enough about God to commit your life to him?"

"I've always believed God existed, uh, sort of. I mean, I don't know if I fully understood what I believed, but, thinking there was a God out there somewhere has always made more sense to me than there not being one, if you know what I mean."

"But that's what I'm talking about," Jack said. "There are tons of people out there that think God exists and do certain ritualistic things just in case, things they think will keep him off their backs. You know, like giving to charities or going to church. What I'm talking about is a commitment, just like you committed your life to Cliff here. I'm talking about spending time to get to know him, to find out what he really wants. God says in the first chapter of Isaiah that He's tired of the sacrifices and wants a relationship. It says something similar in Jeremiah and Psalms and in other places in the Bible too.

"If you're uncomfortable making that commitment in front of me, that's okay. But I beg you to consider doing it in front of God. There's nothing wrong with going to church. I suggest doing it as often as you can. But it can't replace the one-on-one love that God can pour out on you once you get that close to him. If Cliff here ever wrote an autobiography, you know that no one could read it enough times to know him as well as you do. Even you couldn't share enough things about Cliff so that someone could know him like you do. It's the same with God. You can know him personally, which is greater than his autobiography, the Bible, or gleaning information from someone else that knows Him."

Cliff and Ralph turned and stared at each other. Then they looked at Jack and Ralph asked, "You don't know, do you?"

"Know what?"

"That we are writing Cliff's autobiography."

"Really? That's great! I want a copy."

"We're in the middle of writing the last chapter even as we speak," said Cliff.

"So you weren't kidding about rewriting the last chapter, eh?"

"Well, no, I wasn't kidding. In fact, if I could, I would still erase the suffering part. But even the suffering seems to have been worth the outcome it produced."

"Sounds like something Jesus would have said," Jack pointed out. The room then fell silent as all four of them, each in their own way, pondered the grace and the love of God in their lives.

20

"Well, we should probably be going." Barbara said as she looked at her watch. She felt so comfortable with these two that she knew she could have spent many more hours with them. And she knew Jack could talk for many more hours. But she could see that Cliff was getting fatigued again, and wincing with pain every so often. She decided it would be best for them to leave Ralph to deal with Cliff's condition however they had determined to.

In order to display his willingness to be there for them, Jack said to Ralph, "If either of you two need anything whatsoever, please call us."

"You can be sure of that!" exclaimed Ralph. "Thanks for everything. You have no idea how great it has been to get together again after all these years. Let's make a point to do it again soon."

Since Cliff was still looking at something in the Bible, Jack decided to continue the conversation with Ralph. "Sure Ralph, let's keep in touch. Oh, by the way, I never asked you my last question."

"You didn't?" he asked rather hesitantly. "What is it?"

"Well, you don't have to answer it if it's too embarrassing, or if you don't want to talk about it in front of Cliff."

"I…I suppose I don't have any more secrets from him," he said, realizing Cliff wasn't paying attention to them anyway. "What's the question?"

With a real somber look on his face, Jack asked him, "Why

does Cliff call you Ralphy?"

Ralph just started laughing. "Oh, you got me there Jack. Well, when I was a kid, my mom used to yell for me, but she never seemed comfortable with the name Ralph. So when she was real serious, she would sort of call me Raphael, only it sounded more like RALPHY-el. Mr. Preston never heard the el at the end. He thought I liked being called Ralphy. I was too shy to correct him."

"You weren't too shy to correct me."

"No, and I won't be again if you need it. But I do appreciate you calling me Ralph."

"You got it, Ralph," he told him. "Cliff, you take care of yourself, okay?" As he saw Cliff give him only a barely perceptible nod, he decided to try to see what had caught Cliff's attention. He noticed he was looking at Jeremiah 29:11. Then he was turning to a concordance sitting next to the Bible.

"What are you two looking at now?" asked Ralph, not wanting to be left out of something again.

Cliff didn't answer. He just pointed something out to Jack, and then looked up at him to see if he understood. "Can I tell him?" Jack asked Cliff, knowing Cliff's fatigue might restrain him from fully sharing the multitudes of relevant information that were in the one word they were looking at. Cliff nodded as he pushed back from the table.. "Do you remember the verse I showed you in Jeremiah," he asked Ralph. "About God having good plans for us? Come see how it reads in King James."

Ralph looked at the verse and then read it out loud, *"Jeremiah 29:11 For I know the thoughts that I think towards you saith the Lord. Thoughts of peace and not of evil, to give you an expected end.* It does say it a bit differently doesn't it?"

"Yes it does," Jack said. "Now think of it with Cliff in mind."

Ralph was silent for a while and then his jaw dropped. "God

is giving Cliff an expected end. Then I guess his autobiography won't end as a mystery."

"Now look at what the word 'end' means in Hebrew." Jack pointed to the definition in the left column on the concordance. "See where it says the word means 'last or end, hence the future'. That's what I have been trying to tell you two. Cliff is approaching the end of his life, but he is also now approaching the beginning of his future. This is precisely why I say to look up what the writers were originally trying to say, to find out what the author truly wanted to convey."

"When you told me God wrote a book that was personally designed for each individual that read it, I didn't believe it," said Cliff. "Now I see what you mean. Did you notice at the end of the definition it also talks about reward."

"Just like we were talking about earlier. That's why I like to use the concordance. The Hebrew and Greek words have such fuller meanings than the English can portray. A person misses a lot if he only uses the English to understand God's Word."

As much as Jack was excited to continue this conversation, he could see that Cliff was fading fast. He also noticed Barbara looking repeatedly at her watch. He decided he should leave these two to discuss all that had happened at their own convenience. "Both of you, ask God for help getting through these last days. I'll be praying for you as well," he said as he scooped up his Bible and Ralph started pushing Cliff out of the room. Jack knew they needed to let him get Cliff off to bed. "We'll let ourselves out, okay Ralph?"

"Sure, thanks Jack. See ya Barbara. Thanks," Ralph said as he was wheeling Cliff away.

"Yeah. Bye Ralph. Bye Cliff." Barbara said back. She did not even get a movement from Cliff with that, but she didn't expect one either.

As the two of them slipped gingerly past the dogs, Jack thought about all that had happened since he received the invitation. He painfully recalled the horrible death that he had wished on Cliff. In his heart he now cried out to God to forgive him for that, and for Cliff to go peacefully. He had seen too many horrible cancer deaths in his life. He didn't wish that on anyone now, especially Cliff.

Barbara, on the other hand, was praying desperately for Ralph. She knew that those who didn't think they needed any more of God than they already had were the hardest to convince that they did. She was in that camp herself at one time. She was convinced that regular church attendance, being baptized, and partaking of the Lords Supper guaranteed her a place on the other side of the pearly gates. Those activities allowed God to look past her need to party at the pub on occasion. Or on a regular basis.

She still shuddered when she recalled waking up to an empty bed with no idea of where Jack was. She had been too drunk the night before to comprehend it when he told her where he was going. She made quite a few promises and commitments to God by the time he called three days later. Meanwhile, Jack had made quite a few himself, as he attempted to solidify his newfound faith in God with fasting and prayer. Their marriage, and their personal habits, were never the same after those three days. Barbara often thanked God for that.

Barbara was excited for Jack and his newly formed friendship with Ralph. Jack didn't have many friends. In fact he sometimes told people that she was his only true friend, other than certain family members. Jack seemed to rub everyone he knew the wrong way eventually, and neither one of them knew why. No one ever admitted to having a problem with Jack, but no one ever called to chat either. It didn't seem to bother him;

he always seemed content with Barbara's company. She liked that.

"So how do you think it went?" Barbara asked Jack.

"Great. They asked a lot of questions, and I answered them with a lot of questions. I loved it."

"Seriously Jack, how do you think Cliff is doing?"

"From what I saw before, I thought he was really quite strong and alert most of the time, considering. But I don't know. He looked pretty beat by the time we left. Ralph's got his work cut out for him."

"How much longer do you think?"

"I think the pain is getting pretty bad."

"I know. I caught him wincing a number of times."

"He doesn't say much, but you know Cliff. He's going to hide it if he can. If it goes like other people we've known, the pain will put him in the hospital soon for drugs, and then it won't be quick enough. Barbara, we..." Jack had a hard time continuing. "We need to pray for them," he finally said.

"I know we do," Barbara agreed, her face contorting with emotion.

As they held each other in the car and wept, Jack began to pray, "Father, please give Ralph the strength and wisdom to care for Cliff properly. And please, Father, grant Cliff the freedom from pain and the strength to endure his last days peacefully. We ask that the cancer not be allowed to have its way with him, but that instead you would guide his way as the day's progress. We ask that when you have determined that his time here is finished, and he is prepared to see your face, that you keep him here not one moment longer. Thank you so much for allowing me to be a part in what you did in him..."

"And for what you did in Jack, Lord," added Barbara.

"Amen to that. Father, we want to release Cliff to your care.

We make ourselves available if you need us or can use us any more with Cliff or Ralph. Thanks again for your faithfulness. Amen."

It was six thirty Sunday morning when the telephone startled Jack awake. It was times like this that he wished the phone was on Barbara's side of the bed. "Hullo," he said in his best why-did-you-wake-me voice.

"Good morning Jack. Sorry to wake you. This is Ralph."

"Ralph, hi, what's up?" Jack asked as he scrambled to a sitting position in bed.

"I just thought you would want to know. Cliff passed away last night."

"Oh, Ralph, I'm sorry. How are you doing?"

"I'm doing okay. I mean, it really is for the best you know."

"I know, but it's still not easy."

"No it's not."

"How did it happen anyway?"

"As near as I can tell, he died peacefully in his sleep. You know, it was interesting. For most of this past week since you were here last he was actually doing pretty well. He's been too weak to get out of bed, but the pain subsided quite a bit. We could talk for quite a while before he would have to stop."

"What did you talk about?" Jack asked without knowing why. He was curious, but he felt somewhat prompted to ask.

Ralph was quiet for a while, and then said "Gloria."

"You talked about Cliff's wife?"

"Yeah. It was good. We had never talked about her before, not before that last night you were here. We spent quite a bit of this past week just comparing notes about what we remembered. It was hard for both of us, but it felt good at the same time. Last night I said something though that seemed to send him downhill fast. I don't know why, but it sure did."

"What did you say?"

"Well, he happened to say that he really missed her. I told him that he'd see her again on the other side. I guess he'd forgotten about the fact that he might see her again in heaven. That seems odd considering that was the whole point of all of the, you know, hoopla. I guess…once I reminded him of that…he no longer had a reason to live."

Jack could tell Ralph was struggling with either emotion or guilt. "I think it was even more than that Ralph."

"What do you mean?"

"I think Cliff finally had a good reason to die." Jack heard some scuffling noise in the phone, and realized Ralph had covered the mouthpiece. "Ralph?" he asked, but got no answer. When he noticed that Ralph was sobbing he waited a bit. When he thought that Ralph might have the receiver to his ear again, he asked, "Are you okay?"

"I'm just so happy for him!" came the reply. After a few more moments Ralph said, "You reminded me of something Mr. Preston said."

"What was that?" Jack asked.

"He confided to me many years ago that the only time he felt a lot of fear was just before he left on a new adventure. He was afraid of the authorities in a region more than he was the natives. He worried about passports and visas and permits and papers. For some reason the fear always left him as soon as he got off the plane and met his contact person."

Jack could hear Ralph start to sob again. "Jack," he said through the sobs, "I just got a picture in my mind of Gloria meeting him as he got off the plane."

As Jack gave Ralph a few moments to weep, he thanked God

for giving Ralph that vision. Then he said to him, "Ralph, I think that is precisely what you reminded him of, who his contact person was. But now you're going to have to wait."

"Wait for what?" asked Ralph.

"To talk to Cliff about this latest adventure of his."

"Yeah, I guess you're right."

"I know I'm right," Jack joked. "But you know what?"

"No, what?"

"Gloria is going to get an ear full."

"Ralph just started laughing and said, "She'll love that!"

21

There were a lot of people at Cliff's memorial service. Since he had no living relatives, and few friends, most of the people were there just because he was famous. Some were from the media wanting a story. Some were groupies wanting to be seen at a famous dead person's funeral. Others were former employees paying last respects, respectful or not. There was one face in the crowd that Jack was looking for though; a formerly freckled one.

He had seen her when he was giving the eulogy. He quickly looked away when he saw her though; he was having a tough enough time just saying what he had to say. He had never given a eulogy before, and felt he would never want to. On this occasion he was glad to. A lot of people in the audience probably didn't believe all the nice things he said about Cliff. He didn't care. He always enjoyed declaring the truth.

He also enjoyed all the time he got to spend with Ralph preparing to give the eulogy. He learned a lot of things about Cliff he didn't know. He also learned something about Ralph. The day after the last time the three of them were together, Cliff challenged Ralph about the status of his relationship with God. Without really realizing it, Cliff led Ralph to the Lord. He made Ralph swear on a stack of Bibles his allegiance to God. Somehow Jack could picture that very well. What got Jack the most excited though was the fact that with their conversations he could tell Ralph really meant it. He didn't just do it because Cliff said to. It was real.

There was something else that Ralph discussed with him that got Jack real excited. It seems that before Cliff died, he and Ralph finished the final chapter of Cliff's autobiography. They needed someone to proofread the book and do any rewrites that were necessary. Cliff said that Jack was the only person in the world that he ever trusted with that job. Ralph wanted to know if he would do it. Jack thought it ironic that a mere two months earlier he would have said 'Not on your life'.

"Jack?" he heard someone say, and felt a tap on his shoulder blade.

"Jenny?" he asked, almost before he saw her. "I was looking for you."

"You've gotta look a little lower," she said, laughing. "Lucky for you I could see your head sticking over the crowd looking for somebody."

"Yeah. So, how are you doing? I take it you heard about Cliff?"

"My husband did."

"And he told you about the memorial service?" he asked, not hiding his doubts very well.

"Yes he did, eventually," she answered. Then she asked rather seriously "Jack, I need to talk to you about something that happened to me."

"Sure. What happened?"

"Well, two days ago I got this letter from Mr. Montgomery, I mean, you know, Mr. Preston. Anyway, here, you gotta read this," she said as she handed Jack the letter, obviously written by Ralph on Cliff's behalf. It read:

Dear Jennifer Lynn;
*   I ask that you please accept this gift from me. I know I cannot in any way repay the debt I owe you for your years*

of service to me and the shameful way I treated you for it. I sincerely thank you for forgiving me and that debt, even before I asked you to. Please accept this check as a belated bonus, severance pay, or a wedding present for you and the man who loves you. You certainly deserved all three, but sadly received none of them until now.

I know your husband is bitter with me, and I don't blame him. I know what it means to hate someone for hurting someone you love. Hopefully someday he will learn that forgiveness has a way of healing old wounds.

Inform him that it is impossible to return the money to me, and that Mr. Huntley does not need it. If he will not accept the reasons I gave above for giving this to you, then he probably won't accept the truth either. The truth is, God told me that you needed it, and I was more than happy to give it. Hope to see you both again someday.

Sincerely;
Cliff Preston.

"Boy, that was really something!" he said, as they both wiped tears from their cheeks. "That sure doesn't sound like the old Cliff we used to work for, does it?"

"No, it doesn't. But that wasn't the good part."

"It wasn't?" he asked.

"No. You know how much the check was for?"

"No, it didn't say. How much?"

"Nineteen thousand two hundred dollars!"

"You're kidding? That's a lot of money."

"But that wasn't the good part either."

"You're kidding? What was?"

"Well, Robert had been out of work for five months. We had

a pile of bills. When I got the check, I was so afraid he'd make me give it back, I didn't tell him about it. I went straight to the bank and put it in our checking account. Then I went to Costco and loaded up on groceries and stuff. I mean, I loaded up. Over $600.00 worth. Plus, I got a book of stamps so we could mail off checks to cover our bills as we paid them.

"When I got home I raced in with the groceries, hoping to surprise him. I thought he would be happy, but instead he went ballistic. He had been sitting there, adding up our bills on his spreadsheet, just so he could yell at me about it. Before I could tell him about the check, he started ranting and raving about bankruptcy and my stupid ideas.

"So what did you do?" he asked, noticing she was starting to get emotional over the whole incident.

"I got mad right back at him. I grabbed the Costco receipt and threw it on the table with the bills and demanded that he add it to the amount we owed. Then I threw the stamps at him and told him to add that to it as well. I think he did it just because he was mad at me. And then I said--you'll love this--and then I said 'Oh, by the way, you better factor this in to your little spreadsheet as well!' and I threw the deposit slip on the table by the computer. At first he yelled 'What's this?' at me, and I went 'Just look at it!' and his eyes bugged open...and he...he..."

Jenny couldn't continue. Jack could tell she wanted to, as if she had rehearsed this speech so she could, but she couldn't. Finally, out of curiosity, he asked her, "What is it? What did he do?"

All she could do was shake her head no and hold up her hand. Finally she stammered "The amounts...the amounts."

"What about the amounts?" he asked.

"They were the same...on the deposit slip...and what the

spreadsheet said we owed. They were the same," she said be-tween sobs.

"Before or after Costco and the stamps?"

"AFTER!" she yelled.

"But...how could...how did...they couldn't have known what you needed, could they? You hadn't talked to them, had you? I mean...how could...with the stamps...and Costco...?" Now Jack was stammering.

"No. I talked to Mr. Huntley about it, just a few minutes ago, when I thanked him for it. I asked him how he came up with such an odd amount. He says the two of them added up how much they would have given me if they would have been so wise back then. After that they tripled it for inflation, and then doubled it again just because."

"So, did you tell Mr. Huntley what happened?" he asked.

"No, I didn't. I thought about it, but I didn't know what he would think. I wanted to talk to you first."

"I'm honored. Ralph has changed a lot since you knew him. He has a few stories that will shock you as well. Ask him if he would want to play Monopoly with you sometime."

"What?"

"Monopoly. Just tell him to tell you the story about Monopoly. He'll know what you mean."

"Okay, if you say so," she said, not totally convinced that Jack wasn't setting her up for something.

"I assume that was the good news you were trying to tell me, about the amounts being the same?" he asked, trying to change the subject back to where it was.

"Well, no, it wasn't. I mean, that was sure good news all right. But it wasn't the neatest thing that happened."

"Okay, now you got me real curious. What else happened?"

"Well...I...I sort of need to confess something first. I hope you'll understand. There was a good reason Robert got so mad at me. You know, when I came home from Costco? While we were in so much trouble with money, I, I sort of, didn't do the right thing."

"What do you mean?" he asked

"Well, I don't think it was totally my fault. Where I was going to church they were telling us that we didn't have to worry about finances. They said that God would always take care of us. He would always provide for our needs. He didn't want His children in rags while the world prospered. I mean, He doesn't, does He?" she pleaded.

"Well, no, I don't believe He does, but..."

"Anyway, I really believed that, but Robert didn't because, well, he didn't believe in God. I tried to tell Robert not to worry about the money, that God would take care of it, but that just made him angrier. I kept praying for a miracle, that suddenly we would have the money and Robert would see that God really cares about us and he would get saved."

"So, is that what happened?"

"Not like you think," she said. "I decided to take a leap of faith and started trusting God to provide for us. I started giving money to the church and to other ministries."

"How could you do that if you didn't have any money?" he asked.

"Credit cards," she answered. "I maxed them out. I even got a couple cards without telling Robert about it. Then I started writing checks."

"You mean rubber checks? On an empty account? Jenny! What were you thinking?" he scolded.

"I know, I know. It wasn't right. But at the time I was sure God would provide somehow. I mean, why wouldn't He? He owns the cattle on a thousand hills and the houses in Beverly

Hills. He could afford to give me a few thousand, couldn't He?"

"Well, sure He could, but..."

"Of course He could. He does all the time. We had a lot of people who got up in church and gave testimonies about how God had met their needs once they started tithing regularly. You just had to have enough faith. I guess I didn't have enough faith."

Jack could tell she was still struggling with everything that had happened. He didn't know how to console her, or help her; especially when he couldn't get a word in edgewise. "Did Robert assume that you wrote another rubber check to pay for the Costco stuff?" he asked, knowing that if he was in Robert's place he would have.

"I'm sure he did. He had been calculating our bills all afternoon. He was fully prepared to show me how far my 'faith in God' had put us in debt. What he didn't know was that just that morning I had gotten into a little shouting match with God."

"A shouting match, huh?" he asked. "He's not hard of hearing, you know."

"Very funny, Jack. No, I was just angry. I couldn't understand why God would let me down, even for His own sake. I mean, didn't he want Robert to get saved? Did He want us to go bankrupt? Why did He help so many other people and not me? Was there something I was doing wrong?"

He had some answers for her questions, but he felt that she may have already found some. He wanted to find out what those answers might be. "Did you get any answers to those questions?" he finally asked.

"No, not to those questions. I mostly just got convicted that maybe I was wrong about the whole thing. I finally just confessed to God that whether He provided the money or not, what I really needed...was to...know Him better...and to...love my husband again...and to...have him love me."

Jack had to just grab her and hold her. He knew it was hard for her to say. He was glad they were at a funeral service, where it was common for people to cry and hug. And they both did for a while.

"I feel so silly," she finally said, trying to continue. "I thought I had gotten it all out of my system. I remember when I first got the letter from Cliff. I cried like a baby, but not because we had the money. I was to a point that I didn't care about the money any more. It honestly wouldn't have mattered if we would have gone bankrupt and lost it all. When I saw the check I knew God hadn't abandoned me. And I was so excited for Cliff. You must have had some kind of conversation with Cliff that day."

"I sure did, but I don't think it was what I said that changed Cliff's heart. God did that himself."

"That is just so neat!" she exclaimed.

"You still haven't told me what the good thing was."

"What good thing? Oh, yes, no, I haven't, have I? Okay, well, remember that morning when I was yelling at God? Well, I had decided not to go to my regular Bible study that evening. I was going to stay home with Robert--he never went anyway-- and I was going to try to work out with him how we were going to pay off those bills. I was going to try to find a job, or something. That was quite a change for me. Before, I wouldn't even talk to Robert about it. I would just tell him to trust God and forget about it. Now I was prepared to tell him that I no longer trusted God for it and I was willing to work on it myself. Then the check came, and you know the rest of that story.

"When I threw that deposit slip on the table, it kind of shook Robert up. He was in total shock because the amounts were the same. He didn't know what was happening. The first thing he wanted to know was where I got the money. I just handed him Cliff's letter. When he got to the end and realized it was from

Cliff, he started crying. I mean, I certainly didn't expect that. I had hardly ever seen Robert cry for anything. I expected him to yell at me or something. It was weird.

"Then Robert told me that there was a message on our machine. It was Mr. Huntley telling me that Cliff had died. I was in total shock. He wasn't planning on saying anything to me, just 'cause he was mad at both of us. It was then that we both remembered that Cliff had said in the letter that it would be impossible for us to give the money back to him. He must have known he was going to die. We figured he must have died the day after he mailed the letter."

"Jenny." Jack said, getting impatient, "Have you told me the good part yet?"

"No, no, I haven't. Before I had a chance to tell Robert that I wasn't going to the Bible study 'cause I wanted to stay home with him, he told me he wanted to go, you know, to the Bible study. With me! Jack...Robert gave his life to Jesus that night."

"Seriously?" he asked. "That check must have really gotten to him."

"It wasn't the check, it was Cliff's letter. Something in the letter really got to him. He still hasn't told me what."

"Was that the good part?"

"That was definitely the good part. Robert's heart has changed so much; he actually wanted to come to this memorial service."

"Why didn't he come?"

"He had to work!" she said, beaming all over as she said it.

"Where at?" he asked, trying to locate the source of the glow on her face.

"Back at the publisher. It seems that all of a sudden there is a renewed interest in a number of Cliff's books. The publisher has gotten a lot of orders and needed Robert back. Ironic, isn't it?"

"How is it ironic?"

"Well, years ago we would have loved to watch Mr. Montgomery's demise, because we hated him so. Now we are all profiting at his demise, and yet we love him so."

"I see your point." Jack said as he fought a quiver in his chin. He paused a second to compose himself and then said to Jenny, "I think Ralph would love to hear about Robert. Shall we go find him?"

"Sure, I'd love to!" Jenny exclaimed.

Barbara watched from across the room as the two of them approached Ralph. As she did, she suddenly got a mental picture of a stonemason perfectly fitting together three very different stones into a foundation wall.

22

The sun was barely above the horizon when Jack finally said goodbye to Jenny and Ralph. He found Barbara patiently waiting alone at one of the tables near the punchbowl. "Are you about ready to go?" he said, in a teasingly impatient way.

"Not quite yet. I haven't finished my sixteenth cup of punch."

"I'm sorry hon.' You should have come and joined us."

"It looked like you three were in a pretty wild conversation, judging by the way you were flailing your arms."

"It was a very interesting conversation anyway," Jack responded. "Ralph was telling us a lot of stories about Gloria, Cliff's wife. She certainly sounds like she must have been a godly woman. Not who you would have expected to have been hitched to Cliff back then."

"So you're pretty convinced that she was waiting in heaven for Cliff to show up then, huh?"

"Yeah. In fact, we were making up different scenarios as to what that may have been like the moment when Cliff got there. You sorta know how Cliff was. Kind of like Columbo, seemingly wandering around aimlessly, but in reality he was noticing every detail. I bet he had a lot of details to notice up there."

"I bet if you had something to say about it, it would be quite different."

"Well, some of the scenarios I came up with did have a few interesting details. Such as all of the people that Cliff met on his travels, finding out the truth about what he said behind their backs."

"And forgiving him for it?"

"Well, yeah, after chewing on him for a while. But I gotta tell you the scenario that all three of us came up with," he said, trying to change the tone. "We came up with this great story about what that moment was like for Gloria and some of her love of gardening, along with some of the other stuff we talked about. It may not be theologically correct, but it was great. It went like this:"

Gloria's Moment

"Excuse me ma'am," said the angel Gabriel.

Without even looking his direction, Gloria said, "Well, hello Gabriel. You must have an important message for me."

"You know I do ma'am."

Holding a freshly cut flower in front of her, she said, "Just look at this flower Gabriel. Have you ever seen such color?"

"Yes I have ma'am. In fact, I believe that is the same flower that our Lord gave you when you entered the Garden."

"Yes, I believe you're right. But after all this time, the colors are still so amazing! In the world, we would have called this a Black Eyed Susan, but it would only have been yellow. This one is every color in the rainbow! And much more iridescent...Gabriel, do you think he'll like it?"

"I'm sure he will ma'am, eventually."

Gloria turned to look at the magnificent angel visiting her. "What do you mean?" she asked.

"You forget ma'am that I've met this husband of yours."

"That's right, on a dirt street in the Old West, if I remember right."

"To him it was."

"So what did you mean by 'eventually'?"

"I believe it will be quite a while before he takes his eyes off of you," he replied with a grin.

"Oh, Gabriel, what am I going to do with you?"

"Allow me to deliver my message," he answered.

"Okay sir," she said, standing formally to attention.

Understanding the sensitive nature of his message, Gabriel tried to deliver it with as little emotion as he could. "Gloria Marie Preston, your presence is requested at the arrival of Mr. Heathcliff Montgomery Preston. I have been sent to escort you to our Lord for the reunion."

Gloria had been expecting this day ever since she heard the angels rejoicing at his salvation. She had received congratulatory remarks from so many people and so many angels that she was sure she could handle the news. But when it came, she just collapsed into the angel's strong arms. Gabriel set her down in a lounge chair near them and handed her the flower that she had dropped.

When she saw the flower she suddenly looked at the other lounge chair, and then glanced around the courtyard they were in. Jumping up from the chair she ran to a particular spot on the edge of the courtyard, glanced back at the chairs and said, "Right here would be the perfect spot." She took the cut flower and poked it in the ground. It immediately sprang up to the size of a bush looking very much like a bouquet. "He is sure to see it here. Gabriel, could you turn that chair just a little bit more this direction?"

"Yes ma'am." Gabriel turned the chair toward the

flowers, and then asked, "Ma'am, why such plain chairs?"

"These lounge chairs just happen to be the finest teak, and they are just like the ones we had in the world."

Gabriel looked at the chairs, and then glanced around the courtyard. "This is where he told you his stories."

"That's right, "Gloria answered.

"Do you think I will be allowed to hear one of his stories?" Gabriel asked.

Gloria got a big smile on her face as she looked at him and said, "Eventually."

DELETED SCENES

THE BIBLE SEARCH

Jack hurriedly tried to get the Web session going on his computer. He knew Cliff, Ralph, and Jenny may already be sitting at their desks, trying to logon to it, and were hearing nothing but "hold" music. He quickly dialed the audio conference number on his phone and entered the host ID number. Checking to see if anyone was there yet, he said, "Hello?"

"Hi Jack," responded Ralph.

"Don't yell that in an airport," Jack said.

"What? Oh, right. I think we're ready on this end. I'm just now logging in."

"Yes, I see your name just popped up," said Jack. "Can you see my desktop on your screen?"

"What are all those round rocks you're standing next to?"

"Then you are seeing my desk top," answered Jack. "That is a place called Bowling Ball Beach. It's on the California coast, north of Frisco. All of those big round rocks fall out of the hillside and roll into position on the beach. They are so dense and heavy that the waves don't move them. Barb and I visited there last year."

"I don't see anyone else on the beach."

"There was only one other couple there at the time," Jack commented. "The stairs down the cliff had partially washed out, and it was cold and drizzly. But we thought the balls were worth seeing. Okay, can you see the Bible search program now?"

"Yes, it just popped up. It's kind of small."

"Right. Is that better? I just maximized it."

"Yes, that's much better."

"Jenny, are you on the line yet?" Jack asked.

"Just," Jenny replied. "I heard something about Cliff being partially washed out."

"No, not Cliff. I was talking about stairs being washed out at the beach. They went down a cliff. Never mind, I'll tell you later. Ralph, is Cliff there?"

"I'm going to go get him now. I wanted to make sure you could actually make this thing work."

"Thanks for the vote of confidence, Ralph," Jack replied. "Jenny, while Ralph is doing that, here is the picture of Bowling Ball Beach that I was showing Ralph. Barb and I went there last year."

"Is that where Cliff got washed out?"

"I didn't say... very funny," Jack said, as he heard giggling on the speaker. "You probably heard the whole story, huh?"

"No, but I've been there before. I used to live in Fort Bragg with my folks. Did you get to see the Glass Beach."

"Yes, yes I did. Did you see the spark plugs embedded in the solid rock?"

"You bet. They were kind of a joke amongst the Christians in town. You know, the million year old spark plugs, probably left there by a Comet."

"That's great," Jack responded. "I'll have to remember that. In fact, maybe I'll switch my desktop photo to the one I took of the spark plug. It would be..."

"We're here now," Ralph interrupted.

"Hi Cliff," Jack said, at the same time that Jenny said "Hi Ralph."

"Hi, Jenny," said Ralph.

"Jack, how are you doing?" Cliff added. "Hi Jenny."

Jenny quickly remarked, "He doesn't sound washed out to me."

"What?" questioned Cliff.

"You know, I think I'll change my desktop photo to the one with Barbara's petunias." Jack said. "Shall we get started?"

"*I'll tell you later*," Jack heard Ralph whisper to Cliff.

"Okay, I hear you have a few more questions for me. I'll show you how to use this program to find the answers in the Bible. So, what are the questions?"

Cliff answered, "Since we've started talking with you, you've talked about prayer, God doing a work, being compelled to pray, hearing God's voice. I would like you to try to explain what you're talking about in a language I happen to be familiar with. Ralph, do you have that list?"

"Sure, just a minute, I'll get it, it's right here," Ralph said, his voice trailing off.

"Is that a list of questions, or a list of the languages you happen to be familiar with?" Jack asked, hearing a giggle again from Jenny.

"It's a list of questions," he said, rather curtly. Then he added, "As far as a language, I would prefer American West Coast English, upper class, with a pinch of slang. Colloquialisms are acceptable."

"Would you like that with a touch of humor?"

"Yes," he answered, "Dry, please."

"Are you sure? I'm quite good with the sarcastic kind."

"No, dry is probably bad enough," Cliff said without a flinch.

"I'll take some of the sarcastic stuff," said Jenny.

"You've got it!" Jack exclaimed.

"It'll make me feel at home."

"You are at home, Jenny."

They heard a door bang, and then Ralph said, "Here's the list, Mr. Preston. What part did you want to start with?"

"Communicating with God," he said without looking at it. "Jack, a number of the things on this list I think you've already explained, and some other ones I think I already know. But how about if we go through them all, if you don't mind."

"No, I don't mind. I don't think," he answered, somewhat hesitantly. "Where did you get the list?"

"As we were watching different religious programs, we started writing down things we didn't understand," said Ralph. "We thought we might find the answers someday and put it all together."

"That sounds like a typical Cliff Montgomery M.O."

"Then you should have no problems with it," said Cliff in his usual Cliff Montgomery toughness, only this time he seemed to be mocking himself. "Jack, the last time you were here, you talked about developing a relationship with God. You talked about praying to Him, spending time with Him, getting to know Him, and about God speaking to us through his son. With a real practical application, how does all that happen?"

"This ought to be good," everyone heard Jenny say softly. "Oops, excuse me. Maybe I should mute my phone."

"I wish I could do that with Barbara," joked Jack.

"Speaking of Barbara," said Ralph, "Where is she?"

"I expect her anytime. She said she got a little carried away shopping. I presume that meant stopping at garage sales."

"I understand," said Ralph. "We won't wait then."

"Yeah, no need to," Jack said, wanting to get back on topic. "First of all, think about how you communicate with other humans. You formulate the words you are going to speak in your mind, and then you speak them with your lips. I admit that with some people the first part may not happen, ain't that right Cliff?"

"Why are you looking at me?" said Ralph.

"Because Jack's not here," said Cliff.

"Anyway," continued Jack, "Communication with humans is limited to what can be heard and understood. In other words, if there are language or hearing difficulties, then communication still won't happen. I would imagine that you have first hand knowledge of that problem; huh, Cliff?"

"Oh, yes." he said, nodding his head. "In most places I've been."

"Communication with God is only limited on our end." Jack continued. "We essentially only comprehend what we understand with our mind. God can comprehend what we speak, or think, or even feel. He understands our motives and intentions. So as far as communicating with God, we can do so anyway we desire. Except lying of course. I mean, you could try to lie, and some people do, but he will know it's a lie. However you do it, He will get the message.

"Regarding God communicating with us," Jack continued, "the limitation is on our end. I don't doubt that God could find a way to penetrate our understanding with what he wants to convey to us. Instead, my experience has shown me that He trains us how to listen for His voice. For example, a good parent would train their child to listen for their voice, in case the child got lost in a crowd. Wait a minute. I've got a better example. None of us has kids anyway," Jack said, as he realized that.

Cliff then piped in and said, "I think I might have an example."

Kind of surprised, Ralph asked, "What would that be?"

"The shepherds in the Middle East," he said. "I've watched them gather together, with all of their flocks mingling together around them. Then, when they split up, they would give a command, kind of a shrill noise, and all of their sheep would separate from the others and follow them. It was pretty amazing."

What was amazing to Jack was that Cliff stole his example. "That's what I was going to say!" he said to Cliff. "But I think you said it better. What I would like to show you is that same story in the Bible. Does everyone have their Bibles?" he asked, to which all he got was dead air. "Sorry, guys. It's a church thing. Never mind. I wanted to show you this program anyway." He clicked a few things on his laptop computer and said, "You can set this up however you like. I happen to have one version on each side and the concordance in the middle."

"What's a concordance?" asked Jenny.

Jack was surprised at the question. He knew Jenny had been a believer since she was young, and thought that somewhere over the years she had been taught to use a concordance. He decided not to criticize her in front of everyone. "It gives you a dictionary definition of the Hebrew or Greek words used in the original manuscripts. I'll get to that later. See up here where it says 'search'? You just type in what you want, and it will find where that word or phrase is used in the Bible. For instance, I'll type 'sheep' here in the 'phrase' box and hit 'search' down here. There! The word 'sheep' occurs 187 times in 178 verses, and it lists all the verses."

"Let's narrow down the search a bit," said Cliff.

"I see you've been using this already."

"A little bit," remarked Ralph. "Ours looks different than yours."

"You've got the newest version. I need to upgrade mine. We were talking about the sheep knowing their masters voice."

"We were?" asked Ralph.

"Sort of. Anyway, if I search for the words 'sheep' and 'voice,'" he says as he shows them how to do it, "Now I get only five matching verses." Jack then showed them a number of different ways to cross reference the same information. "See how four of them are in John chapter ten?"

"Could you go to that chapter, Jack?" asked Cliff.

"Sure. I'll just type in John 10 here and...there we are, at John chapter ten."

"Let me read that," said Cliff. Then he changed his mind and said, "Ralph, could you read that to me?"

Ralph said, "Sure, how far?"

Jack piped in and told him, "Why don't you read down to, oh, verse 18. And if you want a little easier reading, read it in the version on the left," he said, moving the cursor around the left hand side of the screen. "It's the same thing, just a little bit more modern English."

Ralph took a few seconds to glance at the two translations and find what he was going to read. "Okay. It says:"

John 10:1 (NLT) "I tell you the truth, anyone who sneaks over the wall of a sheepfold, rather than going through the gate, must surely be a thief and a robber! :2 But the one who enters through the gate is the shepherd of the sheep. :3 The gatekeeper opens the gate for him, and the sheep recognize his voice and come to him. He calls his own sheep by name and leads them out. :4 After he has gathered his own flock, he walks ahead of them, and they follow him because they know his voice. :5 They won't follow a stranger; they will run from him because they don't know his voice."

"Wait a minute," interrupted Cliff. "There was something else about the sheep I saw in the Middle East. The guide told me that the shepherds name all of the sheep, and they all respond to their own name. I thought it was amazing. Okay, keep going," he said, as he flicked his fingers at Ralph.

"Okay, I was at verse six:"

John 10:6 (NLT) Those who heard Jesus use this illustration didn't understand what he meant, :7 so he explained it to them: "I tell you the truth, I am the gate for the sheep. :8 All who came before me were thieves and robbers. But the true sheep did not listen to them.

:9 Yes, I am the gate. Those who come in through me will be saved. They will come and go freely and will find good pastures. :10 The thief's purpose is to steal and kill and destroy. My purpose is to give them a rich and satisfying life.

:11 "I am the good shepherd. The good shepherd sacrifices his life for the sheep. :12 A hired hand will run when he sees a wolf coming. He will abandon the sheep because they don't belong to him and he isn't their shepherd. And so the wolf attacks them and scatters the flock. :13 The hired hand runs away because he's working only for the money and doesn't really care about the sheep.

:14 "I am the good shepherd; I know my own sheep, and they know me, :15 just as my Father knows me and I know the Father. So I sacrifice my life for the sheep. :16 I have other sheep, too, that are not in this sheepfold. I must bring them also. They will listen to my voice, and there will be one flock with one shepherd.

:17 "The Father loves me because I sacrifice my life so I may take it back again. :18 No one can take my life from me. I sacrifice it voluntarily. For I have the authority to lay it down when I want to and also to take it up again. For this is what my Father has commanded."

After Ralph finished reading the verses, he sat in silence, seeing Cliff was thinking about something.

"Thanks Ralph," said Jack.

"Was there something you wanted to point out?" said Cliff, as if reading Jack's thoughts.

"Well, I just wanted to point out that I believe God trains us to recognize His voice, just like the shepherds train the sheep to. I'm sure the sheep don't all respond the same, and neither do we. Plus, in the whole scheme of things, I'm just another sheep. I can show you by example how I follow the shepherds voice, which may be good or bad. Ultimately, God will teach you Himself.

"There is one recommendation I would like to make, though," he continued. "Like I said before, I believe the Bible is God's word, His communication to us in writing, if you will. Throughout the Bible it also talks about His voice, as in these verses. Some people believe that you can not rely on anything but the written verse, and they reject anything supposedly spoken by God to believers nowadays. I mean, I understand the danger of believing a voice you hear is God, if in fact he no longer speaks to his people. But there also is a danger in ignoring His voice if He actually is speaking to us. I don't believe that Jesus would say that we would know His voice, and then not speak to us. It just doesn't make sense. I recommend you learn to discern His voice, and test it, rather than rejecting it."

"Are you going to give us any clue on how to do that?" asked Cliff.

"The best I can," Jack answered, trying to figure out how he would do it. "Remember what I was telling you about humans being a three part being? You know, body, soul, and spirit?" He got an affirmative grunt from both of them that said 'yes, we're listening', but didn't hear anything from Jenny. Assuming she had muted her phone, he continued, "The one thing that I have found to be the hardest thing to grasp, for me as well as a lot of people I know, is the spirit side of our nature. As I said before, that is where God usually speaks to us.

"The difficulty becomes comprehending that voice. Our mind has to convert the communication that our spirit receives into something understandable by our brain, or soul, or whatever. Since it is also possible to receive communications in your spirit from evil spirits, you need to make sure that what you are hearing is from God and only from God."

"You haven't told us how to hear anything yet," said Cliff, suggesting in his way that Jack was beating a dead horse.

"Okay, you're right. I will try to get to the point. It's just that, almost all of the religions and cults in the world have traditions that are in place due to some supposed revelation that someone had. I know for a fact that all of these revelations couldn't have come from God because of the divisions they have caused. I just don't want you to miss the mark."

"And do what?" asked Ralph. "Start our own religion?"

"Exactly!" Jack said, laughing. "We have at least a hundred too many as it is."

"Jack!" scolded Cliff. "Back to the point."

"The point is, if you are born again, of the spirit, God will begin to communicate with you." Jack decided to just blurt out information, hoping that somehow the Holy Spirit would get it to go in the right direction. "You have to accept that concept by faith. The communication you receive will first of all be given to your spirit. The best way to describe what that is like is intuition. Have you ever had to trust your intuition, Cliff?" he asked.

"Once when we got lost in the jungle in Venezuela." he said. "We had to back track. The trail looked different going the other direction. We were losing too much time at each fork in the trail trying to figure out which way was correct. I finally decided to just pick a way to go when I got to a fork, and if I got lost, I got lost. We ended up hiking right out of there. I still don't know how we did it."

"That's a good example," Jack remarked. "Some people would say that the trail was imprinted on your memory, and that is why you found your way out. Others would say you were led by a spirit guide. Some Christians would say 'Glory, hallelujah, God showed me the way!'" Jack said, in his best Pentecostal voice and his hands waving, which no one saw. "Truthfully, it could have been any one of them."

"I thought you were going to say one of them was his intuition," said Ralph.

"Sure, it could have been," he said. "But what is intuition? Have you ever thought about it? Or a hunch? Or a feeling? We have all these terms but no real understanding about what they are. Or who they are," he said, trying to make a point. "That is why it is so hard for me to explain it. The first time it was explained to me, we spent a year and a half in a Bible study. The man teaching us wanted to make sure we didn't get it wrong, even if it took forever to get it right."

"I don't have forever," said Cliff. The weight of that statement sobered up all of them. Thankfully, Jack thought of something.

"Okay Cliff. I've told you what the communication is like. That experience will be unique to you, so I can't be any more precise than that. The origin of that communication is obviously of utmost importance. As I said before, it could be God's Spirit, it could be your spirit, or it could be an evil spirit." Jack said this as his fingers typed away at the keyboard, looking for something in the Bible program. "As I pointed out, God's words are usually spoken to your spirit. By the time they reach your brain where you can comprehend them, and act on them, it will already be sort of second hand information, relayed to your brain by your spirit."

Jack finally found the verses he was looking for in the program. "If the information relayed to you by your spirit is accurate, and from God, it will always be a good thing. That I can guarantee. But to know absolutely that it is from God, you should test it. Here are a few verses that show you how the content of the words might give away the source. "Ralph, would you care to read this for us?" he said, as he highlighted some verses in the program, "It's out of the New Living Translation Bible, which I find is a lot easier to read."

"Okay." Ralph said, as he fumbled with his glasses. "Verse sixteen of...what book is this... oh, Galatians, chapter five. Okay, it says:"

Gal. 5:16 (NLT) *So I say, let the Holy Spirit guide your lives. Then you won't be doing what your sinful nature craves. :17 The sinful nature wants to do evil, which is just the opposite of what the Spirit wants. And the Spirit gives us desires that are the opposite of what the sinful nature desires. These two forces are constantly fighting each other, so you are not free to carry out your good intentions.*

:18 But when you are directed by the Spirit, you are not under obligation to the law of Moses.

:19 When you follow the desires of your sinful nature, the results are very clear: sexual immorality, impurity, lustful pleasures,

:20 idolatry, sorcery, hostility, quarreling, jealousy, outbursts of anger, selfish ambition, dissension, division, :21 envy, drunkenness, wild parties, and other sins like these. Let me tell you again, as I have before, that anyone living that sort of life will not inherit the Kingdom of God.

:22 But the Holy Spirit produces this kind of fruit in our lives: love, joy, peace, patience, kindness, goodness, faithfulness,

:23 gentleness, and self-control. There is no law against these things!

:24 Those who belong to Christ Jesus have nailed the passions and desires of their sinful nature to his cross and crucified them there. :25 Since we are living by the Spirit, let us follow the Spirit's leading in every part of our lives. :26 Let us not become conceited, or provoke one another, or be jealous of one another.

"So in other words, God is not going to tell you to have an affair, get drunk, or read Playboy. Instead, when you receive a communication from the Holy Spirit, its content should be in keeping with the fruits that were listed; love, joy, peace, et cetera."

When Jack said that, Cliff held up one finger, then pushed himself away from the table and turned his wheelchair to face a different direction. Ralph knew this to be Cliff-speak for 'I am out of this conversation for a minute'. On Cliff's behalf, Ralph said, "Hold up for a minute, Jack."

"Sure, no problem," responded Jack, not knowing why, but assuming it had something to do with Cliff.

After a minute of silence, Cliff said, "Let me run something past you, Jack, to see if I understand."

"Okay, what is it?" he responded.

"Ralph, do you remember Dr. Richardson?" he asked.

"I think so. The missionary doctor?"

"Yeah. Do you remember the story he told us, about the native that broke his arm?"

"Yeah, sort of."

"Could you tell it to Jack?" Cliff was getting tired again, but he still wanted to continue.

"Sure. There was this native that went out hunting."

"It was downstream," interrupted Cliff.

"Right, he took a boat and went hunting downstream from his village. He fell out of a tree and broke his arm. He tried to get back to his village, but he couldn't paddle back upstream against the current. He passed out from the injury and floated down the river. When he floated into a city, a fisherman saw him and contacted the authorities. This native woke up two days later in a hospital. He kinda flipped out at first."

"Get to the part about the radio," said Cliff.

"Oh yeah," said Ralph. "This Dr. Richardson happened to be at the hospital as a chaplain and recognized the language this native spoke, and contacted another missionary near the man's village on his ham radio. I guess they had a pretty comical time trying to convince this tribesman that the voice of his wife was going to come out of a box on the table," he said, laughing just thinking about it.

"So what happened?" Jack asked.

"This native was instructed to say something to the box, and he would hear his wife speak back. Translated, he said to the box "Is that you, wife?" and she said "Are you dead? How did you get in that box?" Ralph said, as he bent over in his chair, laughing.

"He recognized her by what she said," interrupted Cliff, trying to bring the conversation back to a serious note.

"Yeah, because I guess the sound from the box didn't sound at all like his wife's voice," added Ralph. "Dr. Richardson said the native told him he knew it was his wife because she would ask that kind of a question. So he told his wife "I am not dead, I am in a healing hut. I will be home soon." Then his wife said, "When you get out of the box, I will see you." Isn't that great?"

"The point I was trying to make," said Cliff, sounding a bit serious, "Is that the sound of the voice shouldn't matter. You should recognize the speaker by the subject matter. Is that what you are trying to tell us?"

"Exactly!" Jack said to Cliff. "Whether it's good or bad, you should be able to recognize the source. If it's bad, it's probably from a demon. If it's good, it's probably from God. If it sounds too much like you, well, it probably is from you, from your own mind." As he looked back at the verses Ralph read, he saw something he wanted to point out. "Here is one of the most common things you will see in any cult," he said, highlighting those verses on the computer screen. "See here in verse twenty? It says 'the feeling that everyone is wrong except those in your own little group.'"

"That sounds like the Jim Jones cult," said Cliff.

"And a lot of others, like Warren Jeff's bunch or those folks down in Waco Texas that the FBI busted. There are even major recognized religions that have that kind of attitude. If you see what list it comes from, you see that it's a bad thing. I have to admit that I almost got sucked into a couple of cultish type groups myself that were, quote-unquote, Christian. Fortunately, I had read this verse, and I walked away from them."

"I also see an element of faith in the story about the native," interjected Jenny, surprisingly serious.

"How so?" Jack asked.

"The wife of the native had to have had at least enough faith in the missionary to be willing to listen to the radio," she said.

"Very astute observation," Jack said, trying to hide the fact that he was also very convicted by it. Over the years he had become very cynical because of the polarization he had seen in the church as a whole. On one side were groups rejecting every hint of spirituality, calling it emotionalism or mysticism. On the other were people seeking a 'touch from God', and not opening their eyes to see who was touching them. He got very discouraged wanting to pray for those in the first group who wouldn't accept it, and praying against the demons that the second group had allowed into their lives. He had already lost his faith in humanity, and now he didn't trust most believers.

"You make it sound like skepticism may be better than blind faith," commented Cliff.

Jack laughed when he heard that and said, "Am I that transparent? Tell you what, Barbara just walked in. I'll let her tell you about my blind faith. Hon', come here a minute. I've got Cliff, Ralph, and Jenny on the line. Tell them about my blind faith."

"Blind faith?" Barbara yelled across the room. "You don't even trust the milk."

Jenny asked, "What did she mean by that?"

"Barb, Jenny wants to know what you mean."

Coming closer to the phone, Barbara said, "Jack has to sniff the milk jug every time before he pours it to make sure it hasn't soured."

"And I've never poured sour milk on my corn flakes, have I?"

"Well, no, you haven't. But sometimes you do it when you first open the jug. And it's embarrassing when you do it when we have company."

"But I've never poured someone a glass of sour milk, have I?"

"No, you haven't," Barbara confessed.

Then Cliff asked, "Are you saying I should sniff the Perrier?"

Jack laughed and said, "I'm not saying that exactly, but you shouldn't be embarrassed if you think you need to. I think a lot of strange ideas are brought forth in churches, and people believe them because they are embarrassed to question the speaker. I say, go ahead and challenge what you hear if you think it's in error, check it out in the Bible, and use your concordance."

Barbara piped up and said, "What I say is, if in doubt throw it out, don't just sniff it." That got a chuckle out of everyone.

"But Jack..." Jenny interrupted, "aren't you afraid of people saying you have a critical spirit? I mean, you wouldn't just interrupt the pastor in the middle of a sermon would you? What if you were wrong? I don't know if I could do that. Have you ever done that?"

Barbara let out with a knowingly nervous laugh. "I don't think you want to get into that story, do you Jack?"

"I didn't bring it up," Jack responded.

"What story?" Jenny asked.

"Well, we sort of got kicked out of a church." Barbara confessed.

"No," Jack corrected. "We left because God told us to. It was a different church that we got kicked out of."

"Oh, you're right."

"You guys!" Jenny exclaimed, "What did you do to get kicked

out of a church? Now you gotta tell us."

"Okay, as long as Cliff is up for it," Jack conceded. "Tell you what, I'll use the story to explain some more about using the software. Besides, it has to do with communicating with God. Is that okay, Cliff?"

"Yeah, that's fine. Keep it concise, no filler, maybe just an outline."

"Okay, I understand. Here goes. I woke up too early one Sunday morning unable to escape the thought of women being silent in the church."

"You're joking, right?" asked Jenny.

"No, he's not," said Barbara. "But hear him out."

"Yeah, I'm with you Jenny," said Jack. "I even told God that I understood that at the time the Bible was written, the women didn't sit with their husbands, so if they talked to them, it was by yelling across the room. They also weren't educated, so they weren't considered to have anything intelligent to say. So I reminded God that the rules didn't apply to the situation in churches today."

"Yeah," chimed in Barbara, "Now the wives sit with their husbands and they know more."

"Yes, well, moving on," Jack stammered. "I couldn't shake the thought, so I thought maybe God wanted to teach me something. So I got up and pulled out my concordance." As he said this, he started tapping keys and clicking on the software. "I thought the verse I was thinking of had to do with marriage. So I looked up 'wives,' but couldn't find it. Then I looked up 'women,' and found the verse in first Corinthians fourteen. Here it is:

1Cor. 14:34 (KJV) Let your women keep silence in the churches: for it is not permitted unto them to speak; but they are commanded to be under obedience, as also saith the law.

"That verse alone didn't resonate with me for some reason,

so I decided to see what else was in that chapter." As Jack said this, he brought up the whole chapter in the software program so they could see it on their screens.

"When you read the whole chapter, it is talking about maintaining order in the church. It is also talking about prophesying and tongues. Now, I'm betting that 'prophecy' and 'tongues' are two of the things on your list of questions for me, am I right Ralph?"

"Uhh, that's right."

"Good, then we can kill two questions with one story," said Jack. "Let's take a look at a few verses:"

1Cor. 14:2 (KJV) For he that speaketh in an unknown tongue speaketh not unto men, but unto God: for no man understandeth him; howbeit in the spirit he speaketh mysteries. :3 But he that prophesieth speaketh unto men to edification, and exhortation, and comfort. :4 He that speaketh in an unknown tongue edifieth himself; but he that prophesieth edifieth the church.

"The first thing I realized was that I didn't know what the word 'edifieth' meant. So in this program, I double-click on the word 'edifieth', and I get the literal meaning of the word in Greek. Do you see what I did?"

"Yes, I see that," said Cliff, "But I can't read it. Ralph, read that to me."

"Well," said Ralph, "it's got some Greek word, then it says…"

"Here, let me," interrupted Jack. "It essentially says to be a house builder. To make sure I understood that, I looked up the Greek word, using the Strong's reference number, which in this case was G3618. I click 'Search' up here, then type in G3618 here, and click the icon over here that looks like a magnifying glass. Now we see 39 verses where that Greek word is used in context, and we see that it is usually translated 'build' or 'built.'"

"Sounds to me like a barn-raising would be a good

description," said Cliff.

"I think that is a good way to understand it, since it can often involve helping to build up someone else. Anyway, let me cut to the chase. The verses imply that prophesying will build up other people in the church, because they understand it, but speaking in an unknown tongue is speaking to God, and only builds up the speaker."

"So what did that have to do with us women staying silent?" asked Jenny.

"I didn't really get that either," confessed Jack. "I tried to figure that out for a while, and eventually understood that prophesying was God speaking to the Church, and that tongues was us in the church speaking to Him. I finally asked God to explain it to me. What I heard Him say to me was, "Who is the Bride? Who is the Husband?""

"Oh my!" exclaimed Jenny.

"I don't get it," said Cliff.

"Let me see if I can find something," Jack said, as he started tapping on his laptop keys again. "Here, in Revelation, it says:"

Rev. 21:9 (NLT) Then one of the seven angels who held the seven bowls containing the seven last plagues came and said to me, "Come with me! I will show you the bride, the wife of the Lamb."

"And the Lamb is Jesus!" explained Jenny. "And the wife is the Church! So what you're saying Jack, I think, is that when we meet together at church, we should want to hear from the husband, not the wife, so the wife should shut up."

"Yes, that's what hit me. When I re-read chapter 14 with that idea in mind, it all made more sense."

"It does!" exclaimed Jenny. "I always kinda struggled with this chapter cause I go to a tongues church..."

"Wait, wait, wait," said Cliff. "What's a tongues church? I said West Coast English, remember?"

Barbara jumped on that one. "It's where people aren't afraid to pray in tongues around other people."

"Should they be?" Cliff asked.

"Possibly," added Jack. "Look at these verses just down from the other ones:"

1Cor. 14:26 (NLT) Well, my brothers and sisters, let's summarize. When you meet together, one will sing, another will teach, another will tell some special revelation God has given, one will speak in tongues, and another will interpret what is said. But everything that is done must strengthen all of you. :27 No more than two or three should speak in tongues. They must speak one at a time, and someone must interpret what they say. :28 But if no one is present who can interpret, they must be silent in your church meeting and speak in tongues to God privately.

"Okay, I understand," said Cliff.

"You do?" asked Ralph.

"Yes. With some of the tribes I visited, the chief wouldn't let me talk in English around him, without every word being interpreted."

"But where I go to church, people talk in tongues a lot when they pray, and I'm afraid to bring some of my friends to church 'cause it'll freak 'em out."

"And that's talked about in this verse," added Jack, as he highlighted verse 23:

1Cor. 14:23 (NLT) Even so, if unbelievers or people who don't understand these things come into your church meeting and hear everyone speaking in an unknown language, they will think you are crazy.

"Right," said Jenny. "And that is why I don't invite them."

"But if you did, and your church was doing things properly, according to scripture, this is what might happen:"

1Cor. 14:24 (NLT) But if all of you are prophesying, and

unbelievers or people who don't understand these things come into your meeting, they will be convicted of sin and judged by what you say. :25 As they listen, their secret thoughts will be exposed, and they will fall to their knees and worship God, declaring, "God is truly here among you."

"That would be so neat!" exclaimed Jenny.

"Jack," said Barbara, "You need to tell them why we were kicked out, so we can move on."

"Yes, right. Well, all of this studying took a couple hours. After that, we got ready and went to church. This church had been struggling for a while with various things. This particular Sunday the pastor did a sermon about how all of the disciples were in one accord, and I don't mean the car."

"Jack," scolded Barbara.

"Okay, anyway, after the sermon, he told us that he felt we all needed to pray in one accord for the church. Then he said, and I quote, "I think we all need to pray at the top of our lungs in our prayer language."

"In other words, in tongues," explained Barbara.

"After all I had been through that morning, it just struck me wrong," said Jack. "So I yelled, "NO. That goes DIRECTLY against first Corinthians fourteen!"

"Whoa!" said Jenny. "What did the pastor do?"

"He said he disagreed with me, and I was kind of embarrassed, so I dropped it. But we never did what he said, so I think it accomplished what God intended."

"But," interrupted Jenny. "But what would it have hurt, if everyone spoke in tongues, as long as everyone was okay with it?"

"Curses," said Cliff.

"What?" asked Jenny.

"That is why the chief didn't want me to speak without an interpreter. He was afraid I would be speaking curses on him.

I didn't know what he meant at the time, but now I get it. If you can't understand what people are saying, they may be saying something evil. Is that right, Jack?"

"Exactly," Jack said, surprised that someone so new to being a believer understood what many long time believers couldn't. "I read a book once written by an ex-Satanist. They used to love to go into 'tongues' churches and speak curses on the church. Most Christians didn't know that Satanists can speak in tongues too."

"So is that when you got kicked out of the church?" asked Ralph.

"Like I said, we didn't get kicked out of that church. We left because God told us to. Plus the fact that they didn't like us any more."

"Boy Jack, if you've actually heard God speak to you that much, you should be eligible for sainthood," said Ralph.

From the sound of Ralph's voice Jack couldn't tell whether he was serious or joking. He decided he had better treat that statement seriously. "No offense, Ralph," he said a bit sternly, "but I think your Catholicism is showing. Man doesn't have the right to determine who is a saint and who isn't. You should know that just by looking back at some of the wicked Popes there have been. Being a saint is a calling from God just like any of the five-fold ministry positions."

"Time out!" said Cliff, holding up his hand. "What is a fifled ministry position?"

Everyone heard a quick giggle from Jenny and then sudden silence. Jack figured she must have hit the mute button. "No, five fold," he said to Cliff, "like in five parts. Let me find a verse here," he said while his fingers started typing away again. "Okay, here is what the church refers to as the five-fold ministry. Here in Ephesians chapter eleven, it says '*He is the one who gave these gifts to the church: the apostles, the prophets, the evangelists, and the pastors and teachers.'* Those are the five different ministry positions that are acceptable to some of the church.

"Now let's look at another verse," he said, as he noticed another verse that popped up in his search for verses containing the word 'apostle'. "Here in first Corinthians chapter 12 it says: *Here is a list of some of the members that God has placed in the body of Christ: first are apostles, second are prophets, third are teachers, then those who do miracles, those who have the gift of healing, those who can help others, those who can get others to work together, those who speak in unknown languages.* Now we have an eight-fold ministry."

"Let me see that," exclaimed Cliff. He stared at the screen for a couple of minutes as the others waited. Finally, he said, "That verse there in Ephesians might not even indicate a five-fold ministry."

"How do you mean?" Jack asked.

"It could be four-fold. It says 'the apostles', that's number one, then 'the prophets', that's number two, then 'the evangelists', that's three. Then number four would be 'the pastors and teachers'. See what I'm saying?"

"I think so," Jack said. "Yes, I see that. I had never thought of it that way before. Interesting. Now look at this other verse at the beginning of Romans. See, in verse one, it says Paul is called to be an apostle? Now, see here in verse seven, it says he is writing to those called to be saints. So some people are called to be saints, just as others may be called to be apostles or prophets and such. In another verse it says many are called but few are chosen."

Cliff cleared his throat and then said haltingly to Jack, "Definition please. Called and chosen. Explain the difference."

"Well, what you did the other day is one example," explained Jack. "You called a lot of people to meet with you, but I was the only one chosen. Another example could be a football team.

Many are called to try out for the team, but only a few are chosen to be on it. Fewer still are chosen to be a quarterback, and only one is in that position in a particular play. Who is called and who is chosen is the coach's decision, not the players."

"Meaning what?" asked Cliff.

"Oh, I just say that because there are Christians out there that stick the title of Apostle or Pastor or something on themselves or on others and you can't see any evidence that God had chosen them to be in that position. I just don't think that it's right to do that."

Ralph had been quiet while the other two talked. As if oblivious to where the conversation had gone, he asked, "So, are you saying the saints of the Catholic Church aren't really saints?"

"No, that's not what I meant," Jack said, realizing Ralph was becoming offended. "I'm just saying that I don't think that a group of humans has the right to say a person can't be called a saint just because that person hasn't lived up to a certain set of human criteria. I also don't believe that a person will be denied access to heaven just because he hasn't been baptized or read his last rites."

"Are you saying a person doesn't need to be baptized?" said Ralph, his voice rising as he was more obviously becoming offended.

"Yes, Jack," added Cliff. "What are you saying about that? Ralph here has been telling me I should get baptized before I die."

Boy, Jack thought to himself, *is that ever a subject I want to avoid.* It wasn't because he didn't think it was important. He knew it was. It was because this one subject had divided the church probably more than any other, and he didn't want it to divide the five of them. Not at this point in Cliff's life. He decided he would use the concordance and show them how to figure it out for themselves. "Okay," he said to them with a sigh. "Let's look it up and see what the Bible says. And let's see if we can drop any pre-conceived notions," he said, "and come to a scriptural conclusion. Agreed?"

"Sure, if that's possible," said Ralph.

"Okay, I'll look in the King James Bible for every single reference to the word baptism," he said as he again tapped away at the keyboard. "Okay, it says that the word baptism occurs 22 times in 22 verses. Now, don't think that I am manipulating the information, but I have studied this out before. All I would like to do is look at all 22 verses in order, starting from the last to the first. Is that okay?"

"I don't see why not," said Cliff.

"Okay, I'll do that," he said. "It doesn't change the outcome, it just makes more sense. You'll see what I mean as we go. The first verse then—which would be the last one mentioned in the Bible—is in first Peter three, verse twenty one. It says *The like figure whereunto even baptism doth also now save us (not the putting away of the filth of the flesh, but the answer of a good conscience toward God,) by the resurrection of Jesus Christ.* This verse likens being saved by baptism to Noah being saved in the ark. See the verse above?" He gave them time to look at verse twenty, and then moved on.

The next is in Colossians two verse twelve. It says *Buried with him in baptism, wherein also ye are risen with him through the faith of the operation of God, who hath raised him from the dead.* So far we get a picture of being buried or immersed. In fact, if we look at the meaning of the Greek word," he said as he clicked on it, "we see that it means, well, baptism. This word—baptisma--is taken from the word 'baptizo' which means to make whelmed or fully wet."

They heard a noise on their speakers, and then Jenny said,

"So that would be talking about water baptism, right?"

"Maybe it could be, or maybe not. Let's not jump the gun. We can come back to this," he said, trying to move on.

"Okay," they all said, almost together.

"Good. This next verse is the one that I think is crucial to understanding baptism. It is in Ephesians four, verse five. It says *One Lord, one faith, one baptism*. I'll let you read the verses around it, but I believe it is pretty clear that there is only one baptism."

Jack let them read the verses surrounding that one. Ralph went quite a ways both directions, whereas Cliff acted antsy to move on. "Why is it important that there is only one baptism?" Cliff finally asked.

"If I recall correctly, on your list of things to question me about was 'water baptism' and the 'baptism of the Holy Spirit'. Which one of those do you think this refers to?" he asked, waiting for an answer.

"I don't think we've seen yet, other than the word seems to mean to be covered with water," said Cliff.

"That would be water baptism then, right?" asked Ralph. "Like Jenny said?"

"Well, let's not jump to any conclusions until we see what the rest of the Bible has to say about it," he said, trying his best to be a good teacher. "Let's look at some more verses. The next one, Romans six, verse four, sounds a lot like the second verse we looked at. But look at the next one, Acts nineteen, verse four. It says: *John verily baptized with the baptism of repentance, saying unto the people, that they should believe on him which should come after him, that is, on Christ Jesus*. Now we have another baptism, the baptism of repentance."

"No, we don't have another one," stated Cliff.

"What do you mean?" asked Ralph.

"This one here is the first one that has been named," said Cliff, with a little smugness in his voice. "The other two we got off the TV shows."

"Well, I suppose so," said Ralph. "But the Catholic church has always talked about water baptism," he added.

"Yes," Jack said. "And the Pentecostal church has always talked about the baptism of the Holy Spirit."

"Our church talks about both," added Jenny.

Jack said, "Let's read some more verses and maybe we'll see where they came from."

"Okay," Jenny said, sounding a little confused.

"The next verse, well, is the verse just before the last one so it refers to the same thing. The next one...Acts eighteen twenty-five...again talks about the baptism of John. Then...Acts 13, twenty-four...again says John's baptism was the baptism of repentance. Then...Acts ten...baptism that John preached...Acts one...is the baptism of John. Am I going too fast for anyone?"

"No," said Cliff

"No, I'm keeping up. I thought John baptized with water," said Ralph.

"He did," Jack answered. "Let's keep going...Luke twenty...is a question about the baptism of John...Okay, Luke twelve, and verse fifty. Here is an interesting one. Jesus says he has a baptism that he has yet to be baptized with. Do you know what is so interesting about it?" Jack asked. All he got was silence. "Its placement chronologically."

"I don't get it," said Jenny.

"If we go to the next verse," Jack continued, "we will see... nope, the next one...yes, here it is, Luke chapter 3. We see in verse three that again it is the baptism of repentance. Now, if we go down to verse twenty-one, here, let me read it. It says: *Now when all the people were baptized, it came to pass, that Jesus also* being baptized, and praying, the heaven was opened, And the Holy Ghost descended in a bodily shape like a dove upon him, and a voice came from heaven, which said, Thou art my beloved Son; in thee I am well pleased."

He paused a second for effect, and to see if any of them caught what he had said. He turned to Barbara and said, "You tell 'em, Barb."

Barbara asked them, "Did you notice the timing? The events in Luke three happened *before* those in Luke twelve. When Jesus was talking about having a baptism that he still needed to be baptized with, it was after he had been baptized by John. Could there be yet another baptism?"

"I hope you are going to explain all of this," said a somewhat frustrated Cliff.

"I will," Jack said, "but I will need to confuse you a couple more times first. Then I'm through. Honest."

"Okay," said Ralph. "We'll hold you to it."

"Fair enough. Look at this point here in verse twenty-two. See where it says the Holy Ghost descended like a dove. That is universally understood to illustrate that he was baptized by the Holy Spirit. We'll go back to that. Okay, back up to verse sixteen. It says: '*John answered, saying unto them all, I indeed baptize you with water; but one mightier than I cometh, the latchet of whose shoes I am not worthy to unloose: he shall baptize you with the Holy Ghost and with fire...*"

"Wait a minute, Jack," said Cliff. "I just noticed something. Let me take it."

Jack relinquished his hosting of the meeting again and let Cliff and Ralph work the screen. They all waited patiently while the gears turned in Cliffs head. Ralph didn't seem to know what to think. Jack, on the other hand, was hoping a little revelation was hitting Cliff like it had done to him many years earlier.

He could see that Cliff had figured out which icon to click on that let him zoom from verse to verse that contained the word baptism. Then he felt his heart race a step when he saw him do a search for the word 'baptize'. Pretty soon he was checking out every verse that contained the word baptize in it. He believed Cliff was getting it. Either Cliff's mind was still as sharp as a tack, or the Holy Spirit was guiding him. He believed both were possible.

"There is only one baptism!" Cliff declared, finally breaking the silence. He spun the laptop around so it faced Ralph and leaned back in his wheelchair, like a chess player saying "check". He was challenging Ralph to find what he had found.

"What?" said Ralph. "What did you find?"

"That Jack's been teasing us, setting us up," said Cliff. "Good job, Jack."

"Thanks Cliff. I had a good teacher." Jack was not sure if Cliff realized he was talking about God and not him.

"C'mon guys, I don't have time for this," said Ralph, feeling like the only one not getting a joke.

"Yeah," said Jenny, "tell us what you found, Mr. Montgomery."

"You can call me Cliff, Jenny. You too, Barbara. Let me give you a clue," said Cliff. "Socialism."

"And I'll give you one," Jack said. "Socialize."

"What?" said Ralph, "What does that have to do with what we've been talking about?"

"Here's another," said Cliff. "Terrorism."

"Terrorize," said Jack, getting a chuckle from Cliff, and only a grunt from Ralph.

Then Barbara quickly added "Communism!"

"Communize," snapped Cliff, who then added, "McCarthyism. Let's see you match that, Jack".

"McCarthy...ize?" Jack said, not knowing if it was a word or not. Cliff just laughed. By now Ralph was looking at the Bible program, trying to see what the other two had seen, and trying to make sense of the clues.

"You're probably going to have to help me with this," he finally said, "or we'll be here all night. But I know it has something to do with the difference between the words baptism and baptize."

"That's actually pretty good," Jack said to him. "I know very few people who have noticed it."

"I went through all of the verses for baptism," said Cliff, somewhat triumphantly. "There is only one baptism ever mentioned. But there are lots of ways to baptize, including being baptized in a cloud and a sea."

"That is exactly the point I was trying...what did you just say?" Jack asked, as his mind suddenly caught up with what his ears had heard.

"You're right," said Ralph, who was systematically going through all the verses. "It's right here in first Corinthians ten. I have a question though," he said. "What exactly is the baptism that Jesus was yet to be baptized with?"

Jack was still wondering about the cloud and sea thing, but he wanted to help Ralph figure out the baptism question for himself. "See if you can find the answer in Luke three sixteen," he told him.

After a moment of reading, Ralph said, "It talks about another way to baptize, by fire, but I don't see another baptism."

"Okay, let me tell you how I see it," Jack finally said. "If we go back to Ephesians four, verse five, we have to either accept that there is only one baptism, or reject it. As a rule, I never reject any scripture just to fit my theology. Instead, I adjust my theology to fit the truth in scripture. If there is only one baptism, it is repentance. It has to be. It is the only one ever named in scripture.

"If we make that assumption, then being baptized in water

has to do with repentance, and being baptized by the Holy Spirit does too. I think it follows that being baptized by fire would also have something to do with repentance."

"Are you saying Jesus needed to repent?" asked Ralph.

"No, I don't think he did. If you look at...well, let's look at Matthew...here let me be the host again," Jack said as he waited for Ralph to turn over control of the meeting back to him. "Okay, here it is in Matthew three, verse thirteen. It says: *Matt. 3:13 (NLT)* '*Then Jesus went from Galilee to the Jordan River to be baptized by John. :14 But John tried to talk him out of it. "I am the one who needs to be baptized by you," he said, "so why are you coming to me?" :15 But Jesus said, "It should be done, for we must carry out all that God requires." So John agreed to baptize him. :16 After his baptism, as Jesus came up out of the water, the heavens were opened and he saw the Spirit of God descending like a dove and settling on him.*' Do you see how John the Baptist tried to stop Jesus, saying rather that Jesus needed to baptize him?"

"I think so," said Ralph, unconvincingly.

"John seemed to know that Jesus didn't need to repent. Jesus didn't correct him and say, 'No, you need to baptize me for I have repented'. He said basically, let's do it anyway, because it needs to be done. That is my translation, by the way."

"I guess I can accept that," said Ralph.

"The important point is that I don't believe it negates the fact that repentance is the one true baptism," Jack continued.

"So what does it mean to be baptized by fire?" asked Cliff.

"I think a study of the word 'fire' would be helpful in understanding that. By the way, do you see what I'm doing? If I have a question about something, I don't try to analyze it with my mind first. Instead, I look for some supporting information in the Bible. You could say I try to find a few more pieces of the puzzle before declaring what the picture is."

"It's a bit tedious at times, but I appreciate you trying not to stuff me with your opinions," said Cliff.

"Let's just see what we get when we search for the word fire," Jack said, as he did just that. "Okay, fire appears 549 times in 506 verses. Do you have time for that?" he asked them.

"Not really," said Cliff, matter-of-factly.

"Then I'll show you what I would do to narrow it down. First, I would eliminate the Old Testament because there wasn't any mention of baptism there. Next, I would just skim the verses for context relative to what I am looking for." As he was talking to them, he was locating the book of Matthew in the list of 549 verses containing the word fire.

"First, let's go to the verse that mentions being baptized by fire. It happens to be the second reference for fire in the New Testament, in Matthew three, verse eleven. If we highlight the word 'fire' by clicking on it...we see the definition of the original Greek word for it over here. We see that the word fire means... fire or fiery, or in special instances it could mean lightning, which makes perfect..."

"Jack," interrupted Cliff. "Go up some."

"What?" he asked.

"Go up a few verses from that one, to verse seven." Jack hit the up arrow until the King James column moved up a few verses. "A couple more," he said. They all started looking for the verses that Cliff was interested in. "Looks like we've found our answer already." Cliff said, after less than a minute.

Not being quite the speed reader that Cliff was, it took Jack a while to see what Cliff saw. He had to go over the verses a few times to try to figure it out. When he finally did see it, he wondered why he had never noticed it before. He had to ask Cliff, "How did you see that was there? The verses weren't even showing on the screen."

"Yes they were," said Cliff with a little smugness. "Over there, in the version on the other side of the screen. Your two versions don't line up. I went to read verse eleven on this side and saw verses eight, nine, and ten instead. Do you see what I was referring to?" he asked.

"*I don't,*" said Jenny

"I believe so," said Jack. "How about if I go through it, and you can interject if you need to."

"Please do," said Cliff.

Jack wasn't trying to steal the spotlight. He could just tell Cliff didn't have the strength to do a lot of talking. "Let's start at verse two. It says: 'Repent ye: for the kingdom of heaven is at hand.' So John the Baptist is telling people to repent. Then, in verse six and seven it says all the people from around there that had gone out to see him *'were baptized of him in Jordan, confessing their sins. But when he saw many of the Pharisees and Sadducees come to his baptism, he said unto them, O generation of vipers, who hath warned you to flee from the wrath to come? Bring forth therefore fruits meet for repentance.'* So in other words, he saw some people in the crowd that he couldn't believe were actually repentant. I personally believe God gave John insight into their hearts like he did the prophets in the Old Testament. That would also explain his conversation with Jesus."

"I like how verse eight reads on the other side," pointed out Cliff.

"Yes, I do too. He tells them to produce fruit in keeping with repentance. In telling them to produce fruit he is likening them to a tree. So in verse ten, he refers to them again, saying *"And now also the ax is laid unto the root of the trees. Therefore every tree which bringeth not forth good fruit is hewn down, and cast into the fire."*

"Oh, man!" exclaimed Ralph, with sadness in his voice.

"What's the matter?" asked Jack, kind of surprised.

"I just thought of something," he answered. "I don't know if it's relevant to what we're talking about or not."

"What is it?" Jack asked.

"You know when it talks about the trees not producing good fruit?" he asked somberly. "They do that when they're dying." They all sat there in stunned silence.

Suddenly, it was as if all of the pieces fit together. Jack had felt for years that 'the baptism that Jesus had yet to be baptized with' referred to his death on the cross. Somehow he had never put it together with these verses before. He again read verse eleven, adding a few words of his own, first silently, then out loud. "I indeed baptize you with water unto repentance: but he that cometh after me is mightier than I, whose shoes I am not worthy to bear, he shall baptize you with the Holy Ghost unto repentance, and with fire unto repentance."

Then Cliff continued, "But he will burn up the chaff with unquenchable fire." After another moment of silence, he asked, "Do you think dying is how you're baptized by fire?"

"I think dying is part of the process," Jack responded. "It says in other places that we are to die to ourselves…"

"I've been crucified with Christ," Jenny started singing, "Nevertheless, I-I live! We sing that in church all the time."

"Very good, Jenny," said Barbara. "and it says in another place that our works will be refined by fire."

Jack tapped away at the keyboard until he found the verse she was talking about. "Here it is in first Corinthians three, verse ten. It talks about laying a foundation, and says; '*1Corinthians 3:10 (NLT) By the grace God has given me, I laid a foundation as an expert builder, and someone else is building on it. But each one should be careful how he builds. :11 For no one can lay any foundation other than the one already laid, which is Jesus Christ. :12 If any man builds on this foundation using gold, silver, costly stones, wood, hay or straw, :13 his work will be shown for what it is, because the Day will bring it to light. It will be revealed with fire, and the fire will test the quality of each man's work. :14 If what he has built survives, he will receive his reward. :15 If it is burned up, he will suffer loss; he himself will be saved, but only as one escaping through the flames.'"*

They all sat silent for a while, then Jack continued, "I really think being baptized by fire is something that occurs throughout your life to refine and purify you. If you remember, I said last time that repentance was a reversal in your thinking from selfish inward thoughts to unselfish desires for God and others. That type of a change in your thinking doesn't come instantly. Being baptized by fire sounds like the refinement process that takes place in a person. Death is just the final process, since after that there is no time left for any more refinement. Even in Jesus' life you can see a change after he was baptized in the water and by the Holy Spirit. And his death on the cross was the ultimate unselfish act."

"Jack?" asked Ralph.

"Yes Ralph."

"A dying tree can be saved," he said.

"How so?" asked Barbara.

"Well, it depends on why it's dying," he answered. "If it is diseased or has a pest problem, it can sometimes be treated. Sometimes dead wood, you know, dead limbs, can sap its energy. They can be cut off so the tree can heal. Sometimes it was just improper care that hurt the tree, like over watering or under fertilizing. If corrected, the tree may recover. If it's an environmental problem, say for instance not enough sunlight, it may have to be moved, or what is blocking its light may need to be removed."

Jack's mind was working overtime, remembering instances in his life where God had done all of those things to him. He wanted to share them, but he knew that Cliff didn't have the energy right now to listen to all of it. Plus, he had a tendency to get carried away telling personal stories. Either he would bore others, or reveal more about himself than he cared to. He decided it would be best to move on. "Have we delved into that subject deep enough for now?" he asked.

"I think so," said Cliff. "I might like to study some more on my own, though."

THE BIBLE SEARCH for GOD'S NAME

"Jack," said Ralph, "there is another question that Cliff has."

"And what would that be?"

"What's his name?" asked Cliff.

"What is whose name?" responded Jack.

"Cliff wants to know if God has a name," added Ralph.

"That's right, Jack," said Cliff. "In India, Africa, South America, there were a lot of gods talked about amongst the people, and they all had names. In Japan they were called demons, but they still had names. At the time, I didn't care about any of that stuff. I was more interested in why they were devoted to such things, and not what it was they were devoted to."

"But now you're interested?"

"Of course," Cliff answered. "I'm going to meet Him. Whenever I met heads of state or the chief of a tribe, it was important that I knew their name, and their correct title. I have heard titles, such as God, or Lord, or Father, but those can be applied generically to others. A name is specific."

Jack thought for a moment and then asked, "Would you like me to tell you his name?"

"No," Cliff stated rather abruptly.

"But Cliff," Jenny protested. "You just asked…"

"I expect him to show me," Cliff responded. "I'm beginning to like this Bible program. I find it to be a lot more solid than opinions. But I do appreciate you showing me what you've learned, Jack. It saves time."

"All right then, I'll show where God stated what His name is." Jack started clattering away at his keyboard until he got to the book of Exodus. "Does everyone remember the movie 'The Ten Commandments'?"

"With Charleton Heston as Moses," added Barbara.

Jack heard various affirmative responses on the phone, so he continued. "If you remember the part about the burning bush, that is when God first met with Moses. Now, I have to say that there are places earlier in the Bible that mention his name, but you won't find it in hardly any of the translations."

"Why is that?" asked Jenny.

"I don't know," confessed Jack. "It doesn't really matter, because with the Concordance, once you know what to look for, you can find it. And these are the verses that will tell you what to look for." When he said that, he moved the text on the screen down to Exodus 3:

Ex. 3:1(KJV) Now Moses kept the flock of Jethro his father in law, the priest of Midian: and he led the flock to the backside of the desert, and came to the mountain of God, even to Horeb. :2 And the angel of the LORD appeared unto him in a flame of fire out of the midst of a bush: and he looked, and, behold, the bush burned with fire, and the bush was not consumed. :3 And Moses said, I will now turn aside, and see this great sight, why the bush is not burnt. :4 And when the LORD saw that he turned aside to see, God called unto him out of the midst of the bush, and said, Moses, Moses. And he said, Here am I. :5 And he said, Draw not nigh hither: put off thy shoes from off thy feet, for the place whereon thou standest is holy ground.

:6 Moreover he said, I am the God of thy father, the God of Abraham, the God of Isaac, and the God of Jacob. And Moses hid his face; for he was afraid to look upon God.

:7 And the LORD said, I have surely seen the affliction of my people which are in Egypt, and have heard their cry by reason of their taskmasters; for I know their sorrows; :8 And I am come down to deliver them out of the hand of the Egyptians, and to bring them up out of that land unto a good land and a large, unto a land flowing with milk and honey; unto the place of the Canaanites, and the Hittites, and the Amorites, and the Perizzites, and the Hivites, and the Jebusites. :9 Now therefore, behold, the cry of the children of Israel is come unto me: and I have also seen the oppression wherewith the Egyptians oppress them. :10 Come now therefore, and I will send thee unto Pharaoh, that thou mayest bring forth my people the children of Israel out of Egypt.

:11 And Moses said unto God, Who am I, that I should go unto Pharaoh, and that I should bring forth the children of Israel out of Egypt? :12 And he said, Certainly I will be with thee; and this shall be a token unto thee, that I have sent thee: When thou hast brought forth the people out of Egypt, ye shall serve God upon this mountain. :13 And Moses said unto God, Behold, when I come unto the children of Israel, and shall say unto them, The God of your fathers hath sent me unto you; and they shall say to me, What is his name? what shall I say unto them? :14 And God said unto Moses, I AM THAT I AM: and he said, Thus shalt thou say unto the children of Israel, I AM hath sent me unto you. :15 And God said moreover unto Moses, Thus shalt thou say unto the children of Israel, The LORD God of your fathers, the God of Abraham, the God of Isaac, and the God of Jacob, hath sent me unto you: this is my name for ever, and this is my memorial unto all generations.

:16 Go, and gather the elders of Israel together, and say unto

them, *The LORD God of your fathers, the God of Abraham, of Isaac, and of Jacob, appeared unto me, saying, I have surely visited you, and seen that which is done to you in Egypt:*

Ralph said a bit sheepishly, "His name is 'I Am'?"

"That's what our Pastor calls Him," piped up Jenny. "He calls Him the great I AM!"

"But that's not really a name, is it?" asked Ralph.

"No," stated Cliff, "And it's not his name either," he added.

"Are you cheating?" Jack asked.

"Not at all," said Cliff. "It's right in front of our noses."

You're right, it is," said Jack. "Does anyone else see it? Not you, Barbara, you already know." When no one else responded quickly enough, he hinted, "Check the New Living Translation on the right."

"I see it," shouted Jenny excitedly. "In verse 15 it says, '*Say this to the people of Israel: Yahweh, the God of your ancestors, the God of Abraham, the God of Isaac, and the God of Jacob, has sent me to you. This is my eternal name, my name to remember for all generations.'*"

"But Jack," said Ralph, "wouldn't Moses have known what God's name was?"

"I don't see anything up to this point that says that he did," answered Jack. "Remember, he was adopted when he was only a couple years old and raised as an Egyptian. He knew that he was a Hebrew, but not anything is said about him knowing any of the Hebrew traditions. Let me show you something else. I'll double-click the words 'The Lord' over here in the King James. What do we see, Jenny?"

"It says… well, it must be Yahweh, cause it's spelled Y-H-W-H. And it says, 'the self-Existent or Eternal; name of God.'"

"That's good," said Jack. "Now let's see how many times that particular name was used in the Old Testament." As he said that, he typed the Key Number for Yahweh into the search field. "Okay, it says it is used 6520 times. But look how it is translated." As he said that, he scrolled down the list of verses.

"It's always translated as Lord," said Ralph.

"Pretty much," said Jack. Let's check and see how often Yahweh is used in the New Living Translation, where we saw it." When Jack did that, all of them saw the list of verses on the screen:

<u>Gen. 22:14</u> *Abraham named the place* **Yahweh**–*Yireh (which means "the LORD will provide"). To this day, people still use that name as a proverb: "On the mountain of the LORD it will be provided."*

<u>Ex. 3:15</u> *God also said to Moses, "Say this to the people of Israel:* **Yahweh**, *the God of your ancestors—the God of Abraham, the God of Isaac, and the God of Jacob—has sent me to you. This is my eternal name, my name to remember for all generations.*

<u>Ex. 6:2</u> *And God said to Moses, "I am* **Yahweh**—*'the LORD.'*

<u>Ex. 6:3</u> *I appeared to Abraham, to Isaac, and to Jacob as El–Shaddai—'God Almighty' —but I did not reveal my name,* **Yahweh**, *to them.*

<u>Ex. 15:3</u> *The LORD is a warrior;* **Yahweh** *is his name!*

<u>Ex. 33:19</u> *The LORD replied, "I will make all my goodness pass before you, and I will call out my name,* **Yahweh**, *before you. For I will show mercy to anyone I choose, and I will show compassion to anyone I choose.*

<u>Ex. 34:5</u> *Then the LORD came down in a cloud and stood there with him; and he called out his own name,* **Yahweh**.

<u>Ex. 34:6</u> *The LORD passed in front of Moses, calling out,* "**Yahweh**! *The LORD! The God of compassion and mercy! I am slow to anger and filled with unfailing love and faithfulness.*

<u>Judg. 6:24</u> *And Gideon built an altar to the LORD there and named it* **Yahweh**–*Shalom (which means "the LORD is peace").*

"Nine times?" asked Ralph.

"I don't understand," said Cliff. "If Yahweh is truly God's name, then it should be in there six thousand, whatever, times. 'The Lord' is just a title, like 'the Prince' or 'the Pope'. Jack, do that click thing on those verses where it says 'The Lord.'"

"In the New Living Translation?"

"Yes, where it has Yahweh and 'The Lord' in the same verse."

"Sorry, it doesn't work that way. That translation isn't tied to the Strong's Concordance. And if you look at the translations that are, it just says 'The Lord' once."

"Then click on one of those."

"Okay, it comes up Yahweh."

"Right," stated Cliff. "And look how it's spelled in the Hebrew. It's spelled yod-he-vav-he. That would be pronounced something like Yahweh, not 'The Lord.'"

Barbara decided to weigh in on the subject and said, "I think most people pronounce it Jehovah."

Trying to make sense of what the controversy was, Jenny asked, "wouldn't that be like the difference between John and Juan?"

"Actually, it probably would," said Jack.

"But not if it was a proper name," countered Cliff. "I'll tell you, during the Cuban missile crisis, the Cuban press didn't call our president Juan F. Kennedy, and they certainly didn't call him 'The Lord.'"

Jack laughed and said, "I'm sure they didn't. But then again, there's nothing wrong with referring to God as Lord, or Father, or Savior, or Almighty God."

"I understand that," countered Cliff. But those are titles, not names. A name is a unique identifier, especially for legal reasons. For instance, everyone called me Cliff Montgomery. But that was my pen name, my title in the literary sense. But on legal documents, I was addressed as Heathcliff Montgomery Preston, because that was my name."

That last statement got Jack thinking about something. He started clacking away on his keyboard again, and Barbara asked him, "Whatcha thinkin'?"

"I just thought of something that I've never looked up before," he responded. "Look at this." He pointed at Exodus 20, verse 7.

"That's one of the Ten Commandments," exclaimed Barbara.

"Now look at this," Jack added, as he double-clicked on the phrase 'The Lord'. "Now read it translated correctly. Does everyone else see what I am looking at?"

"Yeah, you're looking at one of the commandments," said Jenny. "Oh, I see what you did. Can I read it?"

"Sure, go ahead."

"It says… well, if you say it right, it says, 'Thou shalt not take the name of Yahweh thy God in vain; for Yahweh will not hold him guiltless that taketh his name in vain.'"

Then Jack asked Cliff, "Does that answer your question about what God's name is?"

"It seems rather clear to me. But it doesn't look like it is very clear to whoever it was that translated these Bibles."

"And what is it that I say quite often?"

Jack then heard one voice turn into four as they all said, "You have to go back to the source!"

"Right, and there were a couple verses that caused the Hebrews to not want to speak the name of Yahweh. The first one is the one we just read. The other is Leviticus 24, verse 16. If I read it substituting the name Yahweh, it reads, '*Moreover, the one who blasphemes the name of Yahweh shall surely be put to death; all the congregation shall certainly stone him. The alien as well as the native, when he blasphemes the name, shall be put to death*.'"

"That sounds a bit severe," said Jenny. "I can see why they

would be afraid to say it."

Barbara quickly added, "They were probably more afraid of the congregation thinking they had blasphemed the name, than they were about what God would think."

"So once again," Jack continued, "we have religion and tradition warping one of Gods commands. God said the punishment was for blaspheming His name, not speaking it. It's sort of similar to eating the fruit, and not merely touching it. In that era, if you used the name of a king, what you said carried the same weight as if the king had said it. But if you used the king's name without permission, you could be put to death. I believe God expected the same type of respect for his name."

"But Jack, interrupted Jenny. "What about the name of Jesus? Our pastor says that there is no greater name in heaven or on Earth, and there is no other name by which we can be saved, and at the name of Jesus, every knee will bow, and so on. How does that fit in with Yahweh?"

Cliff spoke up before Jack could, and said, "You said that Jesus was God, if I remember correctly."

"You did remember correctly, Cliff," said Jack. "So, Jenny, what does the Bible say?"

"I don't know for sure." Jenny said sheepishly.

"Would you like to look it up for us? I can hand you the reins of this software program."

"I... I could try."

"Good," said Jack before she could change her mind. "Just let me click on this here. Then on your screen, click on the thing in the upper right corner that, yes, you did it."

"I saw what Cliff did," Jenny said proudly. "Now what do I do?"

"Type the name 'Jesus' in the search field and then click on the magnifying glass. Yeah... now double-click on the name

Jesus in the middle column, which is King James. Now, see the window that just opened up? That is the original word in Greek that is the name Jesus. See how it is pronounced?"

"Ee – ay – soos. Sounds like Jesus in Spanish."

"That's right. So we're probably the ones that don't pronounce it right. Anyway, see where it says 'of Hebrew origin', and then H3091?"

"Yes."

"That's telling us that the name Jesus has its origin in the Hebrew language. Now, go back to the search field and highlight it, then go to the top of the screen and click on 'Search' and then 'Enter Key Numbers'. Good. Now see the drop down menu? Under where it says 'Go to', type H3091, and click Enter. Good. Now you have all of the verses that use the Hebrew word that the name Jesus was taken from."

"But it says Joshua," said Jenny.

"So what have we learned?" asked Jack. He wasn't trying to put thoughts in her head, he just wanted her to learn to dig for understanding.

"I don't know. Maybe that the name Jesus comes from the name Joshua?"

Barbara added, "Or maybe Jesus is the name Joshua in Greek?"

"I think either could be correct," said Jack. "Possibly like Juan is John in Spanish. Anyway, go ahead and double-click on the name Joshua in one of those verses."

"It says, Ye–ho–shoo–ah. Oh, look at that, It says Yhwh-saved! So the name Joshua means Yahweh saved! Then so does the name Jesus. So Jesus could be Yahweh! Cool!"

"So Jack," interrupted Cliff. "If I was to put all of this together, when I finally cross over to the other side and meet God, I can call Him Yahweh, or Jesus. Either way."

"That's the way I see it," said Jack. "Others may see it differently. But for a lot of reasons, I believe I'm right."

"Such as?"

"Such as, in the Old Testament Yahweh is called Lord, in the New Testament Jesus is called Lord. In the Old, Yahweh said He was I Am, in the New, Jesus said 'Before Abraham was, I Am'. I could go on and on. What I believe pretty strongly though is, when you do meet him, you will probably know what to call him. If you're not sure, ask Gloria."

CPSIA information can be obtained at www.ICGtesting.com
Printed in the USA
BVOW031659190513

321049BV00004B/10/P